CARDS [_ᴅ ᴛ ʜ BOOK 9

THE NINTH ANGEL

TAMARA GERAEDS

ISBN-13: 979-8-4968-0077-8
Cover design by Deranged Doctor Design
Editing by R.E. Hargrave

FREE SOUL JUMPER ORIGIN STORY!

Looking for a series of stories with just as much action, twists, monsters and magic as *Cards of Death*? Look no further! *Soul Jumper* is the thing for you!

Subscribe to my newsletter now – through www.tamarageraeds.com – and you will receive a *Soul Jumper* origin story FOR FREE!

PREVIOUSLY, IN CARDS OF DEATH

The end is drawing near. Thanks to all the wonderful people who've helped me, we've survived so far, and have managed to keep the Devil in Hell. If you need a reminder of who played a part in this incredible journey, please go to the *cast of characters* at the end of the book.

So many incredible things have happened, both good and bad, and now we're getting ready for the battle against the Devil.

I'm not sure what I fear most. The battle itself, or the inevitable goodbyes that will follow it. Because, whether we win or lose, my Shield will move on. Well, all except one. You see, I died and was offered the choice to move on to Heaven or go back and continue my fight against Satan. I chose the latter, and for that I got something in return—the chance to keep one of my friends here on Earth after the battle. D'Maeo was the only selfless choice I could make. I haven't told the others yet.

Unfortunately, this means I will have to say goodbye to Vicky, too.

Soon.

Dad will try to join us in the final battle, but I'm afraid the Horsemen will take him out before he gets the chance to escape them again. So, even if I see him again, it will be the last time.

And those are not the only things I worry about. We found out Vicky is a direct descendant of Lucifer and his late wife Isabel. Charon, the Ferryman of the Underworld, helped her awaken her inherited powers, which means fire can no longer hurt her and she can move objects with her mind. She will hopefully also be able to create some new circles of Hell to trap Lucifer under, like Isabel did.

The Devil has been trying to take Vicky out; no doubt he knows what she's capable of once she has embraced her ancestral powers. He killed Vicky's mother and grandmother a long time ago, and put a curse on Vicky, which we lifted recently. Then, he sent his right hand, Beelzebub, through the portal in the silver mine. When Vicky made eye contact with him, he planted part of himself inside her, to turn her evil. We removed Beelzebub's evil influence from her with a spell, but I don't think we were a hundred percent successful. Vicky has been acting a bit strange again.

While we keep an eye on Vicky, we prepare for the final battle as best as we can, by gathering more power, freeing the ghosts in my Shield from curses and unfinished business, training, and saving the last souls. Our plan is to lure Satan to Darkwood Manor by leaving the portal in the silver mine open. We'll have a couple of surprises for him when he arrives, such as the Pearl of Arcadia, which contains the original message from God to the angels. It will remind rogue angels of their purpose and can also call new angels to us. In addition, we have a mansion that comes to life to fight, the remnant of the black tree inside Maël, Vicky's ability–we hope–to create the nine circles of Hell, and soon, another powerful magician: Mom. We were about to transfer Charlotte's powers into her when the iele, the fairies we borrowed the Bell of Izme from, knocked on our door. In exchange for keeping the bell a bit longer–which we need to keep the portal in the silver mine closed until we're ready to fight Satan-they asked for our help to defeat the marodium, a dangerous species which feeds on nightmares and shapes hatred. They've taken over the iele's hometown of Affection, which the iele's leader Soimane needs to remind her folk of how loving they are. She hopes to erase the iele's hatred against humanity and other magical creatures to bring them back to better times.

We decided to help them, but when we arrived at Affection, we found more than monsters. Several angels were trapped in a barn, surrounded by nightmares…

CHAPTER 1

It's weird how, even when you're expecting it, everything can spin out of control faster than you imagined.

One second we're watching six angels being tortured in their sleep, and the next, we're faced with six creatures who don't resemble angels anymore, backed by the nightmares that made them that way. When one of them woke up, all aggravated and ready to attack the first human it saw, I assumed there would be plenty of time to either shake it from its hypnosis or make a run for it. I didn't expect the five remaining angels to wake at the same time, and I certainly didn't expect the human forms hovering around them to zoom in on us. I figured they would disappear once their job-to turn the angels against humankind-was done. Instead, they turned into all kinds of other monstrosities.

Gisella and Vicky react before anyone else. The werecat-witch throws her hands forward, creating a force field which knocks our enemies over. Or at least, it should, but the angels merely stumble and stay upright. After being blown back, the figures make a fast recovery and advance with angry snarls and hisses.

Meanwhile, Vicky digs two jars of salt from her endless pocket and tosses them to Dylan and Taylar.

"Create a salt line around the barn. Quickly!" she yells.

The two boys hurry outside while the rest of us form a line of defense in front of the only exit.

Gisella tries another blow, and when that doesn't work, she calls the shadows to her. There are lots of them in here, which means she can send a shadow to almost every angel and nightmarish monster. For a moment, I think it's working. Then the angels open their mouths and breathe out, sending the shadows back to their corners.

"Uh… I need some help," Gisella calls out.

The sliver of panic in her voice sounds unnatural. It sends a shiver down my back. If Gisella is losing faith, then things are looking grim.

There's no time to think of a strategy. The angels and monsters are moving forward as one. Maël slams her staff against the side of a man who looks familiar. Taylar is jumped by his spitting image, save for the gruesome scars that line his face and the burn marks on his hands.

As the other forms approach us, I realize the figures have changed into our worst nightmares. And although I'm afraid to face mine, I'm also curious.

What does my worst nightmare actually look like in the flesh?

I conjure two lightning bolts in my hands and brace myself as I turn my head back to the incoming threats. The figure in front of me changes shape constantly, as if it can't decide what it's supposed to be. Vicky's face changes into Mom's, and then turns into a burning ball. I almost smirk.

I guess there are too many fears in my mind to deal with.

While it tries to find the perfect form to tip me off balance, I shower it with lightning combined with rain.

I'm surprised it works, since I've never managed to create more than one meteorological phenomenon at a time. The nightmare-inducing monster shudders as electricity runs through its shadowy form.

All around me I hear the clanging of metal, Maël's mumbling as she tries to slow down time, the whizz of Jeep's hat and Charlie's grease flying by, and the whoosh of Gisella's catlike moves.

My confidence vanishes into thin air with the realization that none of it is driving the angels back.

Then, a voice calls out from behind us. "The salt is in place!"

"Retreat!" I yell at the top of my lungs.

Everyone backs up, and one by one, we step outside.

Multiple Kessleys melt back into a single one. Then, it's only me and Gisella left. The dark figures have chosen one form as they close in on us: Charlie. A smart move, seeing he's my best friend and Gisella's boyfriend. It's hard to attack, even though we know it's not him.

However, they've miscalculated Kessley's abilities. Both Gisella and I hesitate, and my sixth ghost pulls us back and changes into a dragon the size of a small elephant. In response, the Charlies and the angels behind them charge as one.

I focus on a large wave to hit them from the side, but Kessley opens her dragon mouth and breathes fire. The nightmare Charlies shriek and roll over to extinguish the flames.

Gisella grabs my hand and pulls me out into the sun.

Kessley shrinks back into her human form and follows us outside, where Taylar pulls her close and buries his face in her bleached hair.

"That was so brave."

I don't hear her answer, because at that moment the first angel reaches the line of salt. It bounces back slightly, bares its teeth at us and tilts its head.

"Well, well, you found a way to trap us. But you forgot one thing…" The words come out as a growl and the sunlight moves away from the door. The angel stretches its darkened wings. "We are heavenly beings. Salt will not stop us."

I try to hide the sliver of worry making its way up

to my throat by folding my arms. It takes all my courage to stay where I am, about an inch from the doorway. It's a good thing Gisella and Vicky are standing beside me, or I would've stepped back for sure. If we're wrong about these lines of salt, this angel will crush me. I can see it in its dark green eyes.

A thick cloud filled with hail appears above my side of the wooden door. I'm surprised at my ability to keep the formation in the air.

Then the angel folds its wings and steps forward so sudden I flinch. Some hail escapes from the cloud above me.

It doesn't matter, though. The angel bumps into an invisible barrier and lets out a surprised yelp of pain as it bounces back.

The cloud above me dissolves. My lips twitch toward another smirk, but it's actually not that funny. These are angels, and we need to wake them up somehow.

Kessley seems to read my mind. "Use the Pearl of Arcadia."

There's a loud rumbling from behind us, followed by a squeal of rage. It sounds a bit like a lion coughing up a bone and wheezing at the same time.

"Too late," Jeep says, pushing his hat back onto his head and moving his hands, searching for any skeletons hidden under the perfect lawns around us. "The marodium are coming."

I grit my teeth. "Okay, we'll come back to save the angels later."

"Don't bother, we're fine!" the angel calls from the doorway.

I ignore him. "It's time for our plan, guys. Get ready."

Gisella turns to me, and as soon as I wrap my arms around her neck, she somersaults to the roof of the farmhouse, where I hide behind the chimney.

"Good luck," she says, and she takes off in a blur.

Meanwhile, the others have split up, too. They've scattered so fast that even I don't see them anymore.

"Okay, focus," I whisper to myself.

Even though I can't see the marodium yet, the approaching darkness above the houses tells me exactly where they are. The noise coming from the barn must have alerted them to our presence.

Now, I can only hope our plan will still work; we've got the angels and nightmare monsters to take into account as well. If the marodium manage to free them from the barn, we're in trouble.

If only there was time to use the Pearl of Arcadia

But we can't risk it falling into the wrong hands. We'll need it for the final battle.

The darkness slides toward me, fast. Heavy clouds accompany the sound of wet claws on cobblestones. Light is sucked from the streets bit by bit. Even the trees and flowers shrink back. Leaves and petals fold in on themselves, hiding from the approaching evil. The weird squealing gets louder with every passing second.

I take on a more comfortable position and stare at

the rays of sunlight in the distance.

I can do this, I can do this.

The first marodium rounds the corner and I'm so stunned by its appearance I forget what I'm supposed to do.

Although it has a humanoid body, the creature is moving on all fours. Slime covers its slick, uncovered skin. The head is big and bald, the shoulders muscular. As it pauses and stands tall to sniff the air, I get a good look at it. It has a giant mouth with teeth the size of crayons. Its nose is nothing more than two holes. It lets out a hoarse high-pitched squeal, the muscles holding its jaws together moving on the outside of its skull. The arms and legs look like they've been stretched thin. The fingers are extremely long and bony, with sharp nails at the ends. The spinal cord sticks out of its back, as if it's trying to break free.

I come to my senses when it drops back on all fours. Its arms are so long that the wide shoulders are still pointing up.

Two of its congeners join it, and I close my eyes to concentrate. First, I try to drive the image of the horrendous monsters from my mind. Once I've succeeded, I imagine sunlight breaking through the clouds, shining brightly down onto the streets and into every corner of Affection.

The marodium let out a deafening shriek as the light hits them. They scurry to the side of the nearest house to find shelter, but Gisella pulls the shadows away. Their skin hisses as they burst through the door and disappear inside.

Soon, about two dozen more come sailing around the corner. They dive in all directions, shrieking in pain and fear as the sun burns them. Grease flies through the air, blocking their way, while Kessley appears in dragon form behind them to make sure they don't flee back to the other side of town. The three iele we're here to help come soaring from my left, and with a combined arm gesture, they send the fleeing marodium back to the middle of the road. Taylar, D'Maeo, Dylan, and Maël close in on their retreating forms from the right. With danger surrounding them on all sides, the monsters are left with only two options: stay and fight us as their skin burns away or seek shelter in the house their mates have fled into.

Of course, being monsters, they choose the first option. They lift their faces to the sky and open their mouths wide. Images pour out of their throats and come to life around them. The same figures I saw in the barn, plus some new ones. They spread out and drive my friends back.

Gisella faces a dark version of herself. Jeep is forming a line of zombies between him and a bleeding woman on her knees, who resembles his wife Charlotte.

The rest of the nightmares are blocked by a huge flaming form which rises in front of me. It's taller than the house I'm standing on, and casts a threatening shadow over me. Screaming people flee to escape its giant feet, but it simply steps on them. The earth beneath splits open and flaming figures fall into a bottomless pit. In its hands, people struggle to free themselves. One by one, it squeezes them until they explode. Blood drips from its arms and legs.

Hate fills me, but I push it away, knowing it comes from the marodium.

"You're not real," I say, then conjure some wind, imagining it pulling the shape apart.

The creature dives at me and knocks me over. My feet slip from the roof, and I flail for support. The next thing I know, I'm dangling from one hand.

The nightmare leans forward, over the roof. Instead of wind, this time I use sunbeams to chase it away. Holes appear where the light hits and I fill them with wind. Soon, its whole body is swirling as mini tornados tear it apart from all sides. I imagine the wind ripping it into a thousand pieces and it explodes.

I pull myself back up and look down. On the ground, most of the nightmares have been defeated. Kessley's opponent is a tall gray man with creepy long fingers. Her grandfather, no doubt. He shouts at her, throws bombs, and keeps trying to grab Kess. Meanwhile, behind her, two marodium monsters approach.

I want to call out a warning, but Vicky and Gisella come to her rescue. With a swing of their blades, pieces of monster scatter everywhere. Taylar moves to Kessley's side and, together, they take out her nightmare.

All of a sudden, they all whirl around to face each other, hatred making their movements tight and square. A moment later they relax.

We care too much about each other for the hatred to take hold.

I watch the other marodium try to sneak up on my friends without success. More limbs are cut off, but when I narrow my eyes, I see they're growing back.

Sunlight. They need sunlight. I focus hard and the whole block becomes bathed in light.

The marodium flee into the house where the first two still hide. Taylar and Dylan create a line of salt around it, to make sure they can't escape. They meet at the front and back up slowly. Gisella moves her hands to call the shadows to her from inside the house. At first, only the faint shuffling of slick feet and claws is heard. But the more shadows Gisella pulls out, the more frantic the sound becomes. Soon, the shrieks change into bellows of pain. The dark figures inside the barn respond with howls that make my skin crawl. I can hear the frantic flapping of the angels' wings below me as they try to find a way out to help their new masters.

I'm in the middle of the thought, *Well, this worked out better than I expected,* when two more marodium slide onto the street.

CHAPTER 2

I send an extra bright ray of sunshine down on them, and they cringe.

"No!" Gisella looks up at me over her shoulder and gestures wildly at the house. "Keep focusing on the ones inside, Dante!"

As the thrashing behind the walls gets louder, I envision light seeping into every room again. Loud moans drift through the air. The smell of burning skin reaches my nose.

The two marodium monsters in the street straighten their backs and let out a shrill sound, like a tea kettle, but hoarse, as if it has a cold. They lock eyes with each other and their teeth chatter.

Is this some kind of communication?

It would appear so, because a second later they each jump in a different direction. One targets Taylar, D'Maeo, Dylan, Maël, and Kessley, who have gathered on the right side of the house. The other approaches Gisella, Charlie, Vicky, Jeep, and the iele on the left.

I try to follow the fights below while I keep the inside of the house illuminated to take out the marodium trapped in there. I expect an easy kill on the street, since the monsters are greatly outnumbered and the sun is still shining down on them. But, the naked creatures are still strong. The one on the left knocks Charlie over. He hits it in the face with a grease ball, which it shakes off without much effort. Maël swings her staff against the back of its head multiple times. It doesn't even seem to notice as the slime from its skin splatters all over the place.

"Step back," Vicky commands, and when they do, she stares at the monster until it starts to move.

At first, it's only a twitch.

The marodium opens its mouth wide enough to cover its whole face and Kessley yells, "Hurry up! It'll rip Charlie's throat out."

While I can only see the side of Vicky's face, I can tell she's concentrating hard. Her jaw is set, and her hands are balled into tight fists. She's trying to use her telekinetic powers.

The monster bends forward and Charlie screams. Then, the slick body is thrown sideways with force and I cheer inside. Jeep wastes no time aiming his hat at it. It hits the monster in the belly as it gets up again. The tattooed ghost hurries over to it and plants his foot on the rim of the hat.

Vicky sways a bit on her feet and, for a moment, I lose my focus.

Gisella notices when she turns back to the house to pull out more shadows. "Keep going, Dante."

Sun, sun, sun, sun, I think while my gaze keeps drifting back to the fights outside.

Jeep drives his hat deeper into the belly of the monster, and the iele fly over to help out the others.

Maël is doing her best to freeze the marodium in time, but it's jumping and slithering all over the place, trying to knock the weapons from the hands of my Shield members. Kess changes from one beast into another in an attempt to find something to take out the marodium. Nothing seems to work, though. Not a bear, a wolf, a lion, or a snake. Each attack, and each piece of skin cut off by Kessley's sharp claws only makes it angrier and more determined to take us all out.

Smoke starts to rise from the windows and my gaze sweeps back to the house. I imagine the light inside becoming even brighter and sweeping into every corner of the house, under the beds, and into the closets.

The squeals from behind the walls get weaker, the hissing louder. It grows until even the marodium outside pause their attacks and turn their ugly bald heads. An explosion follows, making the house shudder. All the windows shatter, the glass blown out by the force of the exploding remains of the marodium. The wind lifts the ash and carries it up into the sky.

Everyone raises their weapons in case a stray monster leaps out of a broken window or through the front door. But there's nothing left of them. They are all gone.

Gisella releases the shadows she's been collecting, and they glide back inside. Then, she joins our friends, who have surrounded the two remaining marodium while they were distracted.

Except for Vicky, whose face is turning dark. She stumbles to the side of the house and leans against the wall. I send a little sunshine over to her, in hopes of chasing the evil inside her away.

The marodium hiss viciously and my gaze swerves back to the fight. The monster with the cut in its belly is hunched over, the other one's jaw is unhinged on one side. The muscle that held it together hangs limp, the dark blood trickling from it the only sound breaking the sudden silence.

I focus all my power on the marodium in the middle of the road and increase the amount of light shining on them while I turn up the heat too.

They make that horrible, sick tea kettle noise again, shake their heads furiously, and hurl themselves at my friends.

Vicky has recovered and is able to catch one of them mid-air with her powers. Taylar takes a step forward and cuts off its head with one clean swipe of his sword. The head bounces against Kessley's legs. She changes into a dragon again and breathes fire onto it. After it has gone up in flames, she steps over to the still wriggling body and burns that too.

The one marodium still standing is squealing like a panicked hog. It slams its raw-boned claws down onto the cobbled stones, making them move. Charlie aims a grease ball at its large mouth to shut it up. When it tries to rip it away, Dylan and Taylar jump it as one, cutting away at the creature with their weapons. Slimy bits and pieces scatter everywhere and the Kessley dragon takes care of them quickly.

Vicky picks up some stray pieces with her telekinetic powers and sets them down in front of Kess. When the last of it has gone up in smoke and ash, we all let out a relieved sigh.

Vicky, Gisella, and Charlie pretty much collapse on the ground, their backs against the wall of the house.

Wondering if I can get down myself, I peer over the edge of the roof. It's freaking high.

My friends are patting each other's backs for the great job they've done. They seem to have forgotten about me.

Clearing my throat, I call down to them. "Eh, hello? Can someone get me down, please?"

No one responds, because at the same moment there's a loud crash from inside the barn.

Everyone turns around and weapons are drawn. The building shudders.

"What's happening?" Kessley cries out. A bit of leftover dragon smoke rises from her mouth.

The iele float closer to the barn and peer inside

before their leader, Soimane, replies, "The shadow shapes are dying."

"Sounds like they're fighting it," Charlie remarks.

"They are, but they cannot win." Soimane floats up to the roof of the house and smiles at me. "Would you like me to help you down?"

I let go of the chimney. "That would be great."

She takes my hand and I wonder if I should wrap my arm around her. When I try to, she moves away from me. Her eyes twinkle as I wave my arms to regain my balance. "I said I'd help you down, not take you down, Dante."

I give her a stunned look.

What is she talking about?

She tilts her head to scrutinize me when I don't move. "You do know you can use wind to lift yourself, don't you? You are a meteokinetic."

With my free hand I grab the chimney again. "You want me to try something new while I'm standing on a roof, with evil angels about to break free below us?"

"Exactly," she says, her grin growing wider. "It will give you the extra incentive you might need to pull it off." She gestures at the other two fairies watching us from the ground. "And, we're all here to catch you if you fail."

"If I fall, you mean."

Soimane shrugs, her shoulders lifting her long locks higher into the air. "Same thing."

"Just try it, babe," Vicky calls up. "They'll catch you."

Seeing her back to her benevolent self boosts my confidence.

"You really think I can do it?" I ask the iele leader in a soft whisper.

"You can do a lot more than you think. You did things today that seemed impossible before, didn't you?"

My mouth falls open. "How did you…?"

She lets out a tingling laugh. "I'm a fairy, I can sense certain things. Now, stop stalling and try it, or I'm pulling you from the roof."

I pull back my hand. "Alright, alright. Give me a sec to concentrate."

The noise from the barn is subsiding and dark smoke drifts up through the cracks in the walls. Now that their creators are gone, the nightmare creatures are dissolving. My gaze follows their remains as they are picked up by the wind.

Pictures of my body being carried off the roof by a breeze formed like a snow board fill my head. Something pulls at my legs, and I rise a couple of inches. Immediately, I start swaying back and forth.

"Trust in your own power," Soimane says. "You can easily create enough wind to carry you."

She's right, I can do this. All I need is… I nearly topple backward, *more wind. A bit to support my back and a bit in front of me. Like a Segway with extra support.*

The air moving around me gives me a gentle push against my back and touches my hands. Standing tall again, I wrap my hands around an invisible edge.

Then, I picture myself floating down to the ground.

"That's it," Vicky calls out. "You got it."

As soon as I smile at her I lose the image of the Segway made of wind. There's nothing for me to stand on anymore.

"Keep your focus," Soimane says close to my ear.

The ground comes closer at frightening speed. *Wind, catch me!* I yell inside my head, and I squeeze my eyes shut.

There's a loud whoosh. Something grabs me and puts me safely on the ground.

When my eyes open, the other two fairies are smiling at me.

"Thanks," I breathe out, trembling a bit.

"No need to thank us," Sfinte says in a bright tone. "You did that all on your own."

Before I can respond, Vicky almost pushes me over in her enthusiasm. She smothers me with kisses. "That was great, Dante. I didn't know you could do that."

Confused, I shake my head. "I didn't do anything."

She gives me a playful shove against my shoulder. "Sure you did, silly. No one caught you. We all saw it. You saved yourself."

"But I didn't have time to build an image in my head."

Soimane hovers closer to me. "You did do something else, didn't you?"

I scratch my chin. "I'm not sure… I panicked, so…"

"You gave the wind an order," the iele leader finishes my sentence.

My eyes narrow, as I try to remember what my exact thoughts were. Then, I shoot her a wide-eyed look. "You're right, I did. Are you saying that will work, too?"

"With things that already exist around you, sure. Other things you will have to imagine before they will do your bidding."

Vicky pats my cheek. "This is good news. You'll be able to respond much faster, and if you control the wind, you can pick up things and—"

"Throw them at our enemies," I finish. Then, I turn to Soimane. "You knew I could do this?"

"I did when you used your powers on the marodium. That's when I knew you could do more."

"Thank you for teaching me," I say with a bow.

"You are welcome. Thank you all for helping us free our town from these monsters."

D'Maeo gestures at the barn behind me. "We're not done yet."

We make for the doorway and peer inside. The angels have gathered in the middle of the barn where they've formed a circle, their wings touching and their hands outstretched in front of them, as if they are doing a group cheer before a game.

"We should use the pearl," Jeep suggests.

Maël nods. Her golden headpiece reflects the sun that is now shining without my help. "I agree. We cannot leave these angels here and risk them escaping."

"We can keep an eye on them, if you like," Soimane offers. "The marodium's influence will probably wear off after a while."

I tap my chin in thought. "What if one of them escapes? Do we really want to risk that?"

"They might tell Satan about Vicky's new powers and your new skills," Taylar says.

"Exactly." My unease about these angels grows with the darkness that's building up around them. We need to make a decision soon.

"We're also not sure the pearl will work at all," Dylan adds rubbing his thick eyebrows. "I mean… not that I question your premonition about it, but there might be some kind of activation we don't know about yet."

The wooden beams groan in protest as the darkness reaches the ceiling. The sound takes away the last of my doubts.

"Okay, we'll do it."

I reach into Vicky's pocket beside me and pull out the Pearl of Arcadia. Although I try to recall Quinn's actions, all I remember is him releasing the relic into the air, as if it were a wounded bird nursed back to health. I mimic his gesture and the pearl floats up. To my relief, it stays on our side of the salt line.

It starts to turn so fast it soon becomes a blur. A pulsing halo of white light forms around it. Its warmth touches my face, and the angels stop moving. They cock their heads, listening intently.

My gaze flicks back and forth between them and the pearl. Slowly, they lower their arms and fold in their wings. One of them shakes his head, as if to get rid of something. With every shake, more of the darkness falls from him. Light seeps back into his wings and creeps up to his face. The others follow fast, some shaking their whole bodies violently with disgusted looks on their faces.

"It's working," Kessley whispers from behind me.

"Let's not jump to conclusions," Jeep grumbles. "They could be trying to fool us."

Gisella leans against the open door. "That's easy enough to test." She gestures at the line of salt at her feet. "If they can step outside, they're good, and if they can't, they're bad."

No one can argue with her logic, so we wait for the angels to come to their senses.

The Pearl of Arcadia stops turning, and I grab it and put it back into Vicky's endless pocket before the relic drops to the ground.

The angel I faced earlier takes the lead again. He looks quite different. The retreating darkness has revealed a thick, brown, trimmed yet full beard. His skin is bronze-colored, and dark-brown hair touches his shoulders. Heavy eyebrows emphasize his now kind light-green eyes. He's strikingly handsome, just like Quinn, or any other angel. My best guess would be that he is somewhere in his late twenties, counted in human years. His expression is soft now, but I'm still on guard.

He stops in front of me, and his smile literally lights up his entire face. "Dante. We are grateful you took the time to free us. Your help will make a big difference in our fight against our fallen brother." He bows. "My name is Mumiah, angel of rebirth."

Without responding, I take a step back to give him room.

He chuckles, a weird low sound with a high tingle in it. "You've grown a bit suspicious. I can't blame you, and it's good to be cautious in these times. You have nothing to fear from us anymore, however."

With that, Mumiah steps over the salt line and into the sun. His brothers follow, then bow before me, one by one.

Before turning to face their leader, I bow back.

"Are there any more angels that we can free, Mumiah?" I ask.

Sorrow falls over his face. "Many angels went missing before we were lured here. We do not know where they were taken, or by whom. Countless evil creatures have chosen Lucifer's side, some because they want power, some out of fear. But, together, we will defeat them all."

He holds out both hands, which I take. Warmth floods through me and my vision becomes lighter. My thoughts clear and the weight of the battle that's drawing near is taken away for a second.

There's nothing but faith and peace in Mumiah's eyes.

My jaw sets in determination. "We'll be ready."

One corner of his mouth moves up.

Can he pick up on my doubts and fears?

He bends closer to me and lowers his voice so only I can hear him say, "Fear and doubt have a purpose. Don't forget that."

I smile back. "I'll try."

CHAPTER 3

"Be careful," I say to the group of angels.

"And please don't get kidnapped again," Jeep adds.

Mumiah laughs. "We'll do our best. Take care of yourselves." And with that, they vanish in a bright light.

The iele shield their faces while the rest of us gape at the beauty of the lingering shapes in the air. Thanks to the divine light Mona fed us, we can now see angels, no matter what form they're in. Also, the light doesn't blind us anymore. It only leaves us breathless.

Vicky leans against my chest. "I wish everything in the world was this beautiful."

"Me too." I plant a kiss on her temple. "But, I'm sure we'll see more of it soon." After a short hesitation, I add, "Are you okay?"

"Fine."

"Are you sure? I saw what happened during the

fight."

"I got tired, that's all."

Relief washes over me. I stroke her cheek before I turn to the iele. "We need to get back; we've got a lot to do. I hope you can guide the rest of your people back onto the right path."

Soimane sends me a radiant smile. "Thank you, Dante. With Affection back in our hands, I am sure it will work out fine."

Everyone says goodbye, and we hurry back to the entrance, where trees of illusion no longer block our way. From all sides, flocks of birds fly into the town, and butterflies burst out of holes in the trees. All the flowers around us seem brighter and the roads cleaner. Bunnies and squirrels frolic around the lawns of the empty houses.

"Look at that." Kessley sighs. "Everything is blooming again."

A sigh escapes me as well. "I could watch this all day."

"But we can't," Jeep says. "We need to start our final preparations."

With an even deeper sigh I follow him back to the cars.

Darkwood Manor looks cold and boring compared to Affection, but I'm still relieved to be back home.

Mom looks better; not so skinny anymore and she has a bit of color on her cheeks. She seems excited to get started, so at least one of us is confident the transfer of Charlotte's powers will work.

While the others fill Mom and Mona in on what happened in Affection, I take another look at the ingredients needed for the transfer spell, and read the words one last time.

Turning to Vicky, I ask, "Shall we go and put everything in place?"

She shakes her head. "I need to rest a bit."

I take her in from head to toe. She might be a bit more transparent than usual, and her eyes flit across the room uneasily. When I caress her arm, she flinches. With gritted teeth, I pull back.

"Sorry," she whispers. "It's not the darkness, and it wasn't before. I'm just really tired. I'll hand you the herbs before I go to bed. You'll be fine on your own."

With that, she stands up and walks out of the kitchen, and into the annex.

My heartbeat quickens. I try to tell myself there's nothing to it. She's tired, which isn't hard to believe. What worries me, is that this normally wouldn't stop her from helping me. She knows her presence helps me focus and gives me confidence. She always stays with me, even when I tell her it's fine to leave. And now…

Was she lying about the evil inside her? Did my spell to remove Beelzebub's influence not work? Or was it my fear of failure that showed me her dark face in Affection? Is there another problem? Did I do or say something wrong? Is her love for me fading, or…?

I sit up straight.

She's creating distance between us because she knows she'll need to move on soon. She probably thinks it will hurt us less if we aren't so close anymore. But, she's wrong. If our final days together have come, I want to enjoy the time we have left as much as I can.

I push back my chair and hurry into the annex. Vicky comes out and almost bumps into me.

"Oops, sorry." She glances up, shoots me a faint smile, and brushes past me.

"Hang on," I say before she's at the top of the stairs.

She stops and throws me an innocent look. "What is it?"

As I move halfway up the stairs, I try to take her hand, which she deliberately keeps out of reach. "Listen. I know what you're trying to do, but… don't. Okay?" My voice trembles a bit. "We need each other more than ever now. And we're not at the end yet. So…" This time, she lets me take her hand. I rub her warm skin and a buzz goes through me, as always. "Let's enjoy our moments together as long as we still have them."

Vicky stares at me without moving or speaking. Then, she presses her hand onto mine. "I need to rest now, but after that, I'll be at your side again."

She pulls herself free and climbs the rest of the stairs. At the end she turns left instead of right, toward her own room, which she hasn't used since… well, a long time.

My heart sinks. Quinn said we don't have much time left before the final battle. Casting that spell to get Beelzebub out of Vicky's head took some time. Defeating the marodium and freeing the captured angels cost us even more time. Letting myself get distracted by Vicky's behavior might be the last thing I ever do. I owe it to my friends, to Mom and Mona and the whole world, to focus on our battle. Vicky will come around. And if she doesn't…

I turn around abruptly, refusing to even think about that possibility.

All the herbs I need are on the floor of the annex, ready for me to grab.

Once this is all over, I'm going shopping for more furniture.

In my head, the picture of a giant couch in front of a huge television forms. But when I imagine who will be sitting on the couch with me, I shake my head and clench my jaw so hard it hurts.

No more thinking about this. I need to focus on our mission. And after that… who knows what will happen.

Assuming a cross-legged position, I place my Book of Spells next to me. After a quick read-through of the instructions I wrote down earlier, I mix the herbs together. Then, I light a match and throw it into the bowl. The small explosion it creates almost makes me drop everything. The smell of burning feces mixed with rotten eggs rises up, and I hold the bowl at arm's length while turning my head the other way.

A second later there's a bit of commotion in the

kitchen. Chairs slide across the floor, curses drift toward me, and someone opens the back door.

Mona is the only one brave enough to stick her head around the doorpost of the annex. "You've mixed something you shouldn't have, Dante." She covers her nose and mouth with her arm. "Do you need help?"

Her eyes tell me she's hoping for a negative answer.

With a cough I put the bowl down. "Some help would be great. I don't know what went wrong."

Mona steps inside and pushes the bowl a bit farther away from us. "Let me see what you put together."

She scans the lines when I hand her my notebook. "Nothing wrong with this, as far as I can see." With a frown she checks out the herbs in front of me. "Hang on." She picks up a sachet containing blue-purple petals, and opens it. The smell of sweet flowers drowns out the horrid stench for a second, and I breathe it in gratefully.

"Agueweed," Mona whispers before sliding it back into the sachet.

"What's that? It's not on my list, is it?"

Mona clutches the sachet. "No, it's not."

She stares through the windows for quite some time, a wrinkle messing up the perfect smooth skin of her forehead.

I'm afraid to ask her what this means, because, deep inside, I already know the answer.

Finally, Mona wakes from her pensive state. She studies the sachet in her hand, then throws it in the air, where it vanishes in an instant. "You need to start again."

"Yes, I deduced that on my own," I say, getting impatient. "What I'd like to know is, what does that agueweed do, and how did you know it was in the mixture?"

Mona starts pacing. "If a mixture creates a bad smell like this, it means there's a herb or plant in it that is used for evil. Something that doesn't belong in a benevolent spell." She presses her temples. "Agueweed causes severe confusion when used on your enemies. It is very powerful."

"That doesn't sound so wrong. We could use confusion." I search for something to cover the bowl with, since the stench is still rising from it, filling up the annex, and making me nauseous. I can't find anything, so I rip a page from Dad's notebook and place that over it. The fuming stops and I look up at Mona.

She stands still and eyes the rest of the herbs. "I agree that the effects of some black magic herbs and plants can be useful, but it doesn't make them benevolent. They will screw up your spell."

"Is agueweed always bad?" I ask, hoping against better judgment that she'll say no.

"Yes, just like absinth, betel nut, and twitch's grass, to name a few." Then, she voices my exact thoughts. "So, why did Vicky have this in her pocket? Is there a chance she didn't know it was evil?"

I bite my lip. Of course, I want to say yes, but that would be a lie. "No. Vicky's knowledge of herbs, spices, and plants, and their uses in spells, is extensive."

"She could have mistaken the agueweed for something else," Mona offers.

My lips turn up in a grateful smile. "Yes, but that's a bit of a stretch, isn't it? I've never seen her make a mistake in any spell. She knows what she's doing, and she must have known what this was when she purchased it. She also must have put it here on purpose."

Mona's shoulders sag. "Which can only mean one thing."

She pretended to be tired, and I fell for it. I made up an excuse for her behavior because that felt better than accepting the truth.

"She's still under Beelzebub's influence," we say in unison.

"Vicky's not cured?" Jeep's startled voice says from the doorway. His nose wrinkles and he waves his hand in front of his face. "Did she cause this awful smell?"

Unable to sit still any longer I bolt to my feet. "Yes. So, we need to come up with another way to free her. My spell obviously didn't work."

Mona's hand touches my shoulder. "It did, Dante, but Beelzebub is strong. Your spell has been fighting his power inside Vicky. It held up for a while, but," she shrugs, "he's one of the most powerful evil beings alive. I guess we should've known it wouldn't hold forever."

I wipe a tear from my eye. I don't want them to see the despair this awakens inside me. "What about Vicky? She's powerful, too. She's the great-great-granddaughter of the Devil, for crying out loud! She must be able to fight off the power of his right hand."

Mona places a finger against her lips. "Shh, keep your voice down. What if she hears you?"

My eyelids slide closed for a second. "You think she would hurt us?"

Pity falls over her face. "She tried to sabotage your spell, Dante. Beelzebub's hold on her is getting stronger. We need to come up with a plan before it's too late."

"Too late?" I gulp. "You think she will die? Or, I mean… move on, get vanquished… whatever you call it when someone is already dead."

Mona looks to Jeep for help.

My heart sinks. I can't believe we've gotten to a point where the truth is so harsh even Mona is afraid to say it out loud.

Jeep clears his throat, but his voice is still hoarse. "I think what Mona is trying to say is that…" he takes a deep breath before he rips my heart farther apart, "Beelzebub's influence is feeding the darkness inside her. It's making the side of her that is connected to Satan, the parts she inherited from him, bigger and stronger. Once his influence on her reaches its peak, she will turn against us... and fight at her great-great-grandfather's side."

CHAPTER 4

The next couple of minutes I spent bent over, gasping for air. Even Mona's sparks don't help much. No matter what I do—squeeze my eyes shut, open them wide, try to speak, even hold onto Mom, who comes rushing to my side—the images keep coming. Images of Vicky kissing me and then pushing her sword through my heart. Of her standing next to the Devil with a menacing grin and glowing red eyes. Of the whole world burning, and all my loved ones turning into ash before me.

It's too much. Vicky was our best hope of trapping Lucifer underneath the circles of Hell again. With her against us instead of with us, we're lost.

My vision starts to blur, and my body tilts to the side. Then, everything goes dark.

"Dante? Babe?"

I keep my eyes closed. I know this is a dream because Vicky is no longer on our side. Which makes me want to cherish this moment so much more.

My hands carefully reach out. The soft skin of her face sends a jolt of sorrow and happiness through me. The feeling is so confusing, that a cross between a sob and a laugh escapes my lips.

"It's okay. I'm not lost yet," she whispers in my ear.

Her words tickle and intensify my longing for her. When I pull her close and feel her lips brush against mine, there's an uncomfortable cough and a lot of shuffling nearby.

Reluctantly, I open my eyes.

And find everyone staring at me.

Jeep, who was the one coughing, has raised an eyebrow, Mom and Dylan are looking the other way, and Kessley, Mona, and Charlie have content smiles plastered on their faces. The other expressions are a mixture of worry and affection.

Once I realize I'm still sitting on the floor in the annex, I push Vicky away from me. Reality hits me like Thor's hammer in full flight. "You've betrayed us!"

Vicky regains her balance and stares at the worn floorboards. Her shoulders are slumped and pain seeps through her words when she speaks again. "I did, and I'm so sorry. I've been fighting Beelzebub's powers, but he got the upper hand for a minute."

I cross my arms over my chest before they reach

out to her on instinct. "Why didn't you tell me before it got out of hand?"

She presses the sides of her nose and my urge to hug her gets stronger.

"I wanted to, but the darkness inside me stopped me. I only woke from my…" she pauses to search for the right word, "possessed state when I came down and saw you lying on the floor unconscious."

"She threw herself at you, so we blocked her way," Mona explains. "We were afraid she wanted to kill you. It's a good thing Vicky isn't the only one here who can sense things."

My gaze flicks to the ghost queen, who is leaning on her staff, watching things unfold as if we are part of a theatrical play. "As soon as I looked at Vicky, I knew she was herself again."

D'Maeo grabs Mona's hand and smiles. "I think the love between you two chased away the darkness."

"That won't last forever," Jeep says.

"I agree. We need a new plan, and fast." the fairy godmother touches Vicky's arm soothingly and sparks jump against Vicky's cheek.

"That helps." Vicky closes her eyes and takes a deep breath as her skin absorbs the sparks.

Mona's eyebrows shoot up. "It does?"

Vicky nods. The glow leaves her face and her shoulders sag again. "But, only for a while."

Mona slams her hands together hard, startling all of us. "That's okay. I think I have an idea." She vanishes in a cloud of light.

I push myself to my feet and approach Vicky carefully.

She shoots me a remorseful look, and I wrap my arms around her.

"Are you really you again?" I whisper.

"For now. Yes." She sighs, and a tear makes its way down my neck.

I pull back and wipe the wet drops from her eyes.

"I'm so sorry," she repeats. "You told me not to approach Beelzebub. I endangered all of you, our mission, and with that, the lives of every human and angel. I never knew I could be so stupid."

"Hey." I put my finger under her chin and lift her face. "Don't beat yourself up about it. You tried to do the right thing. This time I was right, but it would have been just as easy for me to be wrong. It was a brave thing to do." I kiss her before she has the chance to respond.

Jeep coughs again, not so subtle this time. "I love the whole kiss and make-up routine, but Vicky is still dangerous to us. Until Mona gets back with some miracle cure, we need to make sure Vicky isn't able to sabotage us anymore."

Vicky throws up her arms in defeat. "Just cast a spell to lock me inside a circle or something."

I wipe a stray tear from her cheek. "I could, but will that be enough? After all, the power of Satan's strongest warrior is inside you."

"Good point." She slumps to the ground in utter defeat. "I never thought I would be one of our greatest threats."

There's no arguing with that, so instead I sit down next to her and hold her tight until she relaxes.

"We'll figure something out," I promise her.

She smiles and lets me help her up.

Mona returns with a wide smile which gives me hope. "I've got a plan."

Vicky grabs her head and sways on her feet. "You'd better hurry up. His grip is getting stronger again."

While I hold her up, Jeep rushes to her other side. His face is a mask of worry.

"We can't take any risks," he says. "Can you cast a spell on her to make sure she can't hurt any of us?" He holds up his free hand when I open my mouth to protest. "Even if it only works temporarily, it could prevent a disaster."

"He's right," Vicky pants, her eyes half closed. "Do it. Quick."

D'Maeo takes my place holding Vicky and I walk over to the other side of the annex to prevent myself from mixing up ingredients, since the ones for the power transfer spell are still on the floor.

My mind whirs with all the things I could possibly need. Normally, Vicky is here to help me, but it's obvious I can't trust her for that anymore.

I squeeze my eyes shut and try to remember the function of all the different candle colors, and all the different herbs and spices.

The pressure is too much. My mind won't

cooperate.

When I open my eyes to tell the others, Maël's voice right beside me startles me. "You can do it. You have written spells on your own before. You do not need anyone's help. Have faith in yourself."

I nod and try to pull myself together.

No more doom scenarios. Vicky is not the only powerful one here. We can cure her.

Gisella positions herself behind Vicky, who is starting to struggle against Jeep and D'Maeo's hold. "Tell me what you need."

The ingredients pop into my head and Gisella pulls them out of Vicky's endless pocket one by one. Before I get to the candles, Vicky loses it completely.

She goes invisible, apparates away from us, and uses her newfound powers to send the armchair flying. I duck to avoid it, and it hits the wall to the study, leaving four holes where the legs go through.

"Grab her!" I call out.

Of course, that's easier said than done. A ghost that has a lot of experience with going invisible, is hard to catch.

My whole Shield, plus Dylan, is blinking in and out of sight. They return with all kinds of weapons, while Vicky is picking up the ingredients in front of me and throwing them around the room.

I try to hit her with lightning, but keep missing, because she vanishes before I can even move my hand. My heartrate is going haywire, and thoughts bounce around my head as if they're on a trampoline.

I'm losing her. She'll kill us all. We can't stop her. We're already too late. I should never have…

Taylar returns with two bottles in his hands. He stands still in the middle of the annex and waits for Vicky to show herself again. As soon as she reappears, he throws the contents of one of the bottles at her.

Vicky cries out in pain as steam rises from her skin. She drops down on the floor, back in solid form.

Taylar steps up to her and holds the second bottle over her head. "Stay still, or I'm emptying this over your head. It won't be pleasant."

Kessley hurries over to him and takes the first, now half-full bottle from him, positioning herself at Vicky's other side.

"What's in it?" she asks Taylar.

"Holy water."

Kessley's eyes grow wide. "No way! That worked on her?"

Gisella picks up the stray packets and bottles of herbs. "Well, what are you waiting for?" she spits at me. "You need to hurry."

Warmth creeps from my neck into my face. "Right. Sorry."

I sweep the scattered salt into a large circle around Vicky, Taylar, Kessley, and myself, and place the candles in their appropriate places. Two yellow – for protection – and two black, for banishment.

I glance at Vicky. She's eyeing Taylar like she's pondering a way to take the bottle away from him.

It's a good thing Kessley is standing on her other side, or she could've shoved him out of reach without moving.

"Go on." Gisella pushes some sachets into my hands. "No time to waste, Dante."

I try to block out everything and especially everyone around me. I tell myself I'm alone here, and I can do this at my own pace.

My heartrate drops back to normal and the heavy clouds in my head fall apart.

Mona hands me a clean bowl, which I throw everything into that I need. Agrimony oil for banishment, holy thistle to break unwanted connections, blackthorn berries to ward off negative spirits, and crunched acorn for personal power and to strengthen the protection some more.

Once I've mixed them all up, and everything smells good, I light an incense stick which I grab from Vicky's pocket. It will help me strengthen her self-control. She wriggles under my touch, and makes guttural sounds, which I ignore.

"Keep fighting, Vicky," Jeep tells her from a safe distance.

A low sort of gurgling sound which could be meant as a growl answers him.

"I'm… try… ing," she says in that low voice that has scared me before.

"Don't give up," Jeep continues. "You're strong, you can beat him."

"I'm not… so… s-sure."

While I walk around Vicky, inside the salt circle, and cover her with incense smoke, Jeep moves closer and grabs her hand. "I am sure. Trust yourself and your new powers. The good inside you will always win. I know it. I know *you*."

Hidden behind the determination in his voice, I can hear sadness. He's not sure at all that she'll be able to beat this. But his words will help her anyway. And so far, she hasn't shaken him off or growled at him.

I reach the spot where I started and place the incense stick into an empty bottle. With the herbs in one hand and a lit match in the other, I start again. I light each candle and spread the herbs over our heads, citing the words of my spell:

"Beelzebub's powers, hear me now.
To my command you will bow.
Your hold on Vicky will be broken,
as soon as all these words are spoken.
Full control she will regain,
of her body, soul, and brain."

Jeep lets go when she starts to tremble violently.

"It doesn't… want to… leave," Vicky says, her teeth chattering.

"Well, too bad, it has to," I counter.

I make another round, sprinkle the last of the herb mixture onto Vicky, and say the words again.

This time, the candle flames are blown out. Vicky

stops moving and Jeep catches her as she slides sideways.

I set down the bowl, put out the incense stick, and kneel beside them. "Babe, can you hear me?"

She hums a little. Her voice is back to normal.

"Did it work?" Charlie asks.

I look up at him and the others, all of whom are watching us with worried expressions. "I think it worked a bit, just like my last spell. Like I said, Beelzebub is too powerful for me to take on alone." I caress Vicky's cheek. "I didn't see any darkness leaving her body or evaporating, so I probably only sent it to the back of her mind."

D'Maeo starts pacing, rubbing his gray beard. "It's laying low, waiting for another chance to take over, just like the Black Void did inside me."

Mona grabs his free hand when he passes her and forces him to a halt. "That's fine. I can work with that. Don't worry."

Vicky works herself to her feet, and I hurry to get up too. Even though she seems steady now, I hold onto her. Jeep also stays close, just as worried.

"I'm okay now," Vicky says. "You suppressed his influence."

I press my lips on her cheek for a couple of seconds, thanking God, Heaven, and the whole universe that she's still with us, and in one piece. "Good. How fast can you execute your plan, Mona?"

"Right now." She beckons us all closer. "I will transport you all to Affection, where the iele and my fairy godmother friends are waiting to help us. I'm not used to taking several people at once, so I want to ask you all to touch me. That makes it easier for me."

"Can't you just take Vicky?" Kessley asks.

The fairy godmother shakes her head. "If something goes wrong, we could use some backup."

"You mean if Vicky goes ballistic," Charlie says, raising his eyebrows.

Mona sends him a wry smile. "Yes, Charles, that's what I meant. But I'm trying not to scare anyone."

"My bad." He brings his hand to his mouth and zips his lips closed.

I shiver at the thought that Mona thinks Vicky is strong enough to take out the iele and a bunch of fairy godmothers on her own. Normally, this information would make me happy, but now that Beelzebub has got his claws into my girl, that immense power could turn against us at any second.

We gather around Mona, who is holding Vicky tightly against her chest, as if she's afraid she'll make a run for it at the last second. Which is a real possibility. Once everyone is touching her, she lights up, and her yellow sparks spread around us. They envelope me, until I can't see anything anymore. My feet are lifted from the floor. I close my eyes and search for support with my other hand. I find a cape, Maël's, and hold onto it.

From a distance I hear Mom's voice, calling out, "Good luck! Be careful!"

Only now do I realize she'll be staying at

Darkwood Manor alone. And even though, thanks to Mona, no one with evil intentions will be able to find the mansion, an invisible, cold hand wraps around my heart.

Someone should've stayed with her.

It's too late to stop now, though. The annex is already no more than a vague collection of blurry lines and colors. Before I can even open my mouth to call out a "Wait!" we start turning at dazzling speed. Everything goes quiet and I feel as light as a feather. I throw my head back and enjoy the warm wind blowing against my cheeks. It's like sitting in a speedboat on a sunny day, but without the noise of the engine or the wind, and without the bouncing on the waves. I don't think I've ever experienced something so peaceful.

It ends just as fast as it began. Sounds start to trickle in, and my feet touch solid ground. The warmth leaves me as I open my eyes. We're back in Affection, standing next to the barn where we freed the angels.

CHAPTER 5

"Welcome back," Soimane, the iele leader, greets us, floating between her sisters on our right.

I greet them with a bow, which they answer. "Thanks for helping us."

"We are helping ourselves as much as you." She gestures at Vicky. "We need to make sure the Devil's great-great-granddaughter uses her powers to save Earth, not destroy it."

"Agreed," Vicky says.

It's only when I turn my head to look at her that I see the cluster of fairy godmothers behind her. I recognize some of them as the ones who helped us before, but there are also unfamiliar faces. However, there is no time for introductions, and I'm glad to see Mona knows this, too. She is still holding onto Vicky. Together they walk onto the abandoned road.

As far as I can see, the town of Affection is still

deserted, apart from Soimane, Sfinte, and Mandre. I suppose it takes time to convince the rest of the iele to return home. And now, we've come to delay their reunion.

Maël touches my arm. "It is their own choice to help us. With it, they also help themselves. They want this century-old battle to end as much as we do."

I give her a grateful nod.

Mona puts Vicky in the middle of the empty street and steps back. The other fairy godmothers gather around her, and the iele drift upward until they hover above Vicky's head.

As one, the fairy godmothers stretch their arms toward her. Vicky grabs her head. The godmothers shower her with sparks in ten different colors, which spread over her body like a rainbow blanket. She lets go of her head. Her tight shoulders drop back to their normal height. The three iele lock hands above Vicky's head and start to chant incomprehensible words. They sound lovely, with soft tones and timbre. I almost close my eyes to enjoy it only using my sense of hearing. To let it flow through me while everything else around me fades to the background.

I don't, though, because I need to react in an instant if something goes wrong.

The sparks are bouncing all over Vicky, but the iele's words don't seem to do anything.

Until I see a vague shift in the air. A vibration similar to what happens in a puddle of water when something heavy is dropped next to it. Slowly, it makes its way down to where Vicky is sitting, and slides through her like the hand of a ghost.

Vicky doubles over and places her hands on the ground for support. Her whole body is straining against the force of all the love and healing hitting her.

The iele's chanting gets louder and Vicky covers her ears. A low moan escapes her lips as she drops onto her side.

"Is this supposed to happen?" I ask, commanding my feet to stay still.

Maël replies without a hint of worry in her voice. "The darkness inside her is fighting."

Vicky's moaning changes into a rapidly rising "No!" as she pushes herself into a straight position bit by bit. Rage takes over her face and her skin becomes darker as she shakes off the last sparks clinging to it.

"Hit her again!" Mona yells.

Another shower of sparks soars toward Vicky. Before it hits her, she starts turning, fast. The flashes of her face I can see make me sick with worry. *This isn't helping, it's only making it worse.*

With a murderous stare she sends the sparks hurtling back at the fairy godmothers, who stumble to stay upright. Once they've all regained their balance, they gather their sparks into big balls in the palms of their hands.

The iele intensify their attack. The air wobbles wildly between them and Vicky, as if the weight that caused the trembling before is now creating stormy waves. They hit Vicky hard, and she stops turning. She looks up to use her powers on the hovering fairies when the balls of light from the godmothers hit her. Soon she's back on her knees, struggling to get rid of all the love and healing crawling over and inside her. She coughs, and sparks fly from her mouth. Then, she lets out a string of curses I've never heard her use before. She claws at her skin while black smoke escapes her ears. It dives at the iele and wraps around them. The waves in the air come to a halt as the fairies try to fight the smoke off.

"We need more healing power!" Mona exclaims as several balls of sparks miss their target. She looks drained, her face pale and her legs wobbling. D'Maeo steps forward to support her, but she holds out her hand to stop him. "I'll go see if I can find more fairy godmothers to aid us."

"No, wait. I think I can help." Gisella steps forward, much to Charlie's horror, judging by his wide-open eyes.

Sfinte and Mandre keep chanting and sending waves of love and healing down. Vicky has a hard time blocking them, but still manages to avoid several balls of sparks. They hit the road and pavement, and flowers spring up in the colors of the sparks like rockets.

"You can heal?" Soimane asks Gisella.

"I can. And I can try to use the evil powers within me to pull Beelzebub's darkness out of her."

The iele leader is not convinced. A frown taints

her beautiful face. "Can you do that at the same time?"

"I can try."

Mona wipes some sweat from her forehead. "Good enough for me."

She moves aside to make room for the werecat-witch, who takes her place in the circle and starts to pull shadows toward her. The darkness underneath the trees and at the side of the houses respond eagerly. They grab Vicky's head and force it down, making it impossible for her to move anything with her eyes. One sliver of shadow slides into Vicky's ear.

I shiver; it looks creepy and painful.

Vicky moans and struggles against the shadows holding her down. Soon, she's covered in them from the ground up to her shoulders.

"Let go of me," she growls. "You'll regret this. You all will!"

The iele chant a little louder, and the fairy grandmothers throw another load of sparks onto her.

Gisella keeps sending shadows to hold Vicky down by waving her left hand. Meanwhile, her right hand moves slower and makes more of a wriggling motion. I'm not sure what that hand is doing until the sliver crawls back out of Vicky's ear, pulling along a swirl of the darkest smoke I've ever seen. It doesn't even resemble smoke anymore, it's more like a mixture of mud and oil. And the noise it makes… my skin tightens around my bones at the sound of it. A piercing sort of wailing, almost like a siren. Gisella's shadows release Vicky and wrap around the wailing smoke until the sound is finally muffled. Vicky falls onto her side, and Gisella rushes forward. She puts her right hand on Vicky's temple while the other keeps telling the shadows to squash the smoke.

My muscles tense when Vicky no longer moves.

Did they kill her? Did they accidentally go too far and send her to Heaven, or even farther away from me?

Maël's hand on my arm makes me realize I'm almost hyperventilating.

"She will be fine. Gisella removed Beelzebub's influence," the ghost queen says as calm as ever.

I'm afraid to answer, because I'm not so sure. Yes, some of his influence was pulled out of her, but was that all? And did it do any damage inside her? Will she still be Vicky when she wakes up? *If* she wakes up.

I turn away from the scene as Vicky's head starts to go invisible. I've seen Gisella work her healing magic before, but on other parts of the body. That time she made my leg "disappear" it was scary, but this sight makes me sick. It's my worst nightmare come true. Even if I know this is the way her power works.

Jeep chuckles beside me. "She would've been a great addition to the circus I was in."

I feel like punching him, but I know he means well.

After several seconds he nudges me. "You can look again."

When I do, Vicky's head hasn't fully returned yet.

The back and sides are complete, as far as I can tell, but her face is only half formed. However, it doesn't look creepy anymore, more like a digital painting getting filled in bit by bit. An invisible brush paints the soft lines of her lips, then her perfect nose and her eyes, filling them up with piercing blue. Only blue. No trace of darkness inside them. She looks relaxed, peaceful. And one hundred percent herself.

I can't wait any longer, and rush over to her. Gisella steps aside to give us some room and even though I can feel everyone watching us, I press Vicky against me like a lifebuoy.

After about a minute and a half she mumbles something, and I loosen my grip on her.

"What?"

"You're smothering me."

I pull her face against my chest and chuckle. "That's impossible. You don't need to breathe anymore."

She punches my shoulder and I release her. After a short stare down, she bends closer and kisses me on the lips. "I love you."

Pain shoots through me as my heart contracts. "I love you too."

After pushing myself to my feet, I hold out my hand to help her up. She lets me, even though I know she doesn't need it. She looks completely reinvigorated.

Jeep steps up to us and gives Vicky a hug. "I'm glad you're back."

"Me too," she says, giving his hat a playful tap, so it tumbles from his head.

He catches it and smiles, but his serious expression returns instantly. "Do you still have your powers?"

I suck in my breath; I hadn't thought of that yet.

Are the powers she inherited from Lucifer still inside her? Or did they cure her a little too well?

Vicky turns in all directions, searching for something.

Jeep understands what she's looking for before I do. "There are lots of things to throw around in the barn."

Without answering she makes a beeline for the barn where we found the captured angels earlier. She opens the door and stops in the doorway. Everyone gathers behind her to see what will happen next. The fairy godmothers are whispering anxiously and even the iele, hovering above us, seem restless, their hair bouncing around their heads with jerky movements instead of flowing with ease.

Vicky stands motionless in the doorway for a moment before balling her hands into fists. When everything inside the barn remains still, my heart goes into overdrive.

We've lost our best weapon. What are we going to do if we can't create new circles to trap Satan under?

The longer nothing happens, the more nervous everyone is getting. By now, the iele's hair has gone crazy, flapping wildly around their faces. The fairy godmothers have ceased their whispering and are all holding hands. Jeep is fidgeting with his hat. Maël is turning her staff in her hand over and over, creating a hole in the driveway. Charlie is unwrapping chocolate bars at an alarming rate, even for him, and Taylar is rubbing dirt from his shield with such viciousness that I'm afraid he'll push through the material. All the while Kessley is wringing her hands, and mumbling, "Come on, come on, come on". Dylan has started pacing behind us, stopping every few seconds to glance over our shoulders.

The only relaxed person here is Gisella. Our eyes meet and she throws me a lazy smile. *Don't worry,* her expression tells me.

I try not to, but there's still no movement inside the barn.

Then, Vicky lets out a cross between a groan and a yell, and all hell breaks loose. Instead of one thing being thrown around the barn, *everything* is lifted and tossed around.

There's gasping all around me and even Maël, who's not easily impressed, is watching wide-eyed. Charlie drops his chocolate and Kessley's mouth falls open. Even the iele's hair and dresses stop moving.

Gisella winks at me, as if to say, *See? I told you she's fine.*

I'm not sure this is what I would call fine, but at least Vicky's ancestral powers aren't lost.

Remembering our encounter with the gate keepers of Hell, I step forward and carefully place a hand on her shoulder. "I think that's enough. We don't want you passing out again."

"I'm fine." She relaxes her hands and every floating object in the barn comes to halt mid-air. Pitchforks, shovels, ropes, empty barrels, parts of an old tractor, a wheelbarrow, a couple of old chairs, a rusty license plate… I haven't even identified everything yet when it all drifts to the sides of the barn. Without moving, Vicky directs it all into neat stacks and lines. Then, she purses her lips and the layer of dust, which has settled on the floor, is picked up, pushed together into a large ball and lowered into one of the barrels.

Vicky turns around, a content smile on her face. "I've still got my powers."

She's answered by our stunned silence. Kess is the first to break it with a hysterical laugh. She throws her arms in the air and jumps up and down. "That was brilliant!"

Her enthusiasm wakes us all from our bewilderment. Everyone cheers and dances. Laughter fills the air.

I wrap my arms around Vicky again.

"I'm okay. Really," she whispers in my ear.

I close my eyes for a second, letting the electricity between us flow through me. "How did you do that? It must have taken a lot more energy than that one rock you lifted before."

She presses her warm cheek against mine. "Suppressing Beelzebub's influence taught me a lot about self-control."

My lips curl up. "You're becoming more awesome every day."

"You're not so bad yourself," she says as she places both hands on my butt.

"Come on. Celebrate with us!" Kessley grabs my hand and pulls me into the partying crowd.

Taking hold of Vicky's hand, soon we're at the center of the celebration. The fairy godmothers pop in and out of view, showering us in sparkles in the process. They return with all kinds of delicious smelling cupcakes, pies, and cookies. When Dylan drums a nice beat on two barrels he rolled outside, Charlie starts to do a crazy beatbox.

Gisella ends one of her catlike somersaults next to me and pauses for a second. "I didn't know he could do that."

"Me either!" I laugh.

We dance until we're out of breath—at least, those of us who need to breathe. Soon we're all sitting in the grass, enjoying the sun and nibbling on something sweet.

"Hey, Charlie?" Taylar licks the sugar from his fingers. "Can you do other sounds, too?"

"Sure." Charlie stuffs another whole cupcake into his mouth, wipes his hands on his pants, and stands up. He cups his hands in front of his mouth and imitates a trumpet.

It sounds so real that I hold out my hand to him, palm up, and demand to see his phone. He hands it to me, but it's not playing anything.

He takes a deep breath and starts another beat, a slow one this time, with a bass in the background. Kessley changes into a weird monster with strings for hair. She shakes her head and the strings touch each other, creating a soft violin-like sound.

It's easy to lean back on my elbows and let the music flow through me.

As the iele float up and produce the most beautiful melody I've ever heard, I lower myself onto my back and watch their serene faces, and the way their hair and clothes seem to rise and fall in sync with their notes. Everyone is mesmerized by them. Even the birds, rabbits, chipmunks, and butterflies gather around us to listen. Soon, we're all lying at their feet, as if we're in some kind of fairytale. Even the fairy godmothers are stunned.

Vicky's fingers entwine with mine. Her heat fills me up from head to toe. I haven't felt this peaceful in a long time.

CHAPTER 6

We return to Darkwood Manor revived and ready for action. I'm the last one inside.

"Mom, we're back!" I call out while closing the front door behind me.

There's no answer.

"Mom?" I stand still at the foot of the stairs and tilt my head.

Still no answer. In half a second my tranquil state is out the door. I rush up the stairs to the top floor without pausing.

"Mom!"

A voice in the back of my mind tries to convince me I'll find her asleep on her bed. Another voice keeps screaming at me, *You should've listened to me. You should never have left her here alone.*

Her room is empty.

"Dante!" Vicky calls from downstairs.

I almost trip over my own feet in my haste to get back down to the kitchen, where Vicky is waiting for me. She holds up a note.

"What is it? What does it say?"

Vicky swallows. "She went with Trevor."

"She *what*…?"

I snatch the piece of paper from her hand and try to stop the letters from blending.

Dante,

Trevor's here. Says he's got something important to show me. Figured he must have good intentions, or he wouldn't have been able to find the mansion. Went with him to check it out. Will be home soon.

Love, Mom

Her handwriting is all wobbly. She must have been in a hurry.

Or was she forced to write this?

I shove the note under Mona's nose. "Can this be true?"

The fairy godmother nods. "The protection on Darkwood Manor is still up."

Maël taps her staff against the ceiling. "What about the portal to the silver mine? The tornado demons found the porthole. Trevor could have done the same."

I turn around and fly up the stairs again. My Shield apparates next to me the moment I reach the entrance to the secret room. The closet that hides it is closed. I open it and push the top shelf, then wait for the rest of the shelves to drop down. A lightning bolt hovers in the palm of my hand. As the closet wall slides sideways, a dark, empty room is revealed. Ivy covers the window, shadows fill more than just the corners, and the porthole is invisible.

The lightning dies when I fold my fingers around it and I turn back to my friends. "I don't think anyone was here."

Maël walks into the room and stands still for a while. Then, she nods. "You are right. I do not sense any evil."

We step back into the hallway, and I close the secret entrance. Although we didn't find anything suspicious, my heart remains restless.

"Dante?" D'Maeo places his hand on my arm. "I'm sure she'll be back soon."

I bite my lip and close my eyes for a moment. One more setback and I'm losing it.

A warm hand touches my cheek, followed by soft lips, and I open my eyes.

"Remember what you said about Trevor?" Vicky asks.

The lump in my throat blocks the words I want to utter.

"You said he really loves her."

I try a smile, but my lips don't cooperate. My gaze falls upon the note I'm clutching in my left hand without realizing it. It suddenly reminds me of another note.

My heartrate drops and my shoulders relax.

Vicky sees it. "What are you thinking?"

"I forgot to tell you guys before…" I smile. "Trevor was the one who put Mom in the ceiling of the Monastery of Saint Gertrude. He put her there to save her."

Jeep frowns. "How do you know?"

"He left a note in her pocket."

Vicky nods slowly. "Of course. We told him about your premonition. He knew keeping your mother with him would put her in danger."

"He let her go." Mona shoots me an incredulous look.

I slide Mom's note into my pants pocket. "So, why did he take her now?"

We go back downstairs.

"If the note is true, he didn't take her anywhere," Mona says from behind me. "She went with him willingly, and I'm sure…"

She pauses and I whirl around on the bottom step. "What's wrong?"

She raises a finger. "Hang on. I think…" Her face lights up. "Yes. I can sense her again."

My hand tightens around the banister. "You know where she is?"

Her gaze goes distant. "I do." Her lips curl up. "And she's fine. She was right to trust him."

"Can you take me to her?"

She shakes her head. "No need. She'll be back soon. She's already on her way."

"With him?" My hands ball into fists.

"No, he said goodbye to her."

Fear, anger, gratitude, relief, and anxiety fight for precedence inside me. Instinctively, I reach for my notebooks behind my waistband. My hand finds only fabric and I remember I left them behind in my haste earlier. I walk into the annex, pick them up, and stuff them back in place. The feeling of the leather covers against my skin somehow soothes me.

We join the others in the kitchen and wait for Mom to return.

Mona has taken all the leftover sweets back to Darkwood Manor with her, even though everyone but Charlie is stuffed.

I can barely see D'Maeo's face over the large stack of cupcakes.

I've downed two large mugs of tea when Mona interrupts our aimless chitchat. "She's here."

I'm on my feet in less than a millisecond and reach the door before Mom can use her key to get in. I grab her so tight, she lets out a soft oomph.

"Are you okay?" I ask, breathing in the smell of sweet memories.

"I'm fine. Better than ever, actually."

"He didn't hurt you?"

"Quite the contrary." Mom frees herself from my grip and straightens her shoulders. "Come on, I'll tell you all about it." She walks into the mansion and greets everyone enthusiastically. After scrutinizing Vicky for a moment, she asks, "Did it work?"

Vicky presses her index finger and thumb together. "Perfectly."

Mom pulls back her chair and sits down. "As you can imagine, I was surprised to find Trevor on our doorstep. But then I remembered Mona's protection. If he had any evil plans, he wouldn't have been able to find Darkwood Manor."

D'Maeo taps his imaginary watch. "Make it a summary. We've been held up a lot already."

"Of course. I'm sorry." Mom cuts right to the chase and turns to me. "You once said Trevor had powers that an earth elemental normally doesn't have, right?"

I nod expectantly.

"Well, you were right. However, he... lost some of them recently." She gives me a smug smile I have never seen on her before.

"What are you talking about?" I ask when she doesn't continue. "Did Satan punish him for letting you 'escape'?" I make quotation marks in the air at the last word.

"Oh, no. He lost them himself. And he could do more than make creatures speak English. He could also..." She pauses, searching for words. Then, she pushes her chair back and stands up. "It's easier if I just show you." She walks to the back door and beckons us. "Come on. It's best if we do this in the protective circle."

My curiosity goes through the roof.

Does this mean what I think it means? Did he give her

some of his powers?

We gather inside the circle and Mom shakes her hands loose. Everyone is silent, waiting for her big surprise.

Spreading her legs a little more and planting herself in a balanced stance, she closes her eyes. Her arms move up in front of her in slow motion and she takes a couple of breaths. Then, she makes a downward cutting motion and spreads her arms. She brings them back together against her chest and throws them forward with force.

A shimmering circle comes to life in the air before her. On reflex, we all pull out our weapons.

"Relax," Mom says, smiling at me over her shoulder. "Nothing can get through unless I open it completely. Right now, it's only a window into another world."

Carefully, I step closer. "You can create portals?" My voice is no more than a stunned whisper.

"Yes." She nods. "And windows." She slams her hands together and the shimmering circle disappears before she turns around and bows.

After a short hesitation we all clap for her.

"But, that's not all," she says with a smirk. She takes a step away from me and points at my hands. "Throw some lightning at me."

I recoil. "What?"

"You can't hurt me inside the circle, right?" She makes a 'hit me with everything you've got' gesture with both hands.

"O–kay…" I say slowly. I conjure a lightning ball in my hand and when she beckons again, I throw it at her. It's a half-hearted throw, but it could still harm her if it wasn't for the protective circle.

I suppress the urge to close my eyes. Mom watches the ball approach without moving. I wait for her to open a portal to catch it in. What she does instead makes my mouth fall open.

Seconds before the ball hits her, Mom's face changes. A red, rocky layer slides over her head like a helmet. The lightning bounces off without harming her and a smile cracks Mom's solid skin.

"What the hell? He gave you his elemental powers, too?" I shout the words at her, not sure whether I should be grateful or disgusted.

Mom pulls the collar of her shirt down to reveal more rocky skin around her heart. "He gave me part of it, enhanced with a shielding power. It's as good as impenetrable."

"Wow," Taylar mumbles behind me. "He really, really loves you."

Mom gets rid of the armor with a simple shake of her head. "He does, and he didn't want to leave me unprotected. He gave me the ability to shield myself from an attack, and to flee if things get too heated."

"But you'll have Charlotte's powers soon, so you don't need these," Kessley says.

Mom folds her arms. "Well, yes, but that is none of his business, is it?"

Kess giggles. "Brilliant!"

I'm still stumped. "How did you learn to do that so quickly?"

Mom blushes. "It turns out Trevor is a great teacher."

I hide my face in my hands. "Please don't tell me you're falling for him."

"Of course not," she says without hesitation. "I'll never forget what he did to me. Or you. Besides, my heart still belongs to somebody else."

Sadness falls over her face and I walk over to her and pull her close. I want to comfort her, but what can I say? Dad is not coming back. If we're lucky, he'll get the chance to fight with us, but that will be the last we see of him until we die.

Maybe those are the words she needs to hear.

"Eventually we'll all be together." I meet Vicky's eyes while the words leave my lips, and tears form in the corners of her eyes. When I let go of Mom, the jubilant mood has died. We're all thinking about our approaching goodbyes.

We go back inside and sit down at the table.

Taylar is the first to break the silence. "If you needed training, why didn't you stay here and use the protective circle? Why take the risk of going with Trevor?"

Mom shakes her head fervently. "I couldn't show him the circle. The Devil may not know about it yet, and I thought it best to keep it that way."

"So, you risked your life to keep the protective circle a secret?" Kessley asks, incredulous.

Mom shrugs. "Better my life than that of all of you. If Mona's protection wasn't working anymore, I figured it was better to lead Trevor away from the mansion. But I had a feeling that his intentions were good, for once."

"Good call," Mona compliments her. She collects the mugs and fills the sink with dishwater. "When you dropped off my radar, I was afraid we'd really lost you this time."

She has her back to us, to hide her emotions no doubt. It isn't working, though; I can hear her throat tightening.

Mom saves her from an awkward moment by directing the attention back to her, her words cheerful. "No way. You won't get rid of me that easily. I went to Hell twice, and I'm still alive and kicking."

"Hear, hear!" Charlie says, raising his fifth – or so – cupcake.

I rise and rub my hands together, for the first time eager to start the transfer of Charlotte's powers to Mom. I'm finally confident she'll be able to handle it.

Then, it hits me. "What about the empty body we need to transfer Charlotte's powers? That was the whole reason we selected you."

Mom's lips form into a grin again. "The powers that Trevor gave me are…" she searches for words, "on loan. Trevor took his additional powers, the ones that didn't come with his earth elemental package, from a mage he killed a year ago. He was able to borrow other people's powers. Trevor has that ability now, but it is slowly draining his energy. He used it one last time to protect me." Her cheeks turn red again. "I can push the powers he gave me out of my body whenever I want, and take them back in."

"What use are they then?" Vicky grumbles.

"Well," Mom's eyes twinkle. "I thought I could give them to someone else."

CHAPTER 7

Taylar almost slips from his chair when he turns toward me fast. This is his chance to finally have powers, too.

The small nod I give him lights his face up.

I focus on Mom again. "You know how to do it?"

"Yes, Trevor taught me."

Before I can open my mouth again, Gisella clears her throat and puts my next thought into words. "What if it's a trick to get rid of one of us?"

I drum my fingers on the table. "You mean, the powers may be corrupted or something?"

She shrugs. "He could've infected them. Why not?"

"And risk killing me?" Mom shakes her head. "No. Absolutely not. He wouldn't take that chance."

My gaze wanders to Maël, sitting next to Mom. "If he's done something to these powers, would you be able to sense it?"

Maël pushes her golden cape back and stands up. "I think so."

Mom also stands up and turns to face the ghost queen. It's amazing to see how much she's changed since the last time I saw her. These powers have given her the confidence she needed. I can only hope her days of getting kidnapped or cursed are over for good.

Maël stretches her hand out and holds it an inch from Mom's forehead. After a short silence she moves it down, toward Mom's heart.

Mom's breathing is quickening, but she keeps as still as a statue.

Half a minute later, Maël looks her in the eye and smiles. "You are fine."

Mom breathes out audibly. "Thank you, Maël."

I rise to my feet. "I'll go get ready for the transfer spell."

In the annex I find the remains of my last spell. The one that was supposed to save Vicky. My heart cramps up at the sight of it. It reminds me of our inevitable parting. We saved her, for now, but soon she'll move on, and I won't see her again until my life on earth is over too. If I don't end up somewhere else.

Pushing the bitter thoughts to the back of my mind, I kneel and start putting aside all the herbs I need for my next spell. I try to clean up the mess evil Vicky made while I'm at it.

D'Maeo's voice behind me startles me. "Are you

sure it's a good idea to give these powers to Taylar?"

I take in his concerned frown. "Why wouldn't it be? Soon, he'll be the only one left without active powers."

The old ghost glances over his shoulder. "His powers are latent. Giving him new ones might block them."

"True. But, it might also wake them up."

D'Maeo doesn't seem convinced, so I push myself to my feet and walk up to him. "What are you worried about?"

He lets out a sigh. "Every decision we make has consequences. We've already made several mistakes leading to us getting lost, kidnapped, cursed, and hurt in many ways."

I place a hand on his shoulder. "Yes, but it also brought us a lot of good. We got rid of the curses, all of them. We solved Taylar's and Maël's unfinished business, we freed you from the Black Void and Jeep from his ghosts, and Maël and Gisella have received dark powers they can use in the final battle. It has all been for a reason."

D'Maeo brings his mouth closer to my ear. "But what if we're supposed to leave Taylar's powers alone? What if by meddling with them, we throw away our chances of winning?"

I let that sink in and for a moment my throat gets dry. Then I swallow my insecurities and smile at the leader of my Shield. "Everything happens for a reason, right?"

He nods.

"Then Mom got these powers for a reason, too. She can't do anything with them because we need a magic-free body to harness Charlotte's powers. So, we give Trevor's powers to the most logical choice: Taylar. If that blocks his own powers, that's the way it has to be."

The old ghost tilts his head. A grin pulls his lips up. "I can't believe you're reassuring me now. Isn't it supposed to be the other way around?"

I slap him on the back with a wink. "I'm a fast learner."

D'Maeo grabs me by both shoulders, gives me his "proud father" look, and hugs me. "You sure are." He holds me against him longer than he's ever done. "I'm proud of you, Dante. So proud. You'll be fine without us."

Tears fill my eyes. I want to tell him he's right, but all I can think about is how I don't want to say goodbye to them. They're my family now, and it will leave a gaping hole in my chest when I lose them.

D'Maeo hugs me a bit longer, whether to give me some time to swallow my tears or to swallow his own, I'm not sure. After several seconds, I manage to squeeze some words out. "Thank you, D'Maeo. That means a lot to me."

He lets go and walks back to the kitchen.

Vicky passes him in the doorway. Her gaze follows him for several seconds before she steps into the annex. "What was that about? Is everything okay?"

A disobedient tear crawls down my cheek, which she wipes off. "Did you two have a fight?"

I take her hand. "Not at all." I turn away from her and change the subject before I choke up again. "Would you mind helping me clean this up?"

She doesn't press me for answers and kneels beside me, her arm brushing against mine reassuringly.

We fall into our routine of picking out herbs together. As we take turns offering suggestions, I write everything down. Before long, the annex floor is clear again and I help Vicky up.

"Ready?" she asks me.

"I can't wait."

Everyone is eager to start and soon Mom and Taylar are facing each other inside the protective circle.

I'm still a bit nervous about this, and so is D'Maeo. If he rubs his beard any harder, it's going to fall off. The calmness and confidence that have fallen over Mom sooth me, though. Plus, Maël and Gisella are ready to intervene with time freezes and shadows if necessary.

"Close your eyes," Mom instructs Taylar.

He shakes out his hands and obeys.

"Now, imagine your mind and soul are a box filled with emotions, longings, dreams, and memories. Picture it in your head." She pauses and watches the young ghost for a moment. "Can you see it?"

"Yes," Taylar answers.

"Good. Now, at the bottom of your box, there is a secret layer. It is hidden by all the things that fill up your mind and soul. Can you see the layer?"

"Yes."

"There is a hatch in the middle of this layer. Push all those emotions, longings, dreams, and memories to the side of your box, to clear the way. Make sure they stay there."

"Okay." Taylar sounds like he's in some kind of trance.

Mom continues in the same calm voice. "Open the hatch. Whatever is underneath will stay there safely. I will send my powers to you, and you will pull them through the hatch. They will not fight the powers already present. There is enough room for all of them. Are you ready?"

"Yes."

With both hands on her heart, Mom lets out a slow breath, and starts speaking:

"With my heart and with my soul,
I give away my power's core.
Take the magic within me,
let it rise and set it free."

An orange light comes to life under her hands. As she moves her hands up, the light glides with them. It glows under her skin and pops out of her mouth.

"Let these powers find a place,
with lots of love and lots of space.
Find here, in this willing ghost,
a pure and honest host."

The orange light bobs up and down in the air, as if it's listening. When the last words leave Mom's lips, she pushes her hands forward. The light soars toward Taylar, who still has his eyes closed.

"Keep the hatch open," Mom says.

The light hovers in front of him, no doubt checking to see if this host is indeed pure and honest, and full of love and space. Not that it matters much, since it has been inside Trevor, too.

Without warning, the ball of light shoots forward and crawls up Taylar's nose. The white-haired ghost tilts his head back and a shiver goes through his body.

Kessley dives forward with a frightened shriek.

Gisella grabs her before she can touch Taylar. "Leave him, he's fine."

Taylar stops shivering and lowers his head.

"Now, close the hatch and seal the box," Mom instructs.

Taylar's jaw sets and he squeezes his eyes shut. Then, he relaxes his fingers and sighs. "Done."

Mom steps closer and puts her hands on his shoulders. "That's it."

The young ghost looks down at his chest and then at his hands.

"Do you feel any different?" Mom asks him.

Taylar is still staring at his hands and touching his skin. "I do. There's a sort of tingling inside me. As if some sort of charge lies beneath my skin."

Mom tilts her head with a smile. "Well, in a way, it does."

"So, let's give those powers a spin, shall we?" I hop from one foot to the other, apparently more excited than Taylar himself.

"What's wrong?" I ask when he doesn't respond.

The young ghost touches his chest and throat. "I don't feel good."

He starts to flicker before the last word leaves his lips. He gets so pale and transparent that he's almost invisible.

Kessley hurries to his side and grabs him. "What's happening?"

Taylar shakes her off roughly, and Kess blinks in surprise. He's never treated her like that.

"Don't," he says, out of breath. "I need a minute of rest."

Kessley reaches out to him again, but he steps away and sways on his feet.

"Taylar?" Worry has crept up my throat, making my voice sound hoarse and high.

He stumbles out of the protective circle, with Kessley on his heels.

"Don't touch me!" he calls out.

Kessley freezes on the spot, a defeated expression on her face.

"I'll be fine," Taylar assures her, still blinking in

and out of view. He makes for the back door and almost trips over the threshold.

He disappears inside, leaving us behind, speechless.

"Did this happen to you when you received these powers?" D'Maeo asks Mom.

"Not at all," she answers, wringing her hands. "I felt a sort of electrical charge, like he did, as if energy was coursing through me. And then, I practiced. I never felt ill." She presses her fingers against her temples. "This is all my fault. I should never have suggested this."

Jeep wipes some dust from his hat. "We all agreed to this. And he said he was going to be fine."

Kessley bites her lip. She's about to burst into tears.

I walk over to her and rub her back. "Don't worry, we can always use a spell to get it out of him."

A sob escapes her lips. "He pushed me away."

Lifting her chin, I force her to look at me. "To protect you, Kess." A sigh escapes me when tears start rolling down her cheeks. "I'll go see if he's okay. And if he's not, we'll fix him. I promise."

My reassuring smile seems to calm her down a bit, so I turn toward the kitchen door before it falters. Sensing several of my Shield members following me, I stop in the doorway and glance over my shoulder. "Stay here. I can handle this."

They don't seem convinced, but if I give them an order, there's nothing they can do except obey.

I don't want them to worry about this if there's nothing to worry about. Besides, a feeling deep inside me has awoken, telling me that what's happening inside the house is for my eyes only. I'm not sure where this feeling is coming from, but I trust it without a doubt.

"You are right to trust your instinct," a voice says out of nowhere. I recognize it when it continues with, "Keep what you see to yourself."

Quinn? Is that you? I ask in my head.

There's no answer, he's already gone. I know it was him, though. His words give me hope. Hope that Taylar will indeed be fine. These powers won't swallow him or turn him evil.

Although…

Taylar is not downstairs, so I try the second floor. My heart sinks the moment I reach the top of the stairs. "Fine" isn't among the words I'd use to describe what I'm seeing.

Flashes of light come from Taylar's room on the other side of the hallway, interspersed with something that blocks out the slightest glow. The fact that no sound accompanies the weird coming and going of light makes me even more nervous.

Being extra cautious, I walk around the stairs leading to the top floor and approach Taylar's room. The door is ajar. Behind it everything blinks in and out of view at such a dazzling speed it gives me a headache. I think back to what I saw while I was in my astral form. The good and bad parts fighting inside the young ghost. I shouldn't have left him the way he was. Even though holy water didn't hurt him, and Maël and Vicky haven't sensed anything evil in him. Even if Dylan said he isn't cursed, I should've trusted my eyes. Now, it might be too late to help him.

The soundless fight continues inches from where I'm standing. I take a deep breath.

If Taylar is still in one piece, I'll do everything within my power to cure him. I won't give up on him.

I push the door open a bit farther.

Taylar is standing in the middle of the room with his arms wide and his head thrown back. Now that I'm standing closer, I can make out the details of the darkness and light. The glowing parts are hands balled into fists. The dark parts are mouths with rows of sharp teeth, lashing out at the fists.

There must be at least a hundred of them, all circling Taylar, and trying to rip each other apart.

For a moment, I watch them chase each other. Taylar seems frozen in their midst, but he's no longer blinking, and I can see him clearly. The battle raging around him is hurting him. Both the hands and the mouths tear his skin open. Blood is dripping from countless wounds on his arms, chest, and legs. There are blue spots on his cheeks and forehead.

Why doesn't he let them slide through him? Has he lost the ability to turn transparent?

Deciding my best strategy here is to try and freeze his attackers, I focus on them and picture them freezing one by one.

Taylar's voice startles me. "Don't," he says, without moving. "Keep your distance. I've got this."

He no longer sounds weak or in pain, just… struggling. Out of breath, even though he doesn't need oxygen anymore.

"Are you sure? I can help you destroy them."

"No," he says firmly. Then, softer. "Trust me. Please."

"Yes, trust him," Quinn's disembodied voice whispers.

Without noticing, I've taken a step inside the room. One of the glowing hands lashes out at me, and I hurry back into the hallway. It changes course and hits one of the mouths hard, sending it crashing to the floor.

The battle becomes more vicious, with both sides clawing, hitting, and biting with more and more malice.

Taylar's voice echoes through the room. "Stop!"

All the weird creatures come to a halt and Taylar starts to spin. He goes faster with each turn, until he's no more than a blur. The dark and light are pulled together. They wind around each other, and as soon as they're all connected, they are lifted above Taylar's head. Bit by bit, they form a large ball. At first, the two sides pressed together are fighting each other, wriggling to free themselves, but then their squirming subsides, and the mouths and hands start to lose shape.

Taylar is mumbling, and I prick up my ears to make out the words. "A box inside me, where my powers are safe. Go inside the box, go inside the box."

The ball is sucked closer to the white-haired ghost, and disappears inside him.

Taylar keeps repeating his mantra. "Go inside the box, stay inside the box. Go inside the box, stay inside the box."

The flicker of dark and light stops. All the battling good and evil have gone. Taylar spins slower and slower, until he comes to a complete stand still. He ceases his mumbling, lowers his arms and head, and opens his eyes. His gaze meets mine.

I stare back at him, unsure whether to move or speak yet.

Finally, a smile pulls his lips up. "I did it."

The sweat that has formed on my forehead comes away with a swipe of my palm. "You did what exactly?"

"My new powers disturbed the ones I already had. The balance was lost, so they turned on each other, and on me."

My mouth falls open. "But that means your own powers have woken up, right?"

He lowers his gaze. "They woke up a while ago, but I've been struggling to keep them under control."

I swallow the worry rising to my throat again. "There are evil powers inside you." It's a statement, not a question. "I saw them when my astral form was hovering in the annex."

Taylar coughs uncomfortably. "I'm sorry, Dante. I can't… I can't tell you any more than this."

Anger flares up inside me. "What do you mean, you can't tell me? I won't tolerate secrets in this house, Taylar. Now, I order you to—"

"Don't," Quinn's voice interrupts me.

I look up at the ceiling. "You again. What is going on?" Desperation seeps into my words. "And why can't I see you? Mona made sure we could see angels even when they're invisible."

"Because I'm speaking to you from Heaven." He sighs. "Listen, Dante. You will have to trust Taylar and me. Let this go. Taylar's power needs to remain a secret. Thanks to the powers Susan gave him, he can now control his own. We need them to defeat Lucifer. It is already a risk that I know about it. Don't make him tell anyone else. Have faith, Dante. Trust him. Please."

I clench my jaw and take in the white-haired ghost. Taylar has changed. Despite the guilty expression on his face, he stands tall, more confident than I've ever seen him. His normally white, translucent skin has got a bit of color, and determination shines through his light-blue eyes.

"Okay," I agree. "I won't ask for clarification."

Several seconds pass while I wait for an answer from Quinn, but he seems to have left us alone again.

"Well, if you're ready, we can go downstairs." I turn halfway and beckon with my head. "The others are worried about you."

He doesn't move. "You only listen because Qaddisin told you to trust me. You don't actually trust *me*."

I shake my head. "No, Taylar, I trust you one hundred percent. What I don't trust, is evil. You know as well as I do that it can wriggle its way inside someone without anyone noticing. It almost got Vicky to betray us all. That's why we have to be on guard, always. Anyone can be corrupted. You, me, even Quinn. Evil has sneaky ways of getting its way." I step forward and place a hand on his shoulder. "But, so do we. And it seems your powers are of the sneaky kind. The kind that can help us defeat Satan."

He nods. "I think they are."

"That's great news. I knew you were just as important to us as the others. It took you too long to realize that yourself, Taylar. Don't doubt yourself ever again, okay?"

He grins. "I'll try."

CHAPTER 8

We walk into the garden together. Taylar almost runs to Kessley and takes her in his arms. "I'm sorry, I was afraid I would hurt you," he whispers.

I don't hear her answer, because I've turned to the rest of our friends. "He's fine. He got a little nauseous, that's all."

After a long, passionate kiss, Taylar and Kessley break up. The young ghost keeps one arm around her waist. "Yes, I'm sorry if I scared you. I'm ready to try out my new powers now."

Mom smiles and beckons him into the protective circle. Reluctantly, he lets go of his girl and takes his place next to Mom.

She demonstrates the movement to open a portal. He tries it without the thoughts that activate the power first. Mom compliments him and takes a step back. "Now, for real. Focus on opening a portal to a safe world. There's no need for a specific name of a world, thinking of a world that can't harm us is enough."

I ball my fists to control my nerves. I try to remember Quinn's words, but those only applied to Taylar's own powers, didn't they? What if he can't handle these foreign ones?

Someone touches my hand. I expect Vicky, but it's Kessley, standing there. She grabs my hand and bites her lip.

Warmth flows through me. She's seeking comfort and she comes to me for it.

The others seem relaxed. A weight fell from their shoulders when I told them Taylar was fine. They trust me. Maybe I should trust myself, too. After all, my gut tells me both Quinn and Taylar are right. The youngest member of my Shield is better than he's ever been. His powers are awake at last, and he's received a couple of handy ones as a bonus. He is our best fighter with handheld weapons, both in offense and defense. I don't see a reason why it should be any different when it comes to magical powers.

"He'll do fine, as always," I whisper to Kess.

She shoots me a grateful look.

Taylar has taken his time to focus on a benign world. Now, he starts the movement to open a portal.

His gestures are a lot less elegant than Mom's. He lifts his arms in front of himself, then moves them down abruptly and spreads them. With a grunt, he slams them together against his chest and pushes them forward, hard.

A sparkling square appears in front of him.

Mom peers into it for a couple of seconds before nodding. "Great. Now open it."

"Shouldn't it be a circle?" Charlie asks.

Mom shakes her head. "Apparently it's different for everyone. It can manifest itself in different shapes, although for most people it's a circle, a square, or a rectangle."

Taylar brings his arms down as if to squash something with force. The view through the portal gets clearer, and I glimpse a string of colorful butterflies fluttering around a yellow tree.

Once Mom shows Taylar how to close it again, it vanishes in a couple of seconds.

Kessley lets go of my hand and jumps forward, almost knocking Taylar over. "Nice job!" She flings her arms around his neck.

His grin is wide when she lets go again. "Thanks."

"What about the shield? Does that work, too?" Dylan asks.

Taylar steps away from Kessley and opens his arms wide. "Let's test it. Throw something at me."

All heads turn to me, but I take out my athame and walk over to Vicky. "We need something sharp. Can you throw this at him?"

A glint appears in her eyes as she takes it. "No problem."

She enters the circle and waits for Mom and Kessley to join us behind her.

"Ready?" she asks the young ghost.

Taylar nods. "Try to hit me in the head or the heart."

Vicky pulls her arm back. I expect Taylar to close his eyes, but his gaze is glued to my athame. Vicky flings the weapon at him and his muscles tense. It soars straight for his forehead, and although he's standing inside the protective circle, cold sweat trickles down my spine. We've trained here lots of times, and we don't hold back anymore, but none of us has ever gone for the kill.

My heart almost stops beating as the tip of the knife hits Taylar. With a thud, it bounces off the red shield that pops up around his head.

There's a collective sigh of relief as Taylar picks up the athame that has fallen into the grass.

Vicky strolls over to him and touches the rocky layer on his face. "Does it hurt?"

"Not at all. I barely feel it. It's just a little warm."

We all gather around him to congratulate him on his new powers.

After a couple of seconds, the shield recedes to reveal the wide grin on Taylar's face.

Jeep slaps him on the back. "I'm happy for you."

"Thank you, Jeep."

D'Maeo beams at him. "I always knew you were the bravest of us all. You showed amazing confidence by standing so still with that weapon flying toward you."

The white-haired ghost shrugs. "Well, I knew the

circle would protect me."

D'Maeo tuts. "No, no. Don't be so modest. Most of us would at least have flinched. You didn't."

Taylar blushes. "Oh, well."

The old ghost ruffles through his hair. "Come on, let me enjoy my role as the surrogate father here. I'm bursting with pride. And you know what…?" he waits for Taylar to look him in the eye, "I was proud of you before all of this. I hope that pride is finally rubbing off on you."

Taylar shifts his feet in discomfort. "It's starting to."

D'Maeo gives him an amicable punch on his shoulder. "That's a good start."

Once he steps aside, Maël opens her arms wide. Her cape floats up behind her in the summer breeze. "Can I give you a surrogate mother hug?"

"I'd be honored."

As I watch them, I realize my doubts about Taylar have vanished. I can see nothing but good in him, and the love for us shows clearly in his eyes as we compliment him over and over. After a while, he clears his throat.

"Okay, enough with the sucking up already. I say we give Susan the powers that were meant for her."

Everyone agrees, and Vicky, Dylan, and I go back inside to grab everything we need.

I pray there won't be any disturbances this time.

It doesn't take long for us to set everything up.

Overcome by nerves, Mom keeps rubbing her hands and legs.

"You'll be fine," Mona assures her.

"I'm not so sure anymore," Mom confesses. "I'm not as brave as Taylar, as agile and quick as Gisella, or as observant as Dante. I don't have Charlie's wit or Maël's strong mind."

"Stop it," Mona interrupts her. "Doubts are part of our life, and our mission. No one is confident every minute of the day."

Mom is rubbing her arms now. "Chills are running through me constantly."

Mona grabs her upper arms. "Take a deep breath."

While Mom obeys, Mona continues, "You'll be fine. This is the role that was chosen for you, and you will excel in it."

Mom lets out a snort. "You don't know that."

"Yes, I do. Now, stop doubting yourself, or I'm showering you with sparks."

A high laugh escapes Mom's lips. "That's hardly a threat."

"Don't be too sure about that. My sparks can force you to make a fool of yourself."

Putting her hands on her waist, Mom asks, "Really? How?"

"They can make you so happy that all you want to do is hop around, dance, and sing."

"Oh, make her do that. Please," Kessley calls out from the other side of the circle. "No one ever wants to party with me."

Taylar shoves her in the side. "Hey, that's not true."

She gives him a playful wink. "Right. Except for you, love."

Mom laughs. "I'd love to party with you, Kessley. Unfortunately, we have important stuff to do first."

Mona's face lights up. "Does that mean you're going to do it?"

"I never said I wouldn't. I'm just nervous." She rubs her face with both hands. "We're dealing with a lot of power here, which means a lot can go wrong."

Maël opens her arms. "Yes, but we have the protective circle, we have eight people standing by with powers in case something goes wrong, and we have Charlotte's husband. Even if something goes wrong, we can set it right."

Jeep shoots her a smile before turning to Mom. "Listen to her, she's right. Together we can do this. And I couldn't have wished for a more fitting person to take care of Charlotte's powers."

Mom visibly relaxes as Maël and Jeep's words sink in. She answers them with a smile and a bow. "Thank you for your uplifting words, great necromancer and wise queen of Africa."

Jeep gives her a reassuring nod and Maël bows back. "You are most welcome, mighty Susan."

Mom chuckles. "I'm not mighty yet."

"And I wasn't queen of the whole of Africa."

"Well, you should've been." Mom winks, but I can tell she's serious. She's right, too. Maël was a great queen, and had she lived longer, she could've done a lot of good and stopped a lot of bad things from happening.

Vicky interrupts my thoughts by placing a candle next to me. "Okay, I'm done."

Nerves grab me by my throat.

Mom was right. A lot can go wrong here. What if these powers aren't as benevolent as we think? What if Mom's body can't handle this much power? What if...

Vicky places her hands on my cheeks. "You're giving me a headache, babe. Stop worrying." She beckons Mona.

"Everything okay?" the fairy godmother asks.

"Dante is having second thoughts, too."

"More like fourth thoughts," I mumble.

Mona nods. "Okay, I'll fix this." She walks to the middle of the circle. "Everyone gather around me for a second, please."

As soon as we're all facing her, she performs a ballerina-worthy turn and showers us with sparks. Then, she comes to an abrupt halt. "There, that should be enough. I don't want to take away all your worries and fears. You need them to remain vigilant."

Mom rolls her shoulders. "I feel a lot better, thanks."

"Me, too," I say. "I'm ready to begin."

We both look at Jeep, who pushes his hat a bit back on his head. "Yes, I think it's time."

CHAPTER 9

Everyone steps back except Mom, Jeep, and me.

Vicky has put my Book of Spells down, open to the page where I wrote the spell. Mona snatches Shelton Banks' book out of thin air, opens it, and reads out loud.

"Instructions for the transfer of Charlotte's powers." She waves at the candles Vicky put in place. *"The spell caster, husband, and power vessel each choose a random corner of the triangle."*

Since I'm already standing next to a candle, I stay where I am. Jeep takes his place on my right, and Mom walks over to the third candle.

"Now comes the tricky part," Mona says. She turns to Jeep. *"Charlotte's true love is the only one who can call her powers to him. He will know how to do it if he searches deep within his heart."*

Jeep frowns. "It doesn't say how?"

Mona remains calm. "Because it doesn't know. The answer is inside you."

While he shifts his feet and reluctantly closes his eyes, the fairy godmother bends over the old book again. "*Once the powers have descended into the triangle, the transfer can begin. For this you need…*" she scans the lines, "Yes, we know this. Yada yada yada… Ah, here it is. *The power vessel, the one receiving Charlotte's powers, must be blessed by Jeep and have an open heart and mind to be successful. It has to be completely empty, magic-wise.*"

Mom holds up her thumb.

"*A spell needs to be used to strengthen the transfer and to bind the powers to the new body. To reach maximum chances of success it is best that the spell caster has a strong connection with the vessel.*" With a smile, Mona closes the book and pushes it onto a non-existent shelf above her head. "Looks like we've got everything we need." With that, she steps back.

D'Maeo places his arm around her and kisses her on the cheek. There's not even a hint of worry or doubt on his face, and I know it's not only because of Mona's sparks. He has complete faith in us.

Silence descends as all eyes turn to Jeep, who is rocking back and forth in a soft breeze. His frown has broken into an expression of utter serenity. A soft hum escapes his lips. The sound is melancholic, a mixture of heartache and hope. It gives me chills. Then, he lifts his head to the sky and starts to sing, transforming into a rougher, hoarser version of Pavarotti. His voice touches every fiber in my body, but his words have even more impact:

"Memories, both close and far
leave behind a giant scar.
But my heart has room enough
to hold onto your love.

Decades I have faced the world
yearning for your touch.
If only I could hold you once
it wouldn't hurt so much.

After all these years alone
still I see your face.
One day I will feel again
the strength of your embrace.

Till that day I'll carry on
with a heavy heart.
And hope that when our paths rejoin
we'll never be apart."

The last note fades and I wipe a tear from my cheek. Jeep lowers his head and opens his eyes. I avert my gaze, certain I won't be able to keep myself together if I get even a glimpse of the look in his eyes. His grief and longing have broken down part of the wall I've put up to keep my own despair contained. It's as if I heard myself singing years from now. His words hit every nerve I've got.

Fortunately, they reached something else, too. A rainbow comes to life above us. It unfolds into the middle of the triangle and turns into two large wings.

I never thought I'd see anything more beautiful than an angel, but here it is. The colors of the rainbow flow through the wings while flocks of cloud soften the edges. Their soft heaving creates the illusion of a body attached to them. The smell of rose blossom spreads as the wings drift toward Mom.

I'm afraid to move for fear of disturbing this peaceful sight. However, I bend over to pick up the matchbox and the herbs we've mixed. Once more I glance at my Book of Spells lying near my feet. The words settle into my brain, ready to be pulled out at the right time.

I light the candle next to me—orange for encouragement—and sprinkle the herb mixture over the line of salt that leads from me to Mom. The mixture includes knot weed to control movement, bladderwrack to attract powers, and bergamot and carnation to enhance magical powers. Belladonna adds energy to the spell.

When I reach Mom, the wings have wrapped around her shoulders. They cover her whole back, sides, and part of her stomach. Her face is peaceful as colors seep from the wings into her body.

Next, I light the candle behind her, which is also orange, but for attraction this time, and continue sprinkling over the salt line toward Jeep. His candle is red, for love; when I light it, the flame reaches his neck. His right hand is placed firmly on his chest and his expression is a cross between sorrow and bliss. I continue on my path, and resume my place in the third corner of the triangle before starting the incantation:

"Powers called down by our spell,
settle now inside this shell.
Find a home that's safe and strong.
This is where you now belong."

The candle flames jump down and run across the lines of salt and herbs. For a moment, the fire is blinding. Then, the color becomes a rainbow of red, orange, yellow, green, blue, indigo, and violet. They blend until three lines of white have formed, which shoot to the middle of the triangle, where they entwine.

Mom sucks in air as the wings wrap tighter around her and merge with her body. They fade slowly, leaving dancing spots of colored light all over her.

After relighting the candle beside me, I hold it up. Jeep follows suit with his red one. The candle behind Mom ignites on its own.

I call out the next words:

"Flourish and no longer hide.
Feed upon the good inside.
With our love you will survive.
In this body you will thrive."

Jeep and I thrust our hands forward. Under our outstretched arms, the flames from the candles join the blazing fire in our midst, like the flame from Mom's candle had. The fire turns into a giant, orange ball.

Jeep and I drop our arms and the ball shoots toward Mom as if a string was cut. She sways on her feet when the ball hits her chest. The flames engulf her, and, for a moment, I see nothing but fire.

Then, her face becomes visible, followed by the rest of her body. The vibrant colors have disappeared, and her cheeks are a healthy pink. She smiles before opening her eyes.

Jeep and I set down the candles and rush over to her.

"How are you feeling?" we blurt out as one.

She rolls her shoulders and looks down at her body. "Energized."

Carefully, I touch her right hand, expecting to feel a jolt. Nothing happens. "Are you ready to try your new powers?"

She nods.

Jeep pushes his hat a bit back. "Do you even know what you can do?" He sounds as eager and frightened to find out as me.

The corner of her mouth moves up. "I do."

She turns to the others, all of whom have been waiting with apprehension. "Come join us in the circle."

One by one, they step into the protective circle.

Mom gives me and Jeep a gentle shove toward them. "Go on," she says. "I'll be fine."

There's a tiny glow in her eyes, and for some reason it soothes my doubts. She *is* fine. Giving her these powers was the right thing to do. She can handle them.

I shoot her a smile and join the others several paces away from her.

Kessley is hopping on her toes. "I can't wait to see what she can do. She must be the most powerful of us all now, right?"

My head moves up and down in slow motion. I'm not taking my eyes off Mom for a second.

She lifts her hand and beckons. "Attack me. All at once."

Remembering the way Vicky collapsed the first time she used her new powers, I want to tell her to start with something small. However, the others are already charging, so I remind myself to have faith in Mom, and in Charlotte's powers.

Gisella is doing her somersaults in the air while balls of gel fly around her. Kessley has changed herself into three giant bees, which are zooming above Taylar's outstretched sword. He's flanked by D'Maeo and Dylan, both holding knives. A whirl of yellow sparks shoots up behind them. Vicky, Maël, and Jeep are still standing next to me, activating their lifting, time-bending, and necromancer powers. Vicky focuses on a fallen tree lying on the edge of the lawn.

It rises from the ground and with a grunt she throws it at Mom.

Meanwhile, I haven't moved. Even though I know the circle will protect her, I can't get myself to join in the attack. I stand there, frozen with worry and anticipation.

Will she be able to stop all this power aimed at her?

As if to answer my silent question, Mom changes into a blur. She appears again several feet to my right, out of harm's way. Then, she raises her hands and…

All of a sudden I'm lying on my back in the soft grass.

The wind blows the smell of rain into my face, and content, I breathe it in. A weight shifts on my bare chest and as I look down, a wave of happiness crashes over me. Vicky has joined me. I kiss her temple, and she sighs.

"Can you believe it's finally over?"

With my eyes closed, I enjoy the warmth of the sun on my face. "Not really. I never thought we'd be able to stay together."

"And we beat him, babe. We beat Satan."

Grinning like some fool in a romantic comedy, I wrap my arm around her. "We sure did."

Birds are singing above my head and my heart flutters. "Isn't it a beautiful world?" I whisper, opening my eyes to find out what kind of bird is brightening our day.

My heart forgets several beats and my whole body stiffens.

"Hello, Dante," Mom says an inch from my face. The tip of a sword rests against my throat. My own athame almost penetrates Vicky's cheek. "Don't move."

All I can do is stare at her, my whole body cold and my mind racing.

What happened?

The sun loses some of its warmth and something hard presses against my back, throwing me back into the real world.

Was I dreaming?

A wide grin appears on Mom's face. She steps back, and I rub my throat.

"What do you think?" she asks.

I sit up and stroke the sore spot on my back. My other hand touches the bowl I used for the spell. My brain is empty. All rational thoughts have left me. There are no words left.

The bees land at Mom's feet and turn back into a blonde girl in a leopard skin dress. Kessley holds up her hand to Mom. "That was brilliant."

Mom gives her a high five, her grin widening. "So, it worked?"

"I was somewhere else completely." Kess turns to me and starts hopping up and down again. "Where did you go?"

Giving my head a shake, to lose the weird numbness inside, I reply, "I was right here, lying in the sun with Vicky."

Vicky is still sitting next to me, rubbing her cheek

with a vacant expression. "So was I. With you, I mean."

Mom clears her throat. "Actually, you were all still here. I only made you think you were somewhere else. I wrapped you in an illusion, and made you fill it with what you desired most."

Kessley is shaking Taylar's arm. "What about you? What did you see?"

Her voice is filled with excitement, but she calms down when she notices Taylar's grief-stricken face. Without another word, she wraps her arms around his neck and pulls him close, showering his face with soft kisses.

There's no need for him to tell us what he saw. Without a doubt, he was reunited with his brother. Reality must be more of a punch in the face than it was for me and Vicky.

Jeep seems equally shaken. I reach out to him, but he turns his back to us. His hand goes to his eyes, his shoulders are hunched. I bite my lip and look at Vicky for help.

She rubs his back and whispers to him, "You'll see her soon."

"I know," he says, turning back to us and shooting Vicky a grateful smile. "This just brought back memories. Memories I'd pushed to a far corner of my mind."

Plopping down in the grass, I gesture for him to join me. "Tell us."

"There's not much to tell, really," he says, but he

sits down next to me anyway.

The others follow his example, some of them clearly still a bit lost in their own thoughts and memories. D'Maeo and Mona cling to each other even more than usual, and my heart contracts painfully. I should tell them about the deal I made to keep D'Maeo here, but I can't. Every time I think about what I sacrificed to accomplish that, it feels as if the sky crashes down on me. Instead, I observe the rest of the group. Maël has already recovered from whatever it was she saw in her illusion. Dylan, Charlie, and Gisella don't seem affected in the slightest, for which I'm glad. There are enough emotions tumbling over each other here right now.

"When we were together for about six months," Jeep begins, "Charlotte demonstrated this power. To show me what she wanted the most… a quiet life with me." He smiles to himself. "I think what she really wanted was to use it on me, to see what I desired most."

Kessley moves a bit closer to Jeep, her hand never leaving Taylar's. Her eyes are wide with anticipation. "And did you let her use it on you?"

"Of course I did. Because I wanted the exact same thing." He takes off his hat and lays down in the grass, his hands folded behind his head. "We stayed inside the illusion for two whole days."

Kess gasps. "You can do that?"

Jeep sighs. "Most mages can't. Charlotte could, though. Now I know why."

"Because she was very powerful," Charlie says.

"Yes. But other than that one time, she never showed me any of it."

My attention goes to Mom, the only one who hasn't sat down.

"Do you agree that this much power should not be given to one person?" she asks. Doubt flickers behind her eyes.

Jeep shakes his head. "I think she made the right decision by renouncing her magic. Not because it was too much for one person, but because the wrong people were after them. Now, we need it more than ever. Our enemies have tremendous power. We can only fight them with equal strength."

Mom bows her head. "I'm sorry I made you see her. It was not my intention to hurt any of you."

He smiles up at her and pats the space between him and Maël. "It's fine, Susan. Really," he says as she sits down. "You need to train and test out this magic, see what you can do with it."

"You'll see Charlotte soon," I try to comfort him. "When Satan is defeated."

"Or when he defeats us," Taylar adds gloomily.

"That won't happen," I answer in a stern tone. "But, yes, even then."

Jeep sits up and rubs his face. "It won't be the same, though. Our dream will never come true."

Vicky puts her arm around his shoulder. "You know, I don't think the dream is about the where or when. It's about the who. What's important, is that you will be together." Her voice breaks at the end of the sentence, and her free hand searches for mine while the other holds onto the tattooed ghost.

There's an uncomfortable silence, which Mona breaks by standing up.

I swallow a tear or two before raising my hand. "No, don't."

Mona's sparks freeze mid-air. "I only want to take off the emotional edges."

Pushing myself to my feet, I wipe the sand and grass from my pants. "Our grief will only get stronger as we get closer to the end of our mission. We'll need to deal with it eventually. Wouldn't it be better to process it bit by bit?"

She drops her hands at her side and the sparks recede into her body.

"Wasn't it you who said pain and fear have a function? That you should never take all of it away?" I ask with an apologetic shrug.

Mona studies me with her head slightly tilted. "I did say something like that, didn't I?" Grief falls over her face as she looks at D'Maeo behind her. "And I was right." She takes a deep breath. "I've been using my sparks on you all too much lately. I guess I got a little carried away. I'm sorry."

Vicky lets me help her up, and, in turn, she pulls Jeep to his feet.

"No need to apologize," I say. "You wanted to help. And you did. Now that all our unfinished business has been taken care of, it's time to take on our feelings head-on."

Vicky flicks her blonde tips over her shoulders. "Great. I say we start with another illusion. A longer one this time, since Susan needs to practice."

I agree. We won't know where to look for the last soul until the ninth angel brings us the last set of cards anyway.

CHAPTER 10

Vicky stirs on my chest. "I could stay here forever," she murmurs and stretches her arms lazily before snuggling up to me again with a content grunt.

I wrap my arms around her. "Me too, but I'm getting hungry. Do you want to go see how the others are getting along?"

She works herself up on her elbows and examines every inch of my face.

"What?" I ask after several seconds, starting to feel uncomfortable.

Her lips curl up. "Nothing. I was just imagining what you'll look like when you're forty."

"That's probably not so hard to imagine. I'll look like a slightly younger version of my father." I roll onto my side to take in her face. Not that I need to; I know every inch of it like the back of my hand. "Imagining what you will look like at that age is much harder."

"Why? You've seen Isabel."

I dig into my memory for an image of Vicky's great-great-great-grandmother. "That doesn't help. You only vaguely resemble her."

She pushes a red lock behind her ear with a chuckle. "I never thought I'd actually look forward to finding that out. I mean, who looks forward to getting old?"

"Someone who died young and was brought back to life." I grab the lock of hair after it obstinately falls in front of her eyes again. "I think, at age forty, you'll still be super hot. I mean, look at Isabel."

Vicky bends forward until her lips almost touch mine. "You're such a flirt." She pulls back, rises to her feet, and holds out her hand.

I let her help me up, and steal a real kiss. "I only flirt with you."

Her head rests against my shoulder. "For the next seventy or so years, I hope."

"Definitely."

We make our way back through the trees, into the backyard of Darkwood Manor, which I renamed Lightwood Manor after the renovation. Several tables have been placed against each other, creating space for a large group.

I love the buzz around the house. There are always people here, laughing and enjoying their lives—or afterlives—with each other. Our family has grown so much. Maël is the only one from my Shield who doesn't live here anymore. She lives with her tribe in an in-between world we found, but she visits us at least once a week. Right now, she's sitting in the middle of the table with her father, listening to Kessley's jokes. Taylar walks over, arm in arm with his brother.

Vicky yanks my arm. "Are you coming? I thought you were done with all the staring."

With a laugh, I lift her from the ground and swing her around, making the sunlight dance across her solid skin and red hair. "I can't get enough of all these happy faces around me. Who would've thought we would all be together in the end?"

"I sure didn't." She smooths her long green dress before we walk over to where D'Maeo, Mona, and Mom are finishing the preparations for the barbecue.

D'Maeo throws the first hamburgers on as we reach them.

"Wow, that smells good," I say.

The old ghost is about to answer when a song begins to play, "Close to You" by the Carpenters.

Mom whirls around, as do I, and there he is, strolling toward us with a wide smile on his face and looking very much alive.

Dad.

Mom falls into his arms and I swallow tears of joy when their lips meet.

Finally, our family is complete.

Jeep turns up the volume and pulls Charlotte into the protective circle, which has turned into a dance floor surrounded by dozens of candles. Sparks hover above it.

Soon, several couples are dancing inside the circle, holding each other tightly.

Vicky and I join them, but I can't keep my eyes off Dad. He never danced with Mom; he had no sense of rhythm.

Did she use her magic to change that?

For some reason, I'm unable to look away. He seems so… elegant. Except, he was never—

The scene before me changes and I stumble back. The lights disappear, as well as the lively chatter and the smell of barbecued meat. A shudder runs through me, and I shake it off, along with the images of the illusion. Cold spreads through my body with the understanding everything I saw was in my head. None of it was real, and it never will be. The immensity of this realization makes my legs wobble and sinks me to my knees.

Mom is crouched next to me in a flash. She grabs my head with both hands. "I'm sorry."

It takes a couple of deep breaths for me to calm down. "It's fine. I'm fine." She lets go and I look around to check on my friends. They're all a bit shaken, but I seem to be in the worst shape.

As I clear my throat, Mom helps me up. "You dancing with Dad didn't come from my mind, did it?"

She shakes her head, a glint in her eye. "I wanted to try to make you see what I wanted you to see."

Pride washes over me, and I gladly let it drown out the sorrow. "I thought it was weird, Dad dancing so elegantly, but it never crossed my mind that what I was seeing wasn't real. You really are a natural, Mom."

She shrugs. "These powers do most of the work themselves."

Mona gives her a gentle shove. "Don't be so modest, Susan. Some people need months or even years of training to master their own powers, and you handle someone else's as easily as taking a stroll."

Now, Mom blushes. "I'm glad I can finally help."

There's a loud rumbling above us and we all look up at the sky. Dark clouds are pulled together.

"Are you doing that?" Vicky asks me.

"That's not me," I answer with a shake of my head.

Gisella's hands change into blades. "Well, that's not good, then."

There's no doubt about the truth in her statement. Something about the movement of the clouds is unnatural.

"Everyone who has stepped out of the protective circle, get back inside," I beckon. "Get ready."

"For what?" Charlie asks. "It can't be anything evil, right? Darkwood Manor is invisible to anyone who wants to hurt us."

Maël clutches her staff. "Maybe they found a way around that."

The sun gets completely blocked out and I conjure

a large lightning ball. There's another rumble, this one sounding more like a clash. Something falls from the clouds, and I narrow my eyes.

Everyone tenses. It's hard to see what is plummeting toward the ground. Until it passes my lightning ball hovering in the air.

"It's Quinn!" Charlie calls out.

But it's not just our angel friend.

Quinn is fighting a demon more gruesome than everything we've seen so far. It has four spindly legs under a crooked, bony body. Its two long arms are clasped around Quinn's chest and wings, and the large mouth in the hairy face is wide open.

With a heavy thud, they land in the middle of the circle. The blow knocks the wind out of Quinn and the demon folds its mouth around his face.

"Yuck!" Kessley exclaims backing up with haste.

"That's an understatement," Jeep responds.

We watch in horror as the clumps of hair on the demon's head stretch and grab onto the back of Quinn's head. The monster swallows, its pinprick black eyes focused only on its prey.

The angel struggles to break free of the demon's grip, but the force of the suction and the grip of its hairs keep our friend in place. After about a minute, he drops his arms in defeat.

His muffled voice comes through the demon's head. "You know, this is really uncomfortable. Can someone please pull this thing off me?"

"Right," I say, snapping out of my daze and

conjuring a bolt of lightning.

While my bolt hits the demon in the back of the head, Vicky and Gisella kick the monster in the back. Gisella's elbow connects with its head, and with a loud wail, it releases Quinn.

Quinn falls backward, spits dirt, and wipes his face over and over.

"Hurry," I say, hitting the thing in the face with more lightning to confuse and blind it. "Drag it out of the circle where we can kill it."

D'Maeo, Charlie, Dylan, and Jeep each grab a leg. It squeals and kicks, almost freeing itself, until Gisella hits it hard in the throat.

It's halfway out of the circle when Vicky grabs my arm. "Wait!"

I pause my attack. "Why?"

"I need it, to practice on." She pulls a rope from her endless pocket and ties the four legs together, followed by the arms, which she folds around its own body first.

Only now do I remember Vicky's wish to practice creating the circles of Hell. I don't think it's necessary, but if it gives her the confidence she needs, I'm fine with it.

Quinn stands up and wipes at his clothes and then his face again. "Can we at least chop its legs off?"

My eyebrows shoot up. "Since when are you so violent?"

He coughs and spits out some more dirt. "Since that thing breathed its molecules into me and tried to suck out my soul." He shudders a little. "Not to mention it killed two angels seconds after it broke into Heaven."

I need to shake the image of dead angels from my mind. "I see your point. Tell you what, you can kill it once Vicky is done with it."

Quinn waves my words away. "No, it's fine. You do it. I was actually on my way down to you with something important when that thing crossed my path."

My heart beats a little faster. "Something important?"

He holds out his hand, and in it, a new set of Cards of Death appears.

I suck in air so fast I almost choke. When I've recovered, I take the cards from him carefully. "*You're the ninth angel?*"

He shrugs. "We wanted to make sure the cards reached you. A lot has been going on, as you know, and saving this soul is still your top priority."

Charlie scratches his head. "I thought the final battle was almost upon us?"

Quinn glares at the bound demon just outside the circle. "Nothing is set in stone. You might still be able to foil Lucifer's backup plan." He grins at me. "And even if you can't, it won't hurt to make things a bit more difficult for him."

Vicky cracks her knuckles. "Trust me, we'll make it more than a little difficult for him."

Quinn winks. "I know you will." He gives us a

short wave and spreads his wings. "I've got to go. Good luck. I'll see you soon."

CHAPTER 11

We decide to split up, since we've got too many important things to do. Kessley and D'Maeo will keep an eye on Vicky and the demon while she practices in the backyard. The idea to try creating circles of Hell in the silver mine is discarded right away, because it might draw unwanted attention to us. Mona will contact her fairy godmother friends again, to see how many of them she can gather for extra protection, in case it does come to a direct confrontation with Satan. The rest of us try to decipher the Cards of Death.

I haven't given them a decent look yet, and when I put them on the table between us the first thing that shoots through my mind is that Quinn must have made a mistake.

"The symbols aren't hidden," Jeep states the obvious.

"That's weird," Charlie voices my other thought.

"Is it, though?" Gisella leans over the table to study the cards closer. She turns them around.

The backs are like the ones we got before, with moving demonic symbols and skulls. They switch color every few seconds. It makes me feel like I'm tripping.

"Why are these different? Why aren't the pictures on the front hidden, like they always are?" I ask out loud.

Gisella turns the cards back and taps them to emphasize each word she utters. "Because – there – is – no – punishment – in – the – first – circle." She sits down and shoots me a smug mile. Rightfully so, I must say, since none of us had thought of that.

"What do you mean, no punishment?" Dylan asks with a frown. "I thought each type of demon was based on the punishment for the sinners of the circle they guard."

There's a jubilant cry from outside and we all turn our heads. I smile as a circle of light drops into the ground.

"Except in the first circle," Gisella states, making us all turn our attention back to her. "The first circle is for pagans. There is no sin, and therefore, no punishment."

Taylar scratches his head. "What sin will they make the last soul commit then?"

"None, I think." Gisella meets Maël's eyes across the table and the ghost queen nods. "I think they will kill the last soul as soon as they find them."

I bend over and pull the cards back to me. "So, we should really hurry."

A closer look at the pictures on the two cards makes me think we won't need much time to decipher them. On the first card there's only one drawing: of a body, with a head lying next to it. No need to guess its meaning. This is the way the next soul will die if we don't get to them in time. The symbol that would normally hint to the sin they will commit, is missing.

The second card shows the regular amount of five symbols. Not only are they not covered in anything we need to get rid of, they are also self-explanatory.

To start, there's a flag. I'm not sure which country it's from, but that's easy enough to google. The second picture is a church, the third a stack of books. The other two are a summer dress with a wide skirt, and a smiling face surrounded by wild, blonde curls.

Taylar is leaning over to check out the cards. "Okay, we're looking for a woman with blonde curls, in a wide dress, who loves to read and goes to church every Sunday. And she lives in… Where's that flag from?"

Charlie is already tapping away at his phone. "Luxemburg?" He turns his screen to me.

I tap the flag on the card. "No, this blue is much darker."

He tries again. "Oh, yeah, yeah, here it is." He shows me another picture. "The Netherlands."

Dylan leans back in his chair with a heavy sigh. Because of his gangly build, the chair always seems way too small for him. "Isn't that like, thousands of miles away? How are we supposed to get there in time?"

Taylar slams his fist against his chest. "I can open a portal."

"Really?" Jeep stops fidgeting with his hat. "I thought you could only open portals into other worlds?"

"Nope," the young ghost answers, self-confident. "I can take us there."

Charlie puts his phone away and stands up. "Great. I'm ready."

"Not so fast," Maël warns him. "It would be wiser to find out where this person is exactly. The Netherlands might be small, but there are millions of blonde women there, and thousands of churches. We need to narrow it down."

I glance at the pictures again. "The hints are pretty obvious, so maybe you should query something like Netherlands, books, and church?"

It takes Charlie about three seconds to come up with a hit. "*Amazing bookstores in the Netherlands.* Look at this." He shows us pictures of giant gothic arches, ancient frescoes, and colorful stained glass windows surrounding rows of bookcases. "It's a bookstore *in* a church."

Dylan holds out his arm. "Can I see?"

Charlie hands him the phone, and he scrolls

through the pictures. "No way. That place is like Heaven."

Charlie snorts. "Sure. If Heaven were a place filled with nothing but books."

Dylan sighs and lowers the phone. "To me, it is."

"Then you're in luck, because we're going to check this place out," I say. "I'm guessing the girl or woman we're looking for spends a lot of time there."

"Maybe she works there," Dylan muses. "I'm so jealous."

Jeep rolls down his sleeves when a cold breeze blows through the open back door. "I didn't know you were such an avid reader, Dylan."

The young mage blushes. "Well, I don't advertise it. My classmates used to bully me because of it. Said I was boring, stuck-up, that kind of thing." He grinds his teeth. "They used to take my books from me and hit me with them. Or hide them, usually in the garbage or in a pile of dog mess. Once they even tried to flush a book down the toilet."

"I'm sorry," Jeep says. "Whether you read or not doesn't say anything about your value as a person, and it doesn't mean you're boring."

"I know."

"You should not hide your passion," Maël adds. "Especially not from your friends."

Dylan's cheeks turn even redder. "Thanks, guys."

"Anyway," I say, getting to my feet, "You'll see this heavenly place soon, because we're going there immediately after Vicky finishes her training." I walk to the back door. "I'll go see how she's doing."

In the backyard, Vicky, Kessley, and D'Maeo are staring into a hole in the ground.

"Something wrong?" I ask approaching them with caution.

Vicky looks up and shoots me a crooked smile. "Wrong? No. Puzzling, yes."

"Did it work?" I risk a glance down the hole. The demon we captured is stuck in an ice cube. The cube is one of many around it, and it reaches up to its neck. Its arms are free so it keeps pushing to get out, but the ice doesn't budge. Above it, each glowing circle shows its own interpretation of Hell. Boiling pitch, burning sand, fire, a river filled with souls, smelting gold, black and white snow, and the last one we encountered—tornados.

My mouth falls open. "You copied the punishment of each circle, too?"

Kessley slaps Vicky hard on her back. "She did. Isn't she brilliant?"

I smirk at Vicky's light blush. "She sure is." Her cheek is warm under my touch. "I knew you could do it."

She places her hands on her waist. "Thanks for the vote of confidence, babe. Now, tell me, do you also believe I can get rid of the circles again? Because I have no clue how to do that."

My mouth opens and closes without sound.

Kessley giggles and Vicky's serious expression wavers. "That was my reaction, too, the moment I realized I hadn't thought this through."

I find my voice back. "Did you try doing everything you did to create the circles, but in reverse?"

She nods. "I did. And I also tried ordering them to vanish, crushing them with my mind, and even throwing holy water over them. Nothing has worked."

I stare into the depth and scratch my neck. "Maybe they need to be empty first?"

"That could work," D'Maeo says.

Vicky shakes her hands loose and breathes out slowly. I follow her gaze. At first, nothing happens. Then, the demon is lifted to the top of its circle. The ice around it shatters and it throws some wild kicks.

"Get ready to cut off its head," Vicky says.

I pull out my athame and D'Maeo takes out his sword.

"Ready," we say in unison.

Kessley takes a step back when the demon starts to rise to the surface, passing through one circle after another. Each time the light of a circle touches it, smoke rises from its skin, and it howls in pain. It makes me wonder if there will be anything of this monster left by the time it reaches the surface.

It does, however, reach us mostly intact. And pissed off, too. It lashes out and misses my nose by a hair's breadth. I slice its claw off, and aim for the head next, but D'Maeo has already chopped it off.

The body falls forward and goes up in black

smoke before it hits the ground. An image of the shocked face lingers in the air for a second, before the wind blows it apart.

Vicky's eyebrows knot together as she focuses on emptying the circles. The flames go out one by one, the river dries up, and the souls turn to ash. The ice and snow melt, and the tornados pick up the sand and dissipate.

I'm impressed. Within several minutes, the nine circles are all that remain, pulsing calmly and turning as if they're floating in the sea on a peaceful day. Although these circles are small compared to the real ones, they're still the size of the annex.

"Will it be hard for you to create circles big enough for Hell?" I wonder out loud.

Vicky tilts her head a little, without taking her eyes off the hole at our feet. "No, I can expand them with a simple thought."

I tap my chin, afraid to say the next words out loud and be laughed at. "In that case…"

Vicky turns her head my way. "What?"

"What if we kept them?" I continue. "It will save you time in the final battle *and* improve our chances of locking Satan back in Hell."

Vicky shakes her head. "I wish it were that easy."

When she doesn't elaborate, I frown at D'Maeo. He takes a couple of steps back, and I follow him.

"These circles aren't connected to Hell," he explains. "They only serve as a prison, they don't go very deep."

"I see," I say with a disappointed sigh. "Well, it's fine, really. She can do it, that's what counts."

"If she's not able to destroy them, we need to hide them." He scans the trees fencing off the garden. "My work as a magic transporter taught me that no protection lasts forever. Eventually, someone will be able to see into the house and garden. If they discover these circles, we lose one element of surprise."

I shake my head in confusion. "The Devil already knows what Vicky can do, right? That's why he tried to have her killed."

D'Maeo leans closer and lowers his voice to an almost inaudible whisper. "Yes, but I don't think he knows that she embraced her inheritance, which activated these powers. He probably thinks we're still searching for the reason she got cursed by Shelton Banks."

"I don't believe that," I say after a short pause. "We shouldn't underestimate him. He's been one step ahead of us most of the time."

D'Maeo squeezes my shoulder. "Has he? Or have we been shedding every layer that has been blocking us, and gathering power, building up to this moment, in which everything comes together?" He winks and walks back to Vicky.

I follow him, his words echoing through my brain in an endless loop. He makes it sound as if every step on our way has been intentional, while all we did was work with what we had and knew. The Devil and his accomplices have been interfering with our plans and blocking our powers since before I knew magic even existed. Yet, the old ghost is right. We overcame each bump in the road, and got stronger every time. All this sabotage only made us more determined to succeed.

Vicky interrupts my thoughts by breathing out loudly.

"No luck?" I ask, walking up to her and placing a hand on her back.

She throws up her hands in defeat. "I don't know how to do it. I really don't."

I rub her neck. "Don't worry about it. The most important thing is that you can create them. All we need is some sand and a spell, and no one will notice these circles."

She pouts. "Are you sure?"

"Of course. I'll have something to remember you by every time I sit in the garden."

Her shoulders sag and she purses her lips. Kessley jumps between us and pulls us both close to her. "Hey, don't cry. You two will be together again. Nothing can keep you apart forever, you were meant for each other."

Although I try to smile, my lips don't cooperate. "I'm seriously considering letting someone kill me once we've defeated the Devil," I mumble gloomily.

Vicky shoves me away from her with force. "Don't you dare! You've got a great life ahead of you, no doubt filled with love. You are *not* throwing that away for me, do you hear me?" Her nostrils flare in anger.

"You should be grateful that you can have a full life."

I want to tell her it will be empty without her, but she stomps off toward the house. Just before she reaches the back door, she veers right and disappears around the side of the mansion.

"She makes it sound so easy," I whisper.

D'Maeo scratches his gray sideburns. "That's simply a coping mechanism, Dante. She's been falling apart inside just as much as you." He sighs. "And me."

The pain in his eyes is like nothing I've seen in him before.

I should tell him now. It's not right to let him suffer for no reason.

I wipe the tear away that is rolling down my cheek without my permission. "There's something I need to tell you, D'Maeo."

CHAPTER 12

D'Maeo's expression changes to despair, and I hold up my hands. "Don't worry, it's good news. I just couldn't bring myself to tell you sooner, because… well…" D'Maeo furrows his eyebrows, and I take a deep breath. "I was given the opportunity to let one of us stay here after we defeat Satan."

His face lights up. "Vicky can stay?"

Rubbing my eyes to keep the tears inside, I confess, "No. I didn't choose her."

"What?" D'Maeo and Kessley say in unison.

"Why the heck not?" Kess asks.

My gaze stays on the hole in front of me. "It didn't feel right to choose myself over others. Which meant I was left with only one option." I meet D'Maeo's eyes. "You."

His expression changes about ten times in mere seconds. Shock, sadness, disbelief, relief, sorrow,

133

compassion, elation… they all pass over his face. His wrinkles seem to deepen and vanish at the same time.

"You did what?" he finally breathes.

I place my hand on his shoulder and smile. "I choose to save you from moving on. I couldn't bear to tear you and Mona apart."

Kessley stares at me wide-eyed. "That's the sweetest thing I've ever heard. You gave up your true love to save another."

Unable to hold back my tears any longer, I look away. "Yes, well…" I say, my voice hoarse. "That's why it was difficult for me to tell you guys." I swallow the lump in my throat. "Now you know there's no need to worry about saying goodbye."

A new expression has taken over the old ghost's face. It's a mixture of pride and gratefulness. He shakes his head in disbelief and opens his mouth, but only some vague stuttering comes out. He opens his arms wide and pulls me into a hug that's warm, even though his body is cold. "You are truly an amazing person, Dante. I am so proud to be fighting by your side. You have grown into an admirable young man."

"Thank you," I mutter.

We hold each other long enough for it to become uncomfortable, but it still feels nice. I know I've made the right decision, no matter how much it hurts me.

"Do you want to tell the others?" D'Maeo asks when we let go.

I let out a heavy sigh. "I'm not sure I can handle Vicky's emotions on top of my own, or the other way around. She is an empath, after all."

"Too late," Vicky's voice says behind me. "I heard everything."

I flinch and turn around. It takes all my strength to move my eyes up to hers. My hands get clammy at the sight of the emotions whirling inside them. "I'm sorry, babe. I didn't want you to find out this way."

To my surprise a smile curls around her lips. She crosses the distance between us in a flash and places her hands on my cheeks. "Dante Banner, you never cease to amaze me. I adore you even more now. And yes, moving on without you once this battle is over will tear me in half, but I'm happy with your decision to save D'Maeo." She gives me a passionate kiss and I hear D'Maeo and Kessley shuffling away discretely. I gasp for air and Vicky takes my hands. "I never thought I could love anyone this intensely. Thank you for making me feel this way."

"Thank you, too," I whisper.

"I love every smart and stupid choice you've ever made, every perfect and flawed thing about you, but please don't *ever* say you're going to get yourself killed on purpose again."

"I won't," I assure her. "If you promise me you'll enjoy your time in Heaven without me."

She presses her head against my shoulder. "I will."

"But not too much," I add softly.

She giggles.

My fingers move over her lips, but I step back before this turns into something I can't tear myself away from. "Let's hide these circles, shall we?"

It doesn't take long for me to come up with a spell. I use the cloaking spell, which I've cast several times before, but add a couple of words plus several herbs. Mona makes a quick trip to the store to get some wood chips and to stock up on candles, incense, herbs, spices, and salt. She's back in no time and puts everything in the protective circle.

I thank her, and then Vicky and me get to work. We put four candles around the circles Vicky created, one for each wind direction. They're white, to strengthen the whole spell instead of a specific part of it. Then, we gather the herbs and spices. Dried fern leaf, poppy seeds, dill weed, and a few drops of dew.

"Okay, so now we've got confusion, adaptability, and protection against evil. What's missing is…" I glance at my Book of Spells, "something to seal the hole with, something for transformation, and something to prevent people falling in if the hole opens up by accident."

"To prevent good people from falling in," Vicky corrects me.

"Exactly."

She rummages through the supplies Mona brought us and holds up a bag of elongated white flowers. "How about Solomon's Seal?"

I rub my chin. "Will that actually seal the hole?"

"Sure. It's called that for a reason."

I take the bag from her and put it in the bowl with

the other herbs and spices. "Good. What else?"

"We need something strong to create a barrier, plus something that will turn the wood chips into a solid floor to seal the hole with." She grabs another see-through bag. "Here. Yarrow. That will work for the barrier."

She tosses bag after bag aside and doesn't seem too happy with the bottles Mona brought either. In the end, she lowers herself onto the grass with a defeated expression. "There's nothing here for transformation."

There's a soft cough behind us and we both look over our shoulders.

"Maybe I can help," Kessley offers timidly.

"Do you have a stash of herbs?" Vicky inquires.

Kess holds up her hand and a knife. "No, but I have blood."

"How is that going to—" I start to say, but then understanding dawns. "Shapeshifter blood! Great idea." I turn to Vicky, who hasn't responded yet. "Isn't it?"

A smile turns her lips up. "It is."

She beckons Kessley closer. I hold the bowl out in front of her and she pierces the skin of Kess' index finger. A drop of red falls into the bowl.

"Two more," Vicky instructs.

Kessley squeezes her finger, then pulls her hand away as soon as the third drop is added to the mixture.

"Thanks, Kess," I say.

"Anytime." With her finger in her mouth, she walks back to the mansion.

Vicky and I crush everything, mix it, and then head inside to heat it up in the kitchen.

Mona has started cooking and the smells are making my stomach rumble. Which is no wonder, since we skipped lunch.

"Let's get this done," I tell Vicky.

We return to the garden where I read the spell one more time.

Green smoke curls up from the bowl in my hand. I grind the mixture again and walk around the hole, making sure I stay along the edges inside the salt circle Vicky created as I begin reciting:

"Shadows, shadows come to me.
Surround this hole so only I can see."

I sprinkle the contents of the bowl over the hole from all sides.

"Wanted by evil, dark as night
I cloak this hole in magic's light.

Make it unseen, from left to right
Invisible from any height.

Wrap the shadows all around.
Block all motion, touch and sound."

138

Shadows from the trees soar toward me and start to cover the hole and the circles beneath.

I light the candles and keep walking in circles.

"Seal this hole with boards of wood.
Make all evil see what it should."

The flames reach sideways until they form a burning ring. I throw the wood chips inside it, and they are picked up immediately and spread over the hole, blocking the light that rises from the circles below.

"Solid wood will cover all
that lies within the flaming wall.

This wood will now feel soft as grass
when good or evil tries to pass."

The chips of wood melt together to form boards. These lower themselves and click into place as soon as they are level with the grass. The shadows retreat to their places in the forest, and the flames die.

Vicky nods, content. "Well done. Except, you didn't put anything in about evil falling into it."

"I didn't want to. If we bring the fight here and Satan sees his followers fall into these circles, he'll know you've got your ancestral powers."

She places a finger against her lips. "Good point."

We both stare at the boarded-up hole.

"How do we know it worked?" I ask. "We're good, so we can still see it."

"Well, the boards covered up the hole. That should tell us enough. Plus, we can step on them. See if they really feel like grass." She takes off her boots and steps onto the floor without hesitation. With a smile, she looks up. "It feels exactly like grass. So weird."

"I'm still not sure about the invisible part."

She shrugs. "Have a little faith in your own abilities, babe. Everyone else does."

"It worked," Taylar calls out from the doorway.

With a frown, I turn to him. "How do you know?"

He throws up his hands. "Just trust me."

Quinn's words come back to me, and I decide to take them to heart. "Okay, then. I guess we're done here for now."

I bend over to pick up my notebook and to gather all the other stuff. Vicky is already filling her endless pocket.

"What was that about?" she whispers when I squat down to help her.

"I don't know," I say, which is pretty close to the truth. "Forget about it. We've got more important things to do."

Hand in hand, we walk back inside.

"One more thing crossed from the list," I say as I slide into my chair. "After dinner, we're going to find the next soul."

Charlie waves his phone at me. "We can't leave

tonight. We looked up the time difference between us and the Netherlands. It's eight hours later there, so the book shop is closed. We'll have to wait until tomorrow."

Jeep throws his hat in the air. "We can do some more training. I could use the exercise. I've been sitting still for too long."

"After we think of a plan, and a backup plan," D'Maeo says sternly. "We need to go in well-prepared, since we don't have a lot of time to save this soul."

The others look at me for confirmation, and I nod. "First dinner, then some training, and then off to bed. We need to get up early."

CHAPTER 14

At five o'clock my alarm goes off. Vicky is already sitting up in bed. I shake my head at her boots. "Don't you get tired of lying in bed with your boots on? It must be uncomfortable."

She shrugs. "Not really. You get used to it."

My hand rakes through her dark hair. "At least I never have to wait for you to get ready in the morning. Many women would be jealous if they knew you wake up looking perfect every day."

Her eyebrow shoots up. "Jealous of a dead girl?"

The comment makes me chuckle. "I guess you can't have everything."

She lowers her head and swallows. "You sure can't."

"Hey." With my finger under her chin I lift her head until her eyes meet mine. "Eventually we *will* have it all. We will be together again."

Before she can answer, there's a knock on our bedroom door.

"Are you up?" Mom calls out.

"Yes, we're coming!" I answer.

"Good, breakfast is ready."

My stomach rumbles at the thought and Vicky rolls her eyes. "You're almost as bad as Charlie. How can you be hungry again already? You had two full plates for dinner *and* a snack before bed."

I bend over to nibble at her neck. "Don't forget the snack *in* bed."

She pushes herself to her feet. "You're incorrigible."

Leaning on my elbow I watch her walk to the door. "I wouldn't be if you weren't so damn attractive."

She laughs out loud and opens the door, but doesn't walk into the hallway. "Well, are you coming?"

With the cover pulled back I point at my bare chest and legs. "Like this?"

Her lips curl up even farther. "That's probably a bad idea. Anyone would get a heart-attack from one look at those blindingly white legs."

I grab her pillow and throw it at her.

She catches it with ease, jumps back onto the bed, and smothers me. Instead of trying to get the pillow off my head, I take a fistful of shirt from her side in both hands and pull. We both roll over and she drops the pillow. She giggles when I tickle her.

"Do you give up?" I ask, holding my hands still for a second.

She rests her arms above her head, a twinkle in her eye. "I'm all yours."

"Forever and ever?"

Sadness falls over her face again. "For eternity."

My hands wrap around her face and I rest my forehead against hers, wishing I could take her pain away. "You can have me for as long as you want."

Tears drip onto my fingers and I roll onto my side and pull her close. We lay there entwined for several minutes, while the noise from downstairs gets louder.

Vicky nudges my shoulder with hers. "We should get up. After all, you were the one who said we needed to get up early. Remember, mister big leader?"

"Fine, I'll get dressed." I sit up and stretch my arms above my head. "Tell them I'll be down in two minutes. Make sure they save me some breakfast."

At half past five we're gathered in the garden, stomachs full, and ready to go.

"Okay, everyone," I say. "We all know what the plan is. Let's stick to it. We've got a backup plan, too, so this soul is ours."

When I nod at Taylar, he steps away from the group. Mona and Mom watch us from the doorway to the kitchen.

"Be careful," Mom calls out as Taylar opens a portal.

I'm amazed at how easy this is for him. It's only

144

his second time creating one, but it takes him no more than a couple of seconds. I stare at him in awe, and a wide grin appears on his face.

"Nice job," I say, following Vicky through the gateway. Pausing, I stick my head back through and wave at Mom. "Don't worry about us."

Taylar comes through last and closes the gate behind us.

I find myself standing between two stone walls. In front of me there's a steel door, with a rain pipe above it. Behind me, my friends are huddled together.

"Where are we?" I ask Taylar.

"In The Netherlands, of course." He places his hand on the light stone wall to my right. "This is the bookstore."

"Why are we standing in some sort of alley?"

Taylar pulls himself up on the door. "This is a shopping street, and it's the middle of the day. What do you think will happen if we step through a portal in full sight?" He drops himself back to his feet and raises his eyebrows at me.

"Good point," I admit. "I was in such a hurry that I didn't think about that."

Maël pushes her cape back. "Since we do not want to attract too much attention, we will turn invisible."

I nod, but then my eyes fall on Gisella. "I have a feeling we won't blend in, even without six ghosts."

The werecat-witch looks down at her red leather catsuit. "Right. Maybe I should wait here."

Charlie shakes his head. "Absolutely not. What if

something attacks?"

Jeep rolls up his sleeves. "I agree. We should stay together."

"I've got an idea." Taylar moves his hands, and another portal materializes. He peers inside and beckons Gisella. "Come on. Go change. I'll keep it open."

After a short hesitation, Gisella sticks her head through the gateway. "Hey, that's my room." She steps in, and Taylar blocks it until she returns, dressed in camouflage pants and a tight, short-sleeved, green shirt. Her hair is pulled together in a ponytail.

"Wow, you're like a different person!" Kessley calls out.

Gisella takes a small bow and Taylar closes the portal. Then, he peers over the steel door again.

"You know you could just step through, right?" I ask, taking in the strain his weight puts on his muscles.

He blushes and glances at Kessley. "I know."

Chuckling, I slap him on the back, and wink. "Forget I said anything."

The ghosts step through the door first and tell us when the coast is clear. It's a busy street, so Gisella, Charlie, and I need to climb over the door quickly in order to not draw attention to ourselves. One young couple frowns as they turn the corner and see Charlie climbing over, but they don't say anything. I help him with a soft landing and then we make for the entrance of the bookstore.

The church is situated on a small sort of square. There's an outside café to its left. The church itself is an old, gothic-style building, with a high, arched window in the center. A weirdly out of place metal entrance has been put in front of it, decorated with words connected by lines. I can make out the words "books" and "Dominicanen", which I remember to be the name of the shop.

Dylan is the first in. He stops dead at the sight of the full interior of the building. I have to admit, it is absolutely stunning. There are stain-glassed windows and old frescos. Light pours in through the high and narrow arched windows at the back and the ones just under the high vaulted ceiling. In the middle, a two-floor, steel structure has been built and filled with rows of books. Low tables with stacks of books are placed between the columns on both sides.

Dylan gasps. "I could stay here for hours."

"So could I," I answer, pausing beside him, "but we're not here for the church or the books, don't forget that."

He sighs. "Please tell me we can come back here someday."

Since I can't promise him anything like that, I walk farther into the building as I whisper, "Keep an eye out for anything out of the ordinary."

Our group walks around the steel structure in the middle to study the customers and staff while pretending to check out the huge collection of books. When we return to the entrance, we're not even half a step closer to finding the ninth soul. There's no sign of demons either, though; I'm grateful for that.

We choose a quiet corner to retreat to, and I pull out the Card of Death with the five hints on it. The flag, the church, and the books all suggest this is the location. The summer dress with the wide skirt and the smiling face surrounded by wild, blonde curls are the clues that will have to lead us to the person Satan is after.

"I haven't seen anyone who looks like that," Charlie remarks.

"Maybe we should ask the man at the counter," Vicky suggests. "She might not be working today."

Jeep scans the people browsing through the books close to us. "She might not work here at all. Maybe she's a regular customer."

I slide the cards into my back pocket. "I'll go ask."

The cashier hands a bag filled with books to a woman and a little girl before turning to me. "Kan ik u helpen?" He's short and bald and has bright red glasses.

I'm not sure what he asked me, but it must be something along the lines of *"Can I help you?"*

With a smile, I bend forward hoping he speaks English. Keeping my voice low, as if I'm sharing a secret, I explain, "Hi. I'm looking for someone I talked to last week. Maybe you can help me?" I send him my best innocent teenager-in-love smile and hope the woman we're looking for is not a fifty-year-old teacher. "She has blonde curls and was wearing a colorful, wide dress."

The man chuckles and leans closer to me. "That's Wendy. You're in luck; she's single. She'll be in for work any minute. You can ask her out, but don't take too long. It's a busy day, we need her."

My lips stretch into a wide grin. "Thank you so much. I won't take up too much of her time."

He gestures at the entrance. "There she is. Good luck."

"Thanks."

I walk halfway to the entrance, out of earshot from the cashier, and wait for Wendy to approach me. Even without the heads-up from her colleague, I would've known she's the one we're looking for. Her blonde curls dance around her round face with every bouncy step she takes. All eyes are drawn to her, and that's not just because of the red-and-white-dotted dress she's wearing. She greets the customers with joy. Happiness and warmth radiate from her. I can't help but smile when her eyes meet mine.

"Hi," I say as she passes me. "You're Wendy, right?"

She stops and looks me up and down. "Yes. Can I help you?"

Her English is flawless, and she switches to it without effort.

"There's something we need to discuss."

She stiffens. Her gaze locks onto mine. "Really? What would that be?"

I feel my eyebrows move up, surprised at her

149

sudden hostile tone of voice. "It's about your safety. I'd rather not discuss it here. Is there somewhere private we could talk?"

Wendy lets out a shrill laugh. "Really?" She takes me in from head to toe again. "I was warned about the tricks you might use to get close to me, but I have to admit, this is a good one. You're almost convincing." She leans forward. "You'll have to do better than this, though. You don't think I wear these wide skirts only because they look good, do you? I never go anywhere without protection. Holy water, an athame…" She trails off and narrows her eyes when I remain calm.

"You think I'm evil," I conclude. "You think I'm here to kill you." I watch her closely, trying to figure out why she would think this, and wondering how I can convince her I'm trying to do the opposite.

"Obviously," Wendy says. "You're not the first, and you won't be the last. But even if you manage to capture and torture me, I'll never tell you where the book is."

"Book?" My frown deepens.

Wendy straightens up. Doubt crosses her face. Then, the repulsion and determination are back. "Like I said, you're really good. I almost fell for that."

She takes a step away from me. "If you'll excuse me, I need to call the other Keepers. If we're going to fight, I'd like it to be a fair one. I know you lot never come alone, and I do like a chance to stay alive a bit longer."

My admiration for her cockiness is overshadowed by one word she used. 'Keepers'. The reason why she assumes I came to kill her dawns on me.

"You're still denying it?" she asks incredulously when I don't respond. "I could smell your magic the moment you opened your mouth, pal. You can stop pretending."

All I do is look at her with a blank expression and she sighs. My mind is whirring.

Is she who I think she is?

"Have it your way." The irritation in her words is almost palpable. "At least keep the people in here out of it. Meet me at the side of the church in half an hour." She turns, her skirt moving up as if she's dancing. There's not even a hint of fear in the movement.

In reflex, I reach out and grab her wrist. "Wait."

She glances back, rage burning in her eyes. Her voice is no more than an angry whisper, but I can hear every word clearly. "I said not here. However, that doesn't mean I won't kill you in front of all these people." She turns back fast, freeing her arm from my grip. I'm not sure how she grabbed it so fast, or where it came from, but now there's a small bottle in her other hand. She holds it up, her eyes never leaving my face. "I can kill you right here, or we can fight outside. Your choice."

"You're a Keeper of Life?" I ask. My shock seeps through each word. "You've got the Book of a Thousand Deaths?"

"That act of innocence is lost on me," she snaps, but doubt is trickling into her eyes again.

Spreading my arms, I challenge her. "Well, go on then. Hit me with that holy water and see for yourself."

"I *will* do it," she warns, her voice quivering a little now.

"I know."

"You just want to scare the customers."

"I promise I don't. Just hit me with it."

Hurried footsteps approach from behind and Wendy's gaze shifts over my shoulder. "I see your friends are inside already. Do you wish to make the news?"

I remain calm, hoping she'll see the truth eventually. "Not at all."

"If you think scaring me will help you get the book, you're dead wrong." She raises the bottle a little higher. "I've got more of these. And even if you capture me, I'll never give you the book."

A sigh escapes me; I hate the attention we're starting to attract. "Get on with it, please. The real enemy might waltz through the door any second." I wave my arm at my friends who come to a halt in the corner of my peripheral vision. "You can throw some of it on them, too. It won't hurt us."

I expect more backtalk, when I'm hit in the face by a splash. I cough and splutter, then blink the water from my eyes. When I can see again, Wendy is throwing the contents of another bottle at Charlie.

Gisella is already dripping all over the floor. Customers are making a wide arch around us, bafflement and question marks on their faces.

Charlie wipes his face and shakes his head. "What a waste of perfectly fine holy water."

The bald guy from the counter comes stomping over, a dark cloud almost visible above his head. "Wendy! Wat ben je in hemelsnaam aan het doen? Je beschadigt de boeken!"

I have no idea what he's saying, but hold up my hands in surrender. "It was my fault. We're from the radio and we're challenging people all over the world to do something forbidden under the nose of their employers." It's the best explanation I can come up with on the fly. "To see how the employer/employee relationship differs in each country. Don't worry about the books. If any of them were damaged, we'll pay for them." I smile at Wendy, who's stunned expression is hilarious. First, I'm not evil, and now I'm helping her get out of an uncomfortable situation. It's clear she's more than a little confused.

The guy, who appears to be Wendy's manager, rubs his bald head and shrugs. "Well, I guess it's okay then."

I hold out my hand to Wendy. "Congratulations, you just won a small donation for your company."

She shakes my hand, and her boss pats her shoulder. At a loss for words, he stutters something about customers and getting back to work and thanks me for the nice surprise. As he turns to walk away, I call after him, "Do you mind if I borrow Wendy for an interview?"

He smiles. "Of course not. Take your time."

I turn back to Wendy. "You said something about meeting at the side of the church? Can we do that now?"

"Sure." She leads us through the store, down some stairs, and into a small courtyard. She looks around to check for open windows and nods when she finds none. "We can talk here."

CHAPTER 15

I pace up and down the courtyard, wondering where to begin.

Eventually, the thing that's been bugging me since I found out, is the first thing to leave my lips. "You've got the Book of a Thousand Deaths?"

"I never said that."

"You're a Keeper of Life, right?" I press.

She narrows her eyes at me, as if deciding what she can tell me.

I come to a halt in front of her. "I hope you believe me now. We are truly here to keep you safe."

"Most evil creatures react heavily to holy water," Gisella adds. "And we didn't. Even Beelzebub can't handle it very well."

Wendy's mouth falls open. "You've fought Beelzebub?"

The three of us nod.

"How?" she asks. "I mean… why?"

I sigh. "It's a long story. But, I can give you the short version."

She folds her arms over her chest, still not completely convinced we're the good guys. "Okay."

My feet start moving again. "I'm the chosen one. Or rather, we are." I gesture at Charlie and Gisella, and also at Dylan and my Shield, who show themselves to Wendy for a split second. She recoils a bit, but steps closer in the same movement, which I find admirable. She's an excellent Keeper of Life, standing up to evil and those she's not sure about. Protecting the innocents around her from getting caught up in a fight.

As soon as she meets my eyes again I continue. "We were chosen to stand against the Devil, who is trying to break through the nine circles of Hell to reach Earth. To get here, he needs a soul for each circle. He's down to the last soul, and that soul… is you. That's why we're here, to keep you safe."

She lifts her chin. "I don't need protection. I can take care of myself."

Gisella imitates her posture. "Really? Is that why you wanted to call your colleagues before meeting with us?"

Wendy blushes.

Stepping forward and placing my hands on her shoulders, I assure her again, "You can trust us, Wendy. We want to save you, to save the world. And, we also want to make sure the book is safe. Now, I don't know what kind of powers you have, but I don't want to risk them not being strong enough to defend yourself against a small army of demons."

She swallows, but I'm not sure whether it's because of the prospect of demons coming after her, or because she's intimidated by me.

I let go of her and rub my face. "I don't know how to convince you we're on your side."

"The fact that she's not dead yet must tell her something," Charlie grumbles.

Wendy shakes her head, her curls dancing around her face. "That could be a trick to get me to tell you where the book is. I've seen a lot of tricks. And I can tell you, this is the smartest."

"Probably because it isn't a trick," Charlie answers.

My hands move up in defeat. "This isn't getting us anywhere."

Wendy is taking our growing impatience in with a thoughtful expression. "I've got an idea." She leans against the wall of the neighboring building. "Tell me about the other eight souls. Which ones did you save?"

I don't understand why she'd want me to tell her that, but it can't hurt. So, I summarize what we've been through in the last couple of weeks. It's hard to believe so little time has passed. We've gone through enough to fill a lifetime, but summer break still isn't over. We're actually not even halfway through it.

If we defeat Satan, we can chill for several weeks.

"Who else?" Wendy asks, interrupting my

thoughts.

I tell her about the priest, the fairy, the troll, the Mahaha, and the nun.

Before I even finish the story of how we freed the nuns from the demons who were possessing them, Wendy steps forward and throws her arms around my neck. "It *is* you!"

All I can do is slap her on the back awkwardly and wait for her to explain the sudden change of heart.

She lets go, her cheeks a bright red again. "I'm sorry, I'm just so relieved. I've heard a lot about you, Dante Banner."

"You have?"

"Of course. As Keepers of Life, we need to stay on top of the developments of everything evil-related. We've known about the existence of the chosen one since we were founded. I think we knew it was you before you did yourself."

Wendy's eyes are drawn to Vicky, who must have made herself visible again. "But you didn't know where to find him?"

"Unfortunately, no. That would've saved us a lot of time. We only knew your name. You must have been protected by some sort of spell."

I gesture to the windows around us, and the closed door that leads to the bookstore, then give Vicky a stern look.

"Fine, I'm invisible," she sulks.

"So, how did you know we were telling the truth?" I ask, turning back to Wendy.

"We've been watching your progress. We know about the souls."

"That doesn't mean anything," Gisella counters. "Both sides will know all about them."

"True, but you can't fake the way you talk about your winnings and defeats. The way Dante described those fights and the people who got killed, and the souls you lost… if that was fake, then he's the best liar in the world. Besides, you wouldn't be arguing with me about it if you were on the wrong side." She slams her hands together when we nod. "Now, any idea who or what is coming to kill me?"

"Yes, as you might know, for each soul Satan sends the demons of the relevant circle to kill it. Normally, there's also someone who tries to get the soul to commit the sin that's connected to the circle, but the first layer of Hell isn't connected to a particular sin."

"Which is why we suspect they won't waste any time killing you," Charlie finishes my explanation.

"If they can find you," Gisella adds.

Wendy pulls a blonde lock out of her face. "Are you saying I should hide?"

"Yes, at our mansion." I beckon Taylar. "They haven't found you yet. We should leave now. Taylar can open a portal."

"That's great," Wendy says, "but I can't leave the book. If I go into hiding, I either take the book with me, or I hand it over to another Keeper."

I scratch my chin. "Wouldn't it be better to leave it

where it is? What if they know you have the book? They might be waiting for you to take them to it."

She leans forward and lowers her voice. Her curls tickle my cheek as the wind blows them up. "It's hidden in the church. If you found me here, then they will, too, and they'll turn this place upside down to find it."

D'Maeo makes himself visible. "Then we should close the shop, get everyone out."

"And let them tear this beautiful place down?" Dylan calls out.

"I don't see any other choice," the old ghost answers. "Saving millions of lives is more important than saving one church."

"Actually," Wendy interrupts. She beckons the others closer. "The Book of a Thousand Deaths isn't the only powerful book hidden here."

Jeep gives his tattoos a nervous rub. "You put several valuable items in one place?"

Wendy smiles at him with glistening eyes. "Not exactly." She walks back to the door. "Come on, I'll show you."

She takes us back inside, holds up her hand, and whispers, "Give me a sec to clear the building."

With her head lifted to the high, vaulted ceiling she clicks her tongue several times. Clouds of green smoke drift down and an alarm starts to blare. Some customers look up from the shelves irritably. Wendy has to tell them to leave the store. Others panic at the sight of the smoke that billows down so fast it's as if it's trying to grab them. Wendy points the people to the exits and shouts something to her boss I interpret as *"Go on, I'll be fine"*.

When he heads for the main entrance, Wendy turns to me. "We need to hurry. The fire brigade will be here soon." She points at the metal structure in the middle of the church. "Can any of you fly? We need someone to do a quick check for stragglers."

"Fly? No—"

"Gisella can do it," Charlie interrupts, and before I can respond, she takes off.

We watch her soar through the air and climb up the side of the book tower with the ease of a cat. She hops over the railing and is answered by a frightened shriek. Running footsteps come around the corner of the upper floor. A young man, maybe five years older than me, ducks to get away from the green smoke filling up the store. He trips and tumbles over the railing, and I dive forward in a reflex—as if I'll ever be able to catch him in time. He lets out a deafening scream which is cut off when two shadows catch him. They set him down gently and retreat to their corners. The man shivers, wipes off his whole body, and runs for the nearest exit.

I look up to where Gisella is standing, bent over the railing. "Nice catch."

"Thanks."

Wendy strides past me. "We should close the doors. Make sure no one can get in without us noticing."

"I've got it," Vicky says. She turns her head toward the emergency exit and the doors slam shut.

The main entrance closes with a heavy squeal, too, and Wendy stops in her tracks. She glances back with a smile on her lips. "Impressive."

Vicky grins back.

Wendy makes her way to a stairway on our right. "Follow me."

Some of the smoke crawls into my throat, making me cough. "Is this stuff dangerous?"

"Of course not. I chose harmless gas. It's green because that looks more dangerous than white."

I follow her to the back of the storage room. "You can choose what kind of gas you conjure?"

"Sure. I can conjure any kind, toxic, non-toxic, invisible."

"I bet all Keepers have cool powers like that."

"Actually, not all Keepers of Life are magical."

She pushes some crates aside and places her hand on the wall. With a hiss it slides open to reveal a long corridor with metal shutters on both sides. Wendy steps through the secret doorway and pushes a lever down on her right. The shutters open with another mechanical hiss. Behind them are alcoves containing globes the size of bowling balls.

Wendy walks farther into the corridor. "These are the most valuable books of magic in the world. Or, at least, the ones that haven't fallen into the hands of the dark side."

"Why do you keep them all in one place?" Jeep

repeats his question. "Wouldn't it be smarter to separate them?"

She comes to a halt next to the fourth globe. "Oh, but they aren't in the same place."

Frowning like idiots, we all approach her. I glance into every globe I pass. They are all empty.

"This is a decoy?" Dylan asks.

"No. These globes are portals to the worlds where we keep the books. We spread them all over the universe and relocate them from time to time." Once again, she conjures gas—yellow this time—and wraps the globe in it. "Each globe and portal requires a different way of opening. There are several layers of protection, and the details of each globe are only known to two Keepers of Life." She stares at the gas, hard.

It lifts the glass orb and sets it aside.

Then, she squats down. "Duck."

Sharp pins shoot out from the revealed portal. Kessley ducks a little too late, but turns invisible in time for them to go through her. Taylar pulls her close when she turns solid again and she smiles up at him.

Wendy stands up in time for an iris scan that pops up. A red laser rises to eye level and after a soft bleep, it pulls back. The back wall of the alcove slides open, and everyone draws their weapons.

"Easy, this fellow is part of the security system," Wendy says. She smiles at the tiny monster who blinks against the sudden light. It's about ten inches tall and looks like some sort of tiny troll. It has short legs and arms and the brown-greenish skin of a toad, with small spikes sticking out of its back and waist. It's skinnier than the average fairy tale troll and looks rather friendly, apart from the slime dripping from its protruding jaw. With tiny ears on top of its head, small kind eyes, and a cute little nose, I would hug it, if it weren't for the disgusting and pointy skin and the heavy nose breathing.

Wendy holds out her arm and it sinks its teeth into her wrist. She flinches a little.

The troll closes its eyes and rocks back and forth.

"What is it doing?" I ask.

"It's analyzing my blood to see if it's really me, and also looking for any signs of ill-intent in it."

Kessley scrunches up her nose. "It can taste that?"

Charlie goes for the more pressing question. "What if it comes to the conclusion you have bad intentions? Or if it finds out you're not really Wendy?"

She holds up her arm and we all gasp. A green line is making its way from her wrist, all the way up to her shoulder, under her skin. "Then it won't give me the antidote."

"And you'll turn into a troll yourself?" Dylan asks, disgust written all over his face.

"Yes, and die a day later."

The troll grabs her arm and opens its mouth. We all hold our breaths. Although I have complete faith in Wendy and her good intentions, I don't trust this troll. It might read her wrong or sense her stress because of what we've told her. Or, it might have been affected by evil somehow.

It sticks out a tongue that keeps unrolling until it's almost as long as Wendy's lower arm.

While I ball and unball my fists, she remains calm. The tongue slides over the line, which dissolves.

"Thank you," Wendy says and she lightly pats the troll on its head.

It purrs with delight, and as soon as Wendy pulls back her hand, the wall closes again. A shroud is lifted from the portal underneath it and she reaches inside with both hands.

The book she pulls out looks exactly like the fake one we created to trick Gisella's aunt Kasinda. Crossed bones, skulls, and pentagrams are etched into the thick, leather cover, and the Leviathan Cross—the symbol Vicky has in her neck, linking her to Satan— burns in the middle. The pages are chipped and dirty. The only thing that's different from our fake copy is the evil that emanates from it so strongly I can almost touch it.

Charlie, Kessley, Taylar, Jeep, Dylan, and I all take a step back simultaneously. D'Maeo, Maël, Vicky, and Gisella stay where they are, however. Their eyes turn a shade darker. My heart aches at the sight of it.

Oh, no, this can't be good.

CHAPTER 16

"Put it back," I beg Wendy, my voice strained. "Put it back now."

She follows my gaze to my friends and stiffens.

The four of them take a step closer to her, but I block their way. "Stay back. Remember who you are." I conjure a lightning bolt. It illuminates their faces, and a chill creeps up my spine. "Wendy. Put it back now, please." My lips are barely moving.

Four pairs of evil-filled eyes follow the book in Wendy's hands.

All the muscles in my body are strained. Seeing Vicky taken over by darkness is hard, but I'm ready to lash out if necessary.

Gisella grabs the edge of the book before I even realize she moved.

"Why don't you hand that over to me?" she asks in a too sweet tone.

"Never," Wendy whispers.

A sliver of smoke rises from the waist of the werecat-witch. With a somersault, she gets away from it, taking the book with her. In the blink of an eye, she's at the door, a wide grin plastered on her face. Shadows crawl down from the corners of the corridor and hover by her side, like guards.

"Stop her!" I want to go after her, but D'Maeo, Maël, and Vicky block my way. When Charlie tries to push past them, Maël knocks him off his feet with her staff.

The book has gotten a hold on the four of them. Somehow, it must have clung to the bits of evil inside them and given them power.

The werecat-witch turns and walks out of the secret corridor.

"No!" Wendy screams. She digs her fingers into my arm. "We can't let them take the book. They'll destroy the world."

"I know, but I don't know what—" My words stop as I take a sharp breath.

Why didn't I think of this sooner? I can give my Shield orders. They have no choice but to obey.

Fixing D'Maeo, Maël, and Vicky with a stern look, I command, "I order you to stop Gisella now. Get the book back, capture Gisella, and bring her back unharmed, if possible."

Without a word of protest, they turn and sprint after the werecat-witch. Wendy and I follow with the rest of the crew close behind.

Charlie passes me when I enter the back of the bookstore. Gisella is leisurely strolling toward the main entrance, her shadow guards hovering around her like a shield.

"Gis, please stop!" Charlie yells.

She turns around, the Book of a Thousand Deaths held against her chest.

Charlie takes another step toward her. "Please, think about what you're doing," he begs.

She rubs the book as if it's a baby. "I have thought about this… for a long time."

"No, you haven't. These are Kasinda's dark powers talking. You have to fight them."

Gisella cracks her neck. "I've got my aunt's powers under control. I'm fine. Better than I've ever been."

Charlie raises his hands in despair. "This isn't you, Gis. You're a good person."

Black lines crawl under the skin of her face and her grin shows that even her teeth are darker than before. "Not anymore. This is who I was always meant to be." She holds out her arm and her expression softens. "You can join me, if you want."

Charlie shakes his head. "You know I can't do that."

"I thought you'd do anything for me," she says sweetly.

Behind his back, Charlie conjures a large ball of grease in his hand.

I move closer to Maël. "Freeze her," I whisper. "Quickly."

A deep frown appears in the ghost queen's forehead, but she obeys as Charlie continues to distract Gisella.

"This is the only thing I can't do for you. Let's talk about it. You don't want to lose what we have, do you?"

Her gaze shifts to Maël. More shadows dive down from all sides. They knock Maël off balance before I can warn her, and start pulling at her staff.

"D'Maeo, help her!" I yell.

The old ghost seems to snap out of his trance at last. He positions himself between Gisella and us, and raises his hands to block her powers. The shadows move in erratic patterns, fighting him. Maël pulls her staff free and aims it at the dark shapes.

Taylar is creeping past the stacked tables under the arches, and I worry for him. He can't take Gisella on his own. However, he might surprise her, and give the rest of us the opportunity to attack and take back the book.

Kessley is nowhere to be seen. Hopefully, she has a plan of her own.

Maël mumbles her time bending words again, and the shadows freeze. Brownish smoke drifts over our heads. I feel someone moving behind me. Everyone is ready to attack, but no one wants to be the first. We're all hoping Gisella will come to her senses, although it's obvious those chances are slim while she's holding the Book of a Thousand Deaths.

Taylar has worked his way around the werecat-witch and is only two paces away from her now. He holds his shield in front of him, protecting himself, and at the same time getting ready to attack with it.

"Gisella, please," Charlie begs, trying to pull her attention back to him. "Talk to me. What's going on? What happened to the girl I love?"

She taps the side of her head. "She's still in here. I trapped her, like she did with me. It's my turn to control this awesome body."

Taylar tilts his shield and brings it back, ready to slam it against her.

She pushes herself up and twists her body. Her feet land on Taylar's shield with so much force that he's thrown against a table. He slides over it, knocking all the books to the ground. With a deafening growl, a huge troll—a copy of the security troll in the secret corridor—steps out from behind the metal book tower in the middle of the church. At the same time, Charlie releases his gel ball and I throw two lightning bolts.

"Vicky, pull the book from her hands with your powers," I order.

With obvious reluctance, Vicky obeys. The book moves in Gisella's arms, like it's fighting to break free. Several shadows wrap around it to hold it in place.

The werecat-witch raises a finger and tuts. "Don't be greedy. The book is mine now. If you want to use it," she extends one arm, "then, join me."

"I would," Vicky grumbles, "if—"

The rest of her words are drowned out by the

sound of Dylan, Taylar, Charlie, and me attacking Gisella at the same time. Shadows and clouds of gas blur my vision, but I hear footsteps and cries from all sides, and something zooms past my left ear. Storming forward, I release a bolt of lightning with one hand and hold a bolt up in front of me with the other in hopes of at least seeing something in the chaos. Someone bumps into me, and a giant hand covers my face. It pushes me to the floor and cuts off my air supply. I fumble for my athame and stab upward. With a shriek, the hand pulls back. Lightning soars in the direction of the sound, and in the brief light, I recognize the giant copy of the troll.

"It's me, Kessley," I yell, rolling away from the foot she brings down.

It comes to an abrupt halt half an inch above the floor. The troll blinks. "Dante? Oh, I'm sorry." She lifts me up and sets me back onto my feet.

We both turn in search of Gisella. Next to us, there's a knot of bodies, kicking, groaning, and pulling. Smoke and shadows wriggle through it. I squint and come to the conclusion that Gisella isn't a part of it.

"There!" Kessley calls out. She has turned back into her natural form, and points to the main entrance.

"Guys!" I yell as loud as I can. "Stop fighting each other. She's getting away."

The knot unties itself and out tumble the rest of my Shield, Dylan, Charlie, and Wendy. The shadows

171

hover above their heads, waiting for orders from their mistress.

Gisella is already at the door. The dark lines have taken over every inch of her face, making her look more like a demon than a girl. Dark lines crawl over her green shirt and camouflage pants. "You should probably hide in another realm, because this one," she rubs the cover of the book lovingly, "is going to burn."

Charlie sucks in his breath and stumbles. Jeep catches him.

"Take the book back. Now!" I order again.

Everyone except Charlie springs back into action, fighting off the shadows and making their way to the werecat-witch. Her hand is already on the doorknob and she pulls the door open before we can reach her. I expect light to flood in. Instead, three crooked bodies on thin legs block the doorway.

A panicked, "Watch out!" leaves Charlie's lips while the rest of us slow down.

"Come back to us, Gisella," I plead. "Together, we can defeat them."

She lets out a shrill laugh. "You're such a sweetheart, Dante." She takes a step outside and looks up at the middle demon. It reaches down and picks her up.

Charlie pushes past me with his arms outstretched. "*Nooo*! Let her go!"

Gisella is placed on the bony shoulder of the demon. "I'm joining the winning side, Char. You can come, too, if you like." She stares into the distance, her lips curled in a content smile. "We can torture people together, build a house under a flaming city, create devilishly handsome offspring with an appetite for power…" She licks her lips and tilts her head. "What do you say?"

Charlie keeps walking, and all I can do is watch in horror. Not a single part of Gisella seems to be left inside her. She's a copy of her evil aunt. Or worse. Once again, I curse myself for letting her take those powers. I knew they would corrupt her eventually.

Why did I cling to the promise that this would turn out fine? Why couldn't I listen to the much louder voice that said this was a bad idea?

Charlie has reached the demon. He lifts his head to look at his girl.

Her lips curl up farther. "Are you coming with me? Oh, we'll have so much fun together."

"If I must, I will let you go." He pulls a knife from his back pocket. "But you cannot take the book with you."

"Oh, honey," she says. "I can do whatever I want."

"No, you can't. We'll stop you." Charlie raises his knife. His knuckles turn white. "Please don't do this, Gisella. You're a good person."

The werecat-witch unties her ponytail and throws her bright red hair over her shoulder with a laugh. It sounds as if it's coming from a different person. Not from the Gisella we know. "That good person is no longer in charge. And begging won't do you any good. You're either with me, or against me. Either way, I'm leaving, and I'm taking this with me." She holds the book up in triumph. Then, she presses it against her chest and says something to the demon.

It grunts and turns around.

Charlie's desperately whispered, "No," is drowned out by doors that creak in a loud protest as the demon pushes them open.

We all wake from our horrified half-frozen state at the same time, and hurry after it.

Shrieks of fear and panicked footsteps fill the shopping street. Sirens blare in the distance.

We reach the doors with our weapons drawn just as the demons get to the end of the street on our left. Gisella throws one last look over her shoulder. Then, a portal opens and the demons step through. It closes a millisecond later. The people who'd flattened themselves against the walls of the shops gather in the middle of the street hesitantly, staring at the spot where monsters stood seconds ago. They must be wondering if they imagined it all. After all, monsters don't exist, right?

I curse, turn on my heels, and march back into the church. When the others join me, without even a hint of evil on their faces, I fold my arms over my chest. "Well, it turns out making plans and backup plans doesn't guarantee success."

Jeep clears his throat. "Actually, we did succeed in what we came here for." He nods at Wendy. "We

174

kept the ninth soul safe."

"And for what? This will only slow Satan down." My voice rises with each word. I don't think I've ever been this mad and desperate at the same time before. "Keeping the Book of a Thousand Deaths safe should have been our first priority. With it, they'll be even stronger than they already were."

D'Maeo puts his sword behind his shirt. "We didn't know the book was here, Dante. If we had known, we would've done more to protect it."

I push his hand away. "Don't try to comfort me. It's partly your fault we're in this mess."

His eyebrows knot together in concern. "I'm sorry I lost control, Dante. I—"

"You should've told me there was evil left inside of you."

His shoulders sag. "I didn't know."

He looks defeated and guilty, and I want to tell him it's not his fault, but my rage pushes every sensible word aside.

"You're supposed to lead my Shield when I can't," I fume. "You're supposed to be the father figure here, the one we can always lean on. How can we win this if I can't even trust my own Shield? Or my own girlfriend." I spit the last words in Vicky's direction, and for the first time ever, she cringes.

Heat courses through my veins as I continue. "You're all weak. I don't understand why you were even chosen." With a wild gesture I turn everyone's attention to the young mage. "Dylan here has been a screw-up since he was born, but even he managed to fight." With a jerk of my head I look up at the ceiling. "And why the hell didn't anyone from Heaven warn us about this, huh? Where was the premonition that predicted this when I needed it?" My hand shoots out to pick up a book and I slam it against the side of the nearest table as hard as I can, over and over, with every word I shout. "Why… do I… have to do… everything… on my own?"

Pages fly everywhere, satisfying my anger, but it's not enough. The rest of the book needs to go too and it feels good to shred it into little pieces. "I wish this stupid magic didn't exist!" I pick up another book and tear at the hardcover. It doesn't budge, so I conjure a lightning bolt under it. It pierces the book and sets it on fire. Shocked faces surround me while the flaming book is waved at them. "Ever since I found out about magic, everything has gone from bad to worse. I lost my friends, my mom, my… my…sanity." I slam the book on the floor and stomp on the flames with both feet. It feels good to destroy something, even if it's a harmless book.

My heartbeat slows a bit, and I wipe the sweat and tears from my face before I look up. Vicky has turned her back to me. Kessley has her arm around her shoulders in comfort.

What remains of my energy seeps from my body. In three strides, I'm facing Vicky. Kessley steps aside to allow me to wrap both arms around my girl. "I'm sorry. I didn't mean that." My teeth clench for a second. "Well, I meant some of it. Every time we get a break, something else goes wrong. And, we keep losing people." When my heartbeat starts to pound in my head again, I grab it with both hands, wanting to rip it off. "I'm not sure how much more of this I can handle."

Vicky doesn't respond. She just stares at me, her eyes filled with tears. "You wish you'd never met us."

"No!" I grab her again and pull her close. "Of course not. That's the only good thing magic has ever given me. But it will take you all away from me again, too."

Over her shoulder I take in the others. Charlie has dropped to the floor. He's holding his head the same way I did a second ago. It's not difficult to imagine how he must be feeling, after what happened to Gisella.

Wendy squashes the last of the fire consuming the book on the floor. "Your friends weren't the only ones affected by the Book of a Thousand Deaths, Dante."

I frown at her. "What do you mean?"

"Your rage." She gestures at the confetti spread between the stacks of books. "It was magnified by the book. The evil inside it focuses on negative emotions in people nearby. It latches on and amplifies them until they're out of control. What you felt had little to do with your true emotions."

Vicky rests her head against my shoulder. "Good."

Jeep isn't satisfied with this explanation, though.

177

He's gripping his hat like he's ready to throw it at her. "If you knew all of this, then why did you show us the book?"

She blushes. "I didn't know. I contacted the other Keepers of Life."

"When?" Jeep asks, disbelief in his voice.

"When Dante was having his outburst." She lowers her head to hide her face behind her curls. "I was afraid you would all turn evil on me. I called for help, and they listened in. Told me the effects would wear off soon, since the book is no longer here."

"I'm sorry," I say softly. "I should've known better."

She shakes her head and looks at me again. "This is not your fault. I'm the one who should've known better. The risk of showing a book like that to so many people at once, to non-Keepers, is dangerous."

"We all made a judgment call, and we all got it wrong," Maël says. "We should leave it behind us and focus on a way to get the book back."

"Not me," Wendy says with a heavy sigh. "I've been forbidden to interfere. I am no longer a Keeper of Life."

"Are you kidding?" Kessley replies. "They failed to give you decent information about the book you were protecting, and now they fire you because of it?"

Wendy tilts her head in thought. "Well, yes. Basically." She wipes some ash from her dress. "If you say it like that, it's pretty unfair." Her arms cross over her chest in defiance. "I think I'll pretend I didn't hear their last order."

Kessley cheers. She bounces over to Charlie and pulls him up roughly. "Come on. This team never gives up. We're going to find that book, and once we've put it somewhere far away from us, you'll get Gisella back."

"*We'll* get Gisella back," I correct her.

Charlie sends her half a smile, and I hurry over to them to support his other side, dragging Vicky along. "We haven't lost anyone permanently so far, and we won't start now." I prod him in the ribs. "Come on. Since when do we give up so easily?"

His mouth twitches and forms into a determined line. "Since never." He breaks free from our grip and makes for the main entrance with large strides. "Let's go."

My confidence returns and I nod. "That's better."

CHAPTER 17

The small square outside the church is empty. The sirens are closer now, and I hear a lot of shouting. As I search for the source, Wendy nods to the end of the street. "It's the police. I think they fenced off the area."

"Because they saw the demons," I conclude. "They're probably ready to bomb the place."

Her eyes grow wide. "You're right. I can't leave. I need to make sure the church remains intact, so the other books are safe." She reaches under her skirt and holds out a card to me. "This is my number. Call it if you find the book before we do."

I scramble for something to scribble my own number on, but Vicky is already writing it on a piece of paper.

"Good luck," Wendy says as she takes it.

"You too." I turn to Taylar. "Let's go back inside,

so you can open a portal back home. We'll start the search from there."

He nods and we turn back to the metal doors with the words in them.

"Wait," D'Maeo says suddenly.

My eyes close in exhaustion. I don't want to wait anymore. I want to get the book, and Gisella, back.

"We can't leave Wendy unprotected," the old ghost says. "The demons will come back for her soul."

This never-ending spiral of decisions and setbacks is starting to drive me crazy.

What's more important, Wendy or the book?

"How long will it take you to make sure the church is safe?" I ask Wendy.

"I'm not sure. I'll need to check the corridor, to see if they're after any of the other books. And I need to convince the police that there's no danger anymore."

"That will take forever," Taylar says with a sigh. "We can't stay for long. The longer they have the book, the bigger the chances of the world going to hell."

"Aptly put," Jeep mumbles, turning his hat around in his hands.

"Hang on," Vicky interrupts. "Who says the Devil is still after Wendy? Maybe they changed their plan the moment they got the Book of a Thousand Deaths."

"There's an easy way to find out." I pull the Cards

of Death out of my back pocket and hold them up. They crumble to dust instantly.

Jeep puts his hat back on his head and smiles. "Well, that solves it then. We're going home."

"Hang on."

This time it's Charlie who makes us all look around. He points at the specks of dust floating inches above us. "Don't those normally vanish?"

As soon as he utters his last word, the specks move to the left.

As if on cue, everyone draws their weapons. Except me. With a chuckle, I push Vicky's hand down. "Relax, guys. The cards are made by angels, remember? Angels who want to help us. They are benevolent objects. Maybe Quinn built something extra into this set?"

"Do you think they'll lead us to Gisella?" Charlie looks up at the dust with longing. His voice is strained.

Maël carefully lifts her hand to the specks. "They might."

The dust shoots away from her fingers and comes to a halt about two feet away.

"I think it wants to lead us somewhere. We should follow it." I turn to Wendy. "Will you be okay on your own?"

She shoots me a radiant smile which seems to light up her hair as well as her face. "Of course. Don't worry about me. I'm a Keeper of Life."

Her optimism and diligence rub off on me. "Good

luck."

"You too." She turns and walks back into the church with determined strides.

"The dust is moving," Maël reports.

The policemen gathering at the end of the street worry me. They look like they're ready to blow up half the city to get rid of anything that has even the slightest resemblance to a monster.

"Are you guys invisible to others?" I ask my Shield.

"Of course," D'Maeo answers.

"Good."

We follow the specks an art gallery next to the bookstore. A policeman is calling out to us, but he's speaking Dutch, which means none of us understand what he's saying. Judging by the panic on his face, he's telling us to join him behind his crush barrier, where it's supposed to be safe.

"I don't understand what you're saying," I yell at him.

He frowns, trying to process my words, and the remains of the Cards of Death shoot under the crack in the door, into the art gallery. While the police officer shouts, "Get out of there," I reach for the door handle. To my relief, the door opens, and I step into the narrow hallway of the old building.

The others follow close behind, the cop shouting in the background.

Maël is the last one to step inside.

"Are they coming to get us?" I ask.

She peers around the corner and shakes her head. "No, I think they are too scared to come any closer."

I can't blame them. Before summer break I would've freaked out if I ran into a bunch of demons on the street, too.

Maël closes the door behind her, and we follow the specks farther into the building.

It's not an art gallery at all, it's a tableware shop. Most of the cups and bowls have turned into shards, which cover the floor. Everything has been shattered, except for the porcelain and crystal on the shelves against the far wall.

"Do you think the demons did this?" Vicky whispers, making me jump.

The specks of dust turn back and fly into the main room with the shattered tableware.

"Yes, they must have," I whisper back. "I think the dust is following their scent or something."

We try to stay quiet as we walk to the back of the shop, which is hard for Charlie and me, since there's barely any clear space on the floor. The shards crunch under our shoes and make clinking sounds when we kick them against each other by accident.

"So much for approaching the enemy silently," Jeep says, taking off his hat and aiming it at the door at the back of the store.

Nothing moves in the building, however; no sounds answer the ones we make. The dust floats under the door.

An ominous feeling lands in my stomach.

Something could be waiting for us on the other side.

After several seconds, the specks don't return, which I take to mean the coast is clear. I push the door open with one hand and hold up a lightning ball in the other, just in case something wants to jump us. But there's nothing behind the door, except an old kitchen with lopsided cabinet doors and dirty mugs on the counter.

The dust hovers in front of the sink for a second, before vanishing.

"That's it?" Charlie says, sounding disappointed and heartbroken. "It led us into an empty kitchen?"

Maël pushes him aside and steps past me. "It is not empty."

She waves her hand in front of her and then I see it. There's a disturbance in the air, an almost invisible glimmer. I hold out my arm to prevent the ghost queen from stepping into it. "Be careful."

She smiles at me and backs up.

The others gather around the spot.

"I think it is a portal," Maël says.

D'Maeo narrows his eyes at it. "More like the remnants of one."

"Can we open it? Or find out where it leads to?"

"Probably to Hell," Jeep says dryly.

I shrug. "Or not. Because that's where we'd look first, isn't it?"

Just as I reach for Dad's notebook behind my waistband, something shoots out from the disturbance in the air. Panicked shouts rise from around me, and I step back. Something has grabbed me by the collar. Instead of the notebook, I wrap my fingers around my athame and lash out. The hand lets go, but another one seizes my wrist. I'm pulled off my feet and dragged into the glimmer. A blob of gel latches onto me before my friends disappear from sight. Vicky's scream echoes in my head.

I'm lying on my back on soft ground. It takes a moment for my memories to float to the surface. Once they do, I sit up so fast the world spins around me.

"Oh, good, you're awake," a soft voice says.

When I reach for my athame I find the spot behind my waistband empty.

"It's lying next to you," the voice says.

With a lightning bolt flickering in the palm of my hand, I turn around. My hand drops at the sight of the angel standing behind me. Thick, full beard, wavy hair around his handsome face, light green eyes…

Mumiah.

He smiles and nods at the light in my hand. "You don't need that."

My fist closes around it, extinguishing it with a soft hiss. "Sorry." I take him in from head to toe. "Did you pull me in here?"

His smile widens. "I did. I also called the ash from the Cards of Death to me, hoping you would follow it."

I push myself up from the grass and check out our surroundings. "This is where Gisella took the Book of a Thousand Deaths?" On my left I find Darkwood Manor, the forest is on my right. "She shouldn't be able to find it now that she has turned evil, right? Or does it only work on people who haven't been here before?"

Mumiah shakes his head. "This isn't your house."

"What do you mean? Is it an illusion?"

"Not exactly. More like a copy." He opens his arms wide and turns slowly. "We're standing in a copy of Earth. An exact replica of your world."

I squint at the sky, then at Darkwood Manor again. If Mumiah hadn't told me, I would never have guessed this isn't the real thing.

"Why?" I ask.

Mumiah entwines his fingers in front of his chest. "Do you remember how I introduced myself when we first met?"

The fight in Affection comes back to me, just like the moment Mumiah and the other angels stepped over the salt line at the barn. "The angel of rebirth?"

"Exactly."

When he remains silent, I hold up my hands. "I don't get it."

Mumiah shows me his radiant angel smile again. "I created this world, for the souls who have trouble adjusting to Heaven before they move on to their next lives. Each soul who gets into Heaven has a choice: stay in Heaven or be reborn. Some souls are too overwhelmed to accept what happened to them. Those that are too strong to end up in the Shadow

World, are taken here. They can adjust to the idea of Heaven and reincarnation at their own pace here, in a familiar environment."

I walk to the house and push the back door open. The kitchen is an exact copy of my own, including the smell of Mona's cooking that lingers in the air. "You did a great job."

"Thank you," Mumiah says.

While I walk through to the annex I study every detail. "I can't believe how many worlds there are."

Mumiah flexes his wings. "You haven't even seen half of them."

I scratch the side of my head and put my hands on my waist. "Anyway. You brought me here for a reason. The Book of a Thousand Deaths is here. Do you know where Gisella took it?"

"No, but that's easy enough to find out."

"Good. How?"

A mischievous expression falls over his face. It conflicts a bit with his innocent angel appearance, and sends a chill down my spine. "As soon as Gisella and the demons entered this world, carrying that book, I emptied it."

"You emptied it?" I repeat, not sure what he means.

"Yes, I picked up all the souls in this world, and sent them to Heaven."

"You sent them to Heaven. Just like that."

His grin widens and he opens his arms again. "Well, I *am* the ruler of this world."

I narrow my eyes. "Does that mean you can pick Gisella and those demons up, too?"

"And send them to Heaven?" He taps his bearded chin in thought. "I'm not sure, since they don't belong here. But if I can, it's not a very wise thing to do, transporting a dangerous witch, three demons, and the deadliest book in existence there. I'd rather keep them all here."

"Wait." I drop my arms. "You can do that?"

"I can try. But I need your help."

"*My* help?"

He chuckles. "Can you stop repeating everything I say? Yes, your help. You're a powerful mage, in case you forgot."

A hot blush creeps up my neck. "I'll do what I can."

Mumiah rubs his hands together. "Great! I have a lockdown procedure, but I'm not sure it will keep so much magic trapped. Therefore, I was thinking you could cast a spell aimed specifically at the four we want to keep here, plus the book."

"Or, I could try calling the book to me with a spell," I suggest.

His eyes grow wide. "That's not a bad idea. However, I do believe locking them in this world should be our first priority."

My responding nod is slow as my thoughts are already going into overdrive to come up with a spell to help. "Yes, I agree."

"Great. I'll take care of the lockdown. Meanwhile,

you can write a spell."

I pull out my Book of Spells and realize I don't have a pen. Vicky normally hands one to me. It's clear I take her for granted more than intended.

"Here." Mumiah holds out a pen. "And if you write down the ingredients, I can get those for you, too."

"Thanks," I mumble and take the pen from him, then drop down into the grass, fold my legs and get to work.

Mumiah spreads his wings. "Holler if anything happens while I'm gone."

My "okay" sounds casual, but my chest tightens when he pushes off. Soon, he's no more than a speck far above me. The emptiness of this world presses down on me. Cold creeps up my spine.

What if I was tricked? What if that wasn't Mumiah at all, and I'm stuck here forever?

My breathing quickens and I squeeze my eyes shut.
Don't think like that. Keep it together.

Bent over my book, I start jotting down ingredients. It's almost unbelievable how easy this has become. My mind spits out suggestions like a machine. I do miss Vicky, though. It's nice to have her by my side, double-checking my list for me, giving suggestions if I get stuck. It feels safer, and more natural.

I guess this is good practice, though. Soon, I'll be preparing all my spells without her.

Unwilling to think about that any longer, I shake

my head and focus on the spell. Once I'm able to drown out the eerie silence, inspiration starts to flow again. Several minutes later, it's done. I check the ingredients again and practice the words in my head.

A tremble in the ground makes me freeze. A dark line approaches in the sky to my left. I spring to my feet and look up in search of Mumiah. Before I can decide whether to call out to him or not, another line appears, this one on my right. It cuts through the sky fast, lighting up the forest as it goes. In my imagination birds take off with panicked screeches, but this world is empty so, of course, everything remains silent.

Not sure whether to run for cover, I take a couple of steps back. The lines get closer to each other, one flickering, the other pulsing. It's too late to find shelter now. The two collide with a loud bang. A force field rises from the spot and spreads over the area. I'm knocked backward, into the grass. The earth underneath me moves again as another dark line approaches.

"Mumiah!" I call out.

Getting up, I concentrate on the line in the sky and imagine frost clinging to it, freezing it completely and holding it in place. With a creaking sound, the line slows down. Conjuring more ice, I envision it wrapping around the line. It comes to a halt.

"Yes, great work!" Mumiah's voice calls out. He lands next to me with a loud whoosh. "Keep it like that."

"What… is it?" I ask, trying hard not to lose focus.

"Looks like a force field. I think they know I'm trying to trap them."

"Gisella can throw force fields. But I've never seen it in the form of a line like this."

"Maybe she learned some new tricks." He nods at the sky when I glance at him. "Keep it frozen."

"Sorry." The line moves several inches to the right. I fill my head with nothing but images of ice.

The ground trembles a third time and I almost lose my balance. A second line shoots into sight.

"I need a little more time, Dante. Can you hold them both?" Mumiah says.

Grumbling something under my breath I try to envision both the lines freezing. The image in my head shows me only one. A soft curse escapes me. *If only D'Maeo was here to block this power.*

Then, I remember something.

I can order the ice to do what I want.

The second line reaches the first and slams into it. The ice cracks and both lines push on. Only a couple of feet left until they reach us.

Ice, hold the lines in place! I call out inside my head.

White flecks circle through the air, multiply, and wrap around both lines.

"Dante? Is that you?"

It's as if a cold hand grabs me by the throat. The voice is lower than usual, but unmistakably Gisella's.

CHAPTER 18

"Hurry up," I urge Mumiah.

He flaps his wings with force and raises his hands. A golden ball of light comes to life in his palms. He whispers to it, and it starts to rise.

"Daaante…"

I swallow. She's taunting me, trying to make me nervous. And succeeding.

Ice, ice, ice, I think. *Build a wall between me and Gisella.*

Blocks of ice drop down. They pile up to form a thick, broad barrier.

"Oh, yes, definitely Dante." Gisella sounds smug, her voice muffled by the layer of ice between us.

There's a tap near my face.

"Why are you hiding, Dante?" she asks sweetly.

Build the wall higher, to hide the ball of light, I order, my heart beating a drum solo.

My envisioned wall grows, while the tapping on it

turns into a loud banging which makes the ice crackle.

"This won't hold forever, Dante," Gisella calls out. Irritation is starting to seep through her words. In the background, I can hear the growling of demons.

Meanwhile, Mumiah's golden light is rising above the tree line. With every inch it travels, it grows. The angel pushes his hands up, and the ball opens. It unfolds to form a bright, golden line that takes on the shape of a dome.

A huge crack appears in the ice in front of me. Although I order water to fill it up and freeze, nothing happens.

"Come out, come out, wherever you are!" Gisella muses. Her voice has dropped several octaves. It sends chills down my back.

I imagine water rushing over the wall and seeping into the cracks. *Freeze!* I order it as soon as it appears.

This time it does what I tell it to. A deafening roar makes the wall tremble. *From Gisella or the demons?*

"I'm running out of patience, Dante," she warns, sounding more like a beast than a person now.

I'm thinking about answering her when the sky lights up. It's as if a bomb went off, and I shield my eyes.

The banging on the ice wall ceases. I can make out a muffled, "What was *that*?"

Mumiah lowers his hands. "Are you ready for your spell?"

My gaze goes back to the wall. "Sure, but I can't do that and keep this wall up at the same time."

"Leave them to me." He folds his wings onto his back. "Do you have a list of ingredients?"

As soon as I hand my Book of Spells to him, his eyes scan the lines and, with a nod, he gives the book back to me. "I'll get them for you. Keep the wall up for a couple more minutes."

"I'll do my best."

Mumiah leaves in another flash of light while I tell the ice to stay in place.

"You know…" Gisella taunts from the other side. "If I want to knock this wall down, I can do so in a second."

I'm tempted to call her bluff, but keep my mouth shut. Now that her dark powers are fully awake, there's no telling what she can do.

The wall trembles and creaks when something large and solid hits it. I'm guessing it's a force field, thrown by the werecat-witch.

Fill any cracks that appear, I order the water.

Another blow showers me with shards of ice.

Mumiah gets back in a flash and places a bowl, some candles, a matchbox, and several bottles and sachets on the ground.

"Your turn," he says.

He steps between me and the wall of ice, and I squat down to mix the herbs and spices. The noise around me intensifies and the trembling of the ground returns, almost knocking my mixture over. I grab the bowl, add some grass to it, and press it against my chest, creating a circle of salt with my other hand. Once the ground calms down again, I set the bowl down and hurry to set the candles up.

I'd love to see what Mumiah is doing to keep Gisella and the demons at bay, but there's no time. My focus needs to be on this spell.

Pushing aside the thought that I need Vicky to check for any missing ingredients, I cheer myself on.

I've got this. I can do this on my own. It will work.

I walk around the circle, sprinkling the mixture over the line of salt.

"Powers of the North, guardians of the Earth,
strengthen the force that seals this world.
Keep the—"

My words are cut off by a force field hitting me. It pushes me out of the circle.

Wind, catch me before I slam into the trees! I call out inside my head.

The wind obeys and sets me back on my feet.

I run back to the salt circle, while Mumiah scrambles to his feet.

Another blast hits me. My order to the wind to push back works, and I manage to stay upright.

It's a struggle to get back to the circle. Mumiah opens his arms and brings them together, but before his hands touch, two huge shadows shoot over the ice wall.

Wind, pull Mumiah back!

As he slides away from the wall, the shadows hit

the spot where he was standing a second ago. They slam down with so much force they drill a deep hole into the ground.

Cold air touches my face and the sky turns pitch black.

Gisella rises above the wall, her face darker than I've ever seen it. Like Kasinda's, when we met her, except there are also red lines running along her skin, with bits of red fur springing from them.

Her smile sends a chill through my body.

I tell the wind to stop moving me, and Mumiah backs up.

"No wall can stop me," Gisella gurgles in her unnatural low voice. Shadows lower her to the ground on our side. "I'm offering you a last chance, Dante."

My mind whirs to come up with a way to take her out without killing her. Or, at least, to finish my spell.

"A last chance to join me," Gisella continues. She licks her lips. "I know you like the taste of power as much as I do. Imagine what it will feel like to rule the world, side by side with the Devil himself. You could do whatever you wanted."

"Oh, yeah?" I interrupt. "Let me guess. I could bring my father back from the dead, keep Vicky by my side?"

"Among other things. Sure."

"I can't believe I never thought of this solution before. If I simply join the dark side, all of my problems will be solved." Sarcasm drips from my voice, and Gisella grins.

"I knew you would never give in. I told Lucifer this, but he wanted me to ask you anyway." She flexes her fingers and lets out a deep sigh. "Oh, well, I might as well have a little fun. He wants to kill you himself, but…"

The rest of her words are nothing but distant syllables. Mumiah has reached me, and from one moment to the next, there's only light around me.

"What are you doing?" There's a hint of panic in my words. There's no answer. I drift weightlessly through the air.

A scream of anger pierces the air, and turns into a roar. I brace myself for another attack, but the sound fades. For a second, there's nothing but silence. Then, my feet touch solid ground and the bright light fades.

All of a sudden, I'm pushed over by a warm body.

"Babe!"

"Vicky?"

Two arms wrap around me. "Are you okay?"

"I'm fine."

Her kiss is full of passion and I give into the moment, until I feel several eyes on us. I push both of us up since Vicky refuses to let go of me. I take in the familiar room, with the large kitchen table and the old cabinets. Most of the chairs are filled. There's a painfully empty spot next to Charlie. My heart contracts thinking about the possibility that we won't be able to get Gisella back.

"Is everyone okay?" is my first question.

There's a mutual "fine." Everyone but Charlie

answers, and I put my hand on his shoulder. "We'll do what we can to save her."

He gulps in air. "She's still alive?"

"Yes, she's—"

My answer is cut off by Mom flinging her arms around me, forcing Vicky to let go.

"We were so worried."

D'Maeo pulls a restless Mona onto his lap. "When you were pulled through that portal, we tried to follow, but it closed behind you. The shimmer vanished, and since we didn't know where it led, Taylar couldn't take us there either. We were transported home automatically, because you were no longer with us, and managed to grab Charlie just in time."

Mom pulls up my shirt and examines my chest. "Were you injured?"

I take her hands and force her to look me in the eye. "I'm fine. Mumiah pulled me in, to help him lock the demons and Gisella in his world."

All heads turn to the angel standing in the corner of the kitchen like a statue.

I introduce him to Mom and Mona, and then we tell them what happened.

"You didn't finish the spell?" Jeep asks, rubbing his arms nervously.

"I wanted to, but Gisella attacked and then Mumiah brought us here."

"I had no choice," the angel says. "I'm not sure we could've defeated her. I couldn't risk losing the chosen one."

"I think you made the right choice." Vicky squeezes my hand.

"Me too," Charlie mumbles.

Mumiah unfolds his wings. "I need to go home, to report about the loss of the Book of a Thousand Deaths."

My teeth clench. "Please tell them we're very sorry, and we will do what we can to get it back."

Although this doesn't make the situation any better, Mumiah seems to appreciate the gesture. He nods and vanishes in a flash of bright light.

There's a short silence. Then, Charlie wipes his hands on his pants. "How, eh… how was she?"

I've been waiting for this question since I got back, yet still struggle to find the right words.

It takes me a moment to answer and Charlie lowers his head again. "That bad, huh?"

"I'm sorry, mate. She was… well, worse than Kasinda."

"Which doesn't mean we can't save her," Vicky points out. "We saved Kasinda, too, after all."

Gisella is much stronger, since she already had powers of her own when we transferred her aunt's powers to her, but I can't bring myself to say that out loud.

I search my pockets for my phone, to see what time it is. "It's four o'clock?"

D'Maeo nods. "You were gone for quite some time."

I send a message to Wendy, to tell her the book is locked inside an empty world. For now.

Two check marks appear, but there's no answer. No doubt, she's busy with the other books, the police, or trying to explain to her Keeper of Life colleagues what went wrong and pleading with them to give her another chance.

Now that we've saved the ninth soul, I know we need to work on a plan to help Heaven. We're prepared for our battle to save Earth—if one can ever really be prepared for something like this—but since I don't know much about Heaven, it's far from easy to figure out a way to save it. And, I'm so tired from everything that has happened today, I can't think straight anymore.

"Wasn't there something else we needed to test?" I ask out loud.

Blank stares answer me.

"Test?" Taylar says.

"Yes, like Vicky creating the circles. There was something else, right?"

I can almost hear the wheels inside all their heads turning.

Vicky straightens up. "Oh, I know. We wanted to see if the fairy godmothers could steer me, since I don't really have a body anymore."

"Right." With a smile I turn to Mona, sitting on D'Maeo's lap at the other head of the table. "Would some of your friends be willing to come and test this? You wanted several godmothers to work together on this, right?"

She stands up and sparks whirl around her. "Yes. I'll be back soon."

And with that, she vanishes.

CHAPTER 19

Mona returns before anyone has come up with something to say to break the uncomfortable silence. Three fairy godmothers with equally flawless looks land beside her.

"That was fast," Jeep comments.

"They've been waiting for me to give them a heads-up if the final battle starts, so they were ready to go."

"I'm sorry if we scared you," I say. "This is only practice. For now."

They give me a small bow, and the middle one speaks up. "We're happy to help."

Vicky stands up and rubs her hands. "How do we test this?"

Mona points to the garden. "It's probably best if you fight. Tessa, Noa, and Paula will be watching everything going on around you, and they will try to interfere when your life is threatened." She frowns. "Your afterlife, I mean."

Vicky grins. "Semantics."

The godmother next to Mona speaks up. "This will not only be a test to see if we can move you out of harm's way. We will also be working together for the first time, to protect one protégé."

Kessley hops from her chair and makes a beeline for the back door. "Let's do this! I can't wait."

The fairy godmothers' smooth foreheads wrinkle as they watch her bounce into the garden.

"Don't mind her," Taylar says, a chuckle in his voice. "She gets excited about pretty much anything."

We file into the back garden. Automatically, we gather inside the protective circle, but the fairy godmothers shake their heads.

"That won't work," Mona says. "She needs to be in real danger."

I gulp. "As in… we should actually go for the kill?"

Her lips curl up a bit. "I wouldn't go that far, but yes, try to hurt her. Nothing fatal, just bad enough for us to want to interfere."

I exchange a look with Vicky, asking her permission without words.

She pulls her shoulders back and flexes her arms. "Fine with me. They can heal, too, remember?"

Of course I remember, but that doesn't make me feel much better. I don't like it when someone hurts my girl. However, this is for a good cause. This will hopefully result in protection for her.

The others follow when I step out of the circle.

"Do we all attack her at once?" Jeep asks, sounding as reluctant as I feel.

Mona shakes her head. "No. We need to imitate a large battle, as far as that's possible. Which means several smaller battles. Some of the fighters will turn their attention to Vicky once they've beaten their opponent. Discuss amongst yourselves who will act like the enemies, but don't tell us. That way, we won't be able to anticipate who will attack Vicky."

"Okay." I beckon everyone into a circle.

We divide ourselves into dueling partners and decide who will win and attack Vicky. I think about putting in an extra surprise by also appointing one of the "good guys" as an attacker, but decide it will feel too much like a copy of Gisella, and no one needs to be reminded of that situation right now.

Once everyone knows what to do, we spread out and take our places.

"Ready?" I ask the fairy godmothers.

They nod in unison and we all spring into action.

At first, we're all careful. Fighting each other outside the protective circle is like a whole new world to us. A world in which we can actually hurt one another. It feels uncomfortable.

"Come on," Vicky jeers, before attacking Kessley full force. "We've got to do this, or we will never know if it will work."

"Okay, then," Kess turns into a ten-foot monster

with bulging eyes and sharp teeth.

"Much better." Vicky holds her sword in front of her and waits for the monster to attack.

I can't see what happens next because something knocks me off my feet. A zombie dog grabs my shirt between its teeth and pulls. Several other skeletons jump onto my chest, crawl under my shirt, and start gnawing at my skin.

With a scream, I grab them and throw them away from me. New ones take their places instantly. I try to blow them away with wind, flush them off with water, and set them on fire using lightning. Each time I succeed, they are replaced by new zombies, or simply get back up for another round.

After a while, I realize it's much smarter to attack Jeep. If I take him out, no more zombies will come for me.

There's some water left on the ground from the skeletons I flushed away. I conjure a lightning bolt in my hand, to distract Jeep, and order the water to sneak up on him and wrap around his feet. He's so focused on moving his hands to steer his cats, dogs, squirrels, and other dead animals, and on my lightning, that he misses the water until it's too late. He looks down to see what's touching his legs.

Water, pull now! I shout inside my head.

It obeys and the tattooed ghost hits the grass. I keep him busy by spreading the water over his body, and envisioning more of it to keep him down.

While he struggles to free himself, I kick the last of

the zombies into the forest. Some are holding on adamantly and I have to use sunlight to force them to let go. The smell of burning clings to me, and smoke tingles in my throat. I bend over and cough. A sword flies over my head.

"Hey, watch out!" I turn to see who threw it, and find D'Maeo and Dylan rolling through the grass, punching and kicking.

They're taking this a bit too serious. That sword could've taken my head off.

I'm about to stomp over to them to tell them how I feel when something sharp hits me in the back. I keel over with a shout of pain and reach for the burning spot. Blood seeps from a cut halfway down my back.

Everyone is taking this way too serious.

Ready to get up and tell everyone to stop fighting, I feel someone approaching. Without wasting time, I roll over, pull out my athame, and hold it up. D'Maeo's sword hits the blade of my weapon. Behind him, Jeep turns invisible. The water holding him down seeps into the grass. He reappears, jumps to his feet, and walks over to us, his hat in his hands, ready to throw it at me if I move.

"You lost," the old ghost says. He winks. "But your fairy godmother did a great job, didn't she?"

He pulls back his sword and I lower my athame. "What makes you say that?"

"You ducked in time for my weapon to miss you, and you rolled over a second before I reached you."

With a frown I push myself into a sitting position. "You're right. But Jeep's hat did cut me."

D'Maeo shrugs. "That wasn't fatal."

"Shouldn't you two be attacking our prime test subject?" I nod in Vicky's direction.

They both sigh. "Right."

They sneak up on Vicky, who is still battling Kessley. I straighten my shirt and wipe some sand from my pants.

Good to know they're reluctant to attack her, but have no problem wounding me.

Although I want to see how Vicky is doing, I soon turn away. If I watch this fight any longer, I'll join in. It feels so wrong to stay out of it, to leave her to fend for herself. Each time a sword or magical weapon misses her by an inch, my heart stops. I need a distraction.

On my right, Mom is fighting Maël. Sweat drips down the ghost queen's temples and the hand around her staff trembles. She's facing Mom, but her eyes are focused on something else. An illusion only she can see.

Mom looks stronger than I've ever seen her. There is a blush on her cheeks and some of her wrinkles have vanished. Her shoulders seem broader than I remember, and she has pulled them back proudly. Her hair is less frisky and shines. Also, I could swear she has grown an inch or two.

She approaches Maël, concentration painted on her face.

Behind me there's shouting, and I close my eyes, forcing myself not to turn around. If Vicky's hurt, I don't want to see it.

Mom has almost reached Maël. She reaches for her staff… and freezes.

The ghost queen blinks and narrows her eyes. Her gaze locks onto Mom. "I know that trick. It does not work on me anymore."

My jaw clenches with such fury my teeth squeak in protest. I didn't think it would be so hard not to interfere. Lightning comes to life in the palm of my right hand without me conjuring it consciously. I clench my fist to extinguish it before I fling it at Maël in a reflex.

Mom moves again, but in slow motion. A frown appears between Maël's eyebrows and her eyes flick in all directions. Then, Mom's hand flies forward. Her fist connects with Maël's nose, and a cracking sound draws a hiss from me. The ghost queen doesn't recoil, though. She stays upright and flings her staff forward, knocking Mom onto her back. The tip with the stone is aimed at Mom's throat before she can blink. Mom holds her hands up in defeat and Maël apparates into the fight with Vicky without a word.

I walk over to Mom and help her up. "Nice job."

She wipes the grass from her pants. "Thanks, but it wasn't nearly good enough. She escaped my illusion too easily."

"Don't beat yourself up. You haven't used your powers that much yet. I've had mine a lot longer and

I'm still learning how to control them, along with discovering new things."

She wipes some stray locks from her face. "I know, but we don't have much time left to train. I need to learn fast."

I put my arm around her and pull her close. "I'll tell you what. We'll take a short break and train some more while the others fight Vicky."

She kisses my temple. "Thanks, honey."

We drop down into the grass and inevitably my gaze wanders over to the fight of the "bad guys" against Vicky. She seems to be doing fine on her own. After several minutes, I'm starting to think she doesn't need the protection of the fairy godmothers. Then, I notice her ducking and stepping back just in time to avoid getting staked several times in a row, and realize the godmothers are working literal miracles. Vicky turns around when D'Maeo sneaks up on her. She closes her eyes and the old ghost flies backward. He lands next to us, rolls over twice, and gets up, ready to charge again.

Vicky is pushing each of her attackers back with her mind. They stumble, but they're starting to resist the force, coming closer ever faster. Jeep sends several skeletons to pull her legs out from under her, Kessley changes into a raging bull, Charlie throws his grease balls—all while Maël tries to freeze her.

"She's getting tired," Mom observes. She raises her hands and cheers in a whisper, "Come on, Vicky, you can do it."

Even though it's impossible for Vicky to hear Mom's words from this distance and with all the noise from the fight, all of Vicky's attackers suddenly tilt back.

Mom cheers louder and throws out her fist. "Yeah! Kick their asses!"

D'Maeo, Jeep, Kessley, Charlie, and Maël are lifted from the ground and my laughter gets stuck in my throat. They soar so far back they disappear into the forest. Except for Charlie, who slams against a tree and slumps to the ground, unconscious.

"Shit." Vicky's gaze flits from my best friend down to her hands. Then, she sets off toward the still form under the tree, with me on her heels.

She reaches him first because she apparates from halfway down the lawn.

"Charlie?" She cradles his head with care.

A cloud of sparks lands next to her when I reach them. Mona bends over Charlie and her sparks jump eagerly onto him. While they spread over his whole body, she places both hands on his chest.

It takes me only a few seconds to notice her hands don't move up at all.

Charlie's heart has stopped beating.

My mouth opens to ask Mona if she can save him, but I hold back the words. I don't want to disturb her healing.

The rest of my Shield appears around us, the battle forgotten.

A hand presses down on my shoulder and Mom

whispers, "Step aside, honey. Give them some room."

Only now do I realize the other fairy godmothers have joined us. As soon as I make way, two of them kneel beside Charlie. Their red and green sparks join Mona's as they place their hands next to hers.

Mom holds me close to her and rubs my arm. Only now do I realize I'm trembling. Vicky puts his head back gently and backs up with her hand on her mouth in shock.

My vision gets blurry as tears start to fall, forming a continuous stream down my cheeks.

He's dead. She accidentally broke his neck.

Mom almost crushes my shoulder now, but I don't mind. If she lets go, I'll collapse.

Vicky meets my eyes. Guilt paints her face, and she blinks away tears.

I slowly shake my head. It's not her fault. Her powers surprised her. She would never do this on purpose.

The fairy godmothers work in silence. I don't see any changes. No movement in his chest, no sharp inhale, not even the flinch of a finger.

All of a sudden everything around us gets so bright I have to squeeze my eyes to see anything. My heartbeat drowns out the shocked voices whispering things I don't want to hear anyway.

Relief washes over me when Quinn appears. That is, until the fairy godmothers step away from Charlie without a word and he reaches down to pick up our friend.

A pained cry escapes my lips and I shoot forward. I don't even know what I'm yelling. Something like, "No, don't take him."

Everyone around me is foggy. All I see is the angel standing there with Charlie's limp body in his arms.

"I may be able to heal him in Heaven," Quinn says, his demeanor calm. "Let me try, Dante."

I don't understand why he would ask for my permission until Mom grabs my wrist. I hadn't even noticed my hand gripping his arm.

"S-sorry," I whisper, my voice hoarse.

"I'll do what I can," Quinn says. Then he spreads his wings and disappears.

My hazy gaze sweeps over the defeated expressions of the fairy godmothers and my legs give in. I collapse onto the grass and sob uncontrollably.

CHAPTER 20

The first hour or so after Quinn leaves is a blur. Someone guides me into the mansion and pushes me into my chair. There's nothing but silence, or maybe my hearing has shut down. Someone puts a mug into my hands and when I don't lift it to my lips, they do it for me.

"Small sips."

I obey, and start to feel a bit better. The dull ache in my heart remains, though. One small setback and I will collapse and never get up again.

We lost Gisella and Charlie, in one day. Is this what the upcoming days will hold? Me losing everyone I care about.

I've been trying to prepare myself for the loss of my Shield. Of course, I know the chances of all of us getting through the battle with Satan unscathed are as good as nil, but we're losing people seconds before we even start.

Why does our luck keep changing?

"Is he going to be okay?"

The words reach me, but my brain needs some time to process them. Other sounds start to trickle back in.

Vicky's voice is full of guilt. She's trying to explain what happened.

The fairy godmothers are evaluating their work. From what I can gather, their plan worked perfectly. Bitterness fills me from head to toe.

Too bad we only gave Vicky protection.

Now, someone is stroking my back, but I can't handle it anymore. I shove the hand away and shout, "Leave me alone."

The kitchen falls silent. It takes several blinks to lift the mist blocking my vision. My cheeks itch and I wipe the wet streaks away forcefully. "What the hell happened?"

"I'm not sure." Vicky sounds timid.

I turn my head to look at her, and frown. I've never seen her like this before. Her shoulders are hunched, she avoids my gaze, and her foot is tapping restlessly against the leg of her chair.

"I've told you so many times that I'm not that important," she mumbles. "We shouldn't focus on just one person."

"You *are* important, Vicky," D'Maeo responds. "Without you, we have nowhere to put Satan once we've defeated or captured him."

"Well, we need to defeat him first, don't we?" she replies, her words dripping with venom. "And I can't do that on my own."

"Vicky—" Maël begins.

I cut her off. "No, she's right. We've been approaching this battle all wrong. We've been focusing on who we think are the most important people. We've forgotten the basic rule we live by— everyone is important. We're all in this together. And, we *all* need protection."

"We can arrange that," the brown-haired fairy godmother says. "We can appoint two godmothers to each of you."

With my hand raised I silence Jeep, who wants to protest. "Good. That's what we'll do." I wipe some stray tears from my eyes and continue. "And I don't want to hear anything about this anymore. That's an order."

I wipe the tears on my pants. "You stop feeling guilty," I tell Vicky. "This wasn't your fault." Although I sound harsh instead of soothing, I can't help myself. Anger floods through my veins, and I let it, because right now, it keeps me going. If I let the pain in, it will consume me, which can't happen. We've fought so hard to get this far, and we're almost there. Our next step is facing the Devil, and my friends aren't the only ones who deserve a safe world. There are billions of defenseless people out there who need us. We can't fail them.

I reach out to Vicky and touch her leg. She stops tapping her foot and looks up.

"Any idea what happened? Did you forget you

weren't fighting real enemies? Did you unlock more of your powers?"

She shakes her head. "I was holding back. I used enough power to keep them from getting closer. And then… there was a sudden surge, as if something boosted my power. That's why everyone was pushed away from me with so much force." Her lip disappears between her teeth. "I didn't mean to do that, I really didn't." Despite her efforts to keep them in, several tears escape her eyes.

I get up and press her head against my chest. "I know. It's okay."

"It's not okay," she murmurs. "And I want to know what went wrong."

Mona walks around the table refilling our cups. "Did anything change before it happened? Did you get scared or was anything else different?"

While I drop back into my chair, Vicky wipes her face. "I don't know."

My thoughts go back to what I saw of the fight, which wasn't much. I try to jog my memory as I follow Mona's progress. Mom shoots her a radiant smile and that's when it hits me.

"It was you!" Excited that I've figured it out I jump from my seat.

My outburst startles everyone. All faces turn to me.

"Who?" Vicky asks with a frown.

I point at Mom. "You. You were the thing that changed. You cheered her on a millisecond before…"

My elation wains a little.

"How could that have done anything? I didn't even hear her," Vicky says.

"It has something to do with Charlotte's powers, I'm sure of it." I look around for support. At first everyone is silent. I can almost hear them thinking, *He's gone crazy.*

Maël speaks up. "It is possible. I have heard of people able to enhance the powers of others."

Mom scratches her head. "You have?" She stands up. "Well, then we should test it." Without waiting for a response, she walks out the back door.

When we follow, she's standing in the protective circle. She points to a spot a couple of feet away from her and directs me to stand there, and attack someone with a lightning ball.

"Yes, ma'am." I beckon the others, but they all hesitate.

"Come on," I grumble. "We're inside the circle, nothing can happen to you here."

Taylar lifts his shield and walks up to me. "Let's go, then."

Mom rubs her hands together. "I'm not sure how to do this. Would it be enough to cheer? Do I need to use your name?"

Jeep scratches his cheek. "Actually, I don't think it was the cheering that did the job. It was probably a thought, maybe combined with a movement of the hand."

Mom cracks her neck. "Okay. I'll try that first."

I start throwing balls of lightning at Taylar, who evades them with ease. The third ball nearly scorches my own nose. It's twice the size of the normal balls I conjure, and I almost drop it on my foot.

"Did I do that?" Mom sounds astonished.

"I think so," I reply. "Try again."

This time, I conjure a lightning bolt, and it grows into something resembling a staff, reaching from the ground up to my head. I lift it horizontally and toss it at Taylar, who holds up his shield in defense. The bolt hits it so hard the young ghost topples backward.

"Wow!" he cries out. "Take it easy."

I hold up my hand in apology.

Kessley is jumping up and down on the other side of the line. "That was brilliant, Dante!" She hops into the circle. "Try it on me now."

Mom chuckles. "Okay."

Taylar steps out of the way when Kessley attacks me. Lightning balls zoom past her head. She's too fast so, instead, I focus on a wave slamming down on her.

She dives right in and comes out the other side as a water dragon.

Water, wrap around her and turn to ice.

It tries to obey, but before it gets the chance, the dragon multiplies. Normally, it would turn into two dragons that each split again and so on, until Kessley decides it's enough. Now, the two dragons become a dozen in a heartbeat.

"Woohoo!" Kessley cheers, changing back into her human form and pulling all her copies back inside her. She spreads her arms and out pop a dozen Kessleys again. "Wow! Look at me," she calls out.

I can't help but smile, too.

Mom can enhance our powers.

Kess flings herself around Mom's neck and kisses her on the cheek time and again.

Grinning, I open my mouth to ask Charlie to give it a try. I can't wait to see what his grease balls will turn into.

And what about Gisella's shadows? Will she be able to call them all to her with one simple move of a finger if Mom helps her?

When I search for them in the group, my shoulders sag. My grin fades as I remember they're not with us anymore, and may never be again.

Taylar walks over to me, panting. "This is great, isn't it?"

I try to smile, but my lips won't cooperate. "Yes, it's wonderful."

He nudges my shoulder. "Don't lose hope now. We've seen worse."

He's right, but I can't get rid of the feeling of dread looming over my head.

Taylar leans closer. "You got us through bad times before. You can do it again. We need you as our leader, and as our friend. If you give up hope, everyone will." His eyes beg me to keep it together, to tell him I'm fine. That we'll all be fine.

So, I do the one thing I can think of. I nod and smile. Then, I turn to face the others and beckon them. "Everyone into the circle."

Mom frowns at me over Kessley's shoulder, and I shoot her a grin. "Let's see what you can do with that power."

After splitting the group in two, I instruct Mom to enhance the powers of several people.

"Or of a whole group," Kess suggests, her excitement bubbling over.

"One step at a time," D'Maeo advises. "We don't want to exhaust her."

"See what you can do, and stop when you get too tired," I tell Mom, while we all take positions opposite each other.

She pretends to roll up the sleeves she doesn't have. "I'm ready."

With a smile, I turn to my opponents. *She's actually enjoying this.* Can't say I blame her. I remember what it was like to discover my powers. To feel like a real superhero. Well, almost. I haven't got the matching suit or bravery.

"Focus, babe." Vicky's voice pulls me back to the fight. Something bright soars in my direction and I duck. I imagine the sun burning hotter and hotter on the heads of our friends. All the clouds in the sky move to our side of the circle, casting shadows to keep us from getting burnt.

"Keep your eyes out for zombies," I warn Vicky, Taylar, Dylan, and Kessley. "Jeep is waking them up again."

"You keep focusing on the weather," Vicky

counters. "We'll take care of the rest." She positions herself half in front of me, throwing the next load of Mona's sparks off course.

A weird feeling washes over me. It's as if slime trickles into my brain, slowing my thoughts down and making it impossible for me to focus. My limbs are so heavy I can't move them. I struggle to think straight.

What happened? Did something hit me? Am I unconscious?

I blink in slow motion.

Nope, still standing and awake.

Wind, make me move, I command. There's whistling around me, but I'm still frozen. With my sluggish brain, I try to conjure water to pick me up. Nothing happens.

I want to say that someone shut down my powers, but my voice doesn't obey. My lips don't even move. That's when I manage to put two and two together.

Maël did this. She's frozen us in time. Now, I know how much this sucks.

Although I order my eyes to find the ghost queen, it takes forever. My gaze locks onto her and I focus so hard on a wave to push her over that sweat trickles down every part of my body. I wouldn't mind if this froze in time, too, but it's a sign that I'm breaking through her spell.

A small wave hits her feet, and she looks down, temporarily distracted. Time starts to tick again, and a new wave is created. It knocks the staff from her hand, and she turns to retrieve it.

Meanwhile, the number of zombies joining the fight keeps growing. Seems Mom succeeded in enhancing more than one power at a time. I'm so proud, but don't have time to think about it any longer because the zombies are clawing their way up to my neck.

I order the wind to grab onto Jeep's fingers and keep them still, so he can't control his army or summon more of these obnoxious undead. It works, until D'Maeo steps in front of him to block my powers.

From the corner of my eye, I see Mona turning into a whirling cloud of sparks. It's so bright and big, and it turns so fast, I forget I'm in a fight for a second. In that second the whirlwind crosses the distance between the two groups. I lose sight of her and try to come up with something to stop her.

Too late. The invisible fairy godmother hits me full force. I'm lifted from the ground and fall down several feet. My landing is inelegant and forceful. The wind is knocked out of me, and I gasp for air.

Next to me, Vicky, Taylar, Dylan, and Kessley are tumbling through the air, helpless.

The whirlwind becomes visible and comes to a halt, turning into Mona again.

"Nice job!" I call out to Mom.

"I'm not done yet," she replies.

I wipe the sweat from my forehead and wait for my friends to join me.

Mona steps out of the circle. "Time out."

223

Three Kessley copies jump her as one, knocking her over. She pushes them away with vigor. "I said time out, everyone!"

We all freeze, and this time it's not because of Maël's powers. I've never heard Mona speak like this. There's anger as well as panic in her voice.

Rushing over to her, I help her up. "What's wrong? Did you get hurt?"

"No." Tears form in her eyes as she stares past me into the distance. "It's—"

The door to the kitchen bursts open and the fairy godmothers spill out into the garden.

"Did you get the call, too?" the short one with the blonde curls asks.

Mona takes a deep, shaky breath. "I think we all did."

If my heart beats any harder, it will burst out of my chest. "What's going on? Please tell me."

Mona exchanges a worried look with her sisters. When she turns back to me, the worry and hurt on her face make my stomach flip. "It's the Book of a Thousand Deaths. It has been used."

CHAPTER 21

We all gather around the godmothers.

"Are you sure?" Mom asks.

Deep wrinkles appear in Mona's forehead. "Unfortunately, yes."

Kess keeps pulling the hem of her dress down. "How do you know?"

"If something really bad happens, something that can jeopardize the safety of our protégées, a signal is sent to us."

"And if one of the ten most dangerous objects on earth is used, we'll get a distress call, too," the brown-haired godmother adds.

Mona tries to rub the wrinkles from her forehead. "We call those the Terrible Ten. The Book of a Thousand Deaths is at the top of the list."

D'Maeo wrings his hands. "Does this mean Gisella escaped?"

225

The godmothers all nod while Mona answers, "Yes. The spells inside only affect the world you're in."

I'm afraid to ask, but need to know. "What kind of spells did she cast?"

Mona shakes her head and her skin turns back into its perfect smooth form. "The exact contents of the book are only known to a few. All we know are the results."

I swallow the nausea rising to my throat. "How bad is it?"

Mona tilts her head to the sky, listening. Her jaw tightens. She opens her mouth, but no sound comes out.

"It's horrendous," one of the other godmothers replies.

Mona finds her voice. "Which was to be expected. The book was hidden for centuries for a reason."

"Can you... tell us?" Kessley asks tentatively.

One by one the fairy godmothers shake their heads.

"I'm sorry, I can't." Mona staggers to the kitchen.

D'Maeo and Mom rush to her side to support her. The rest of the godmothers mumble an apology and follow them inside.

Jeep spins his hat in his hands. "That bad, huh?"

Taylar nudges me. "Maybe we can find something on the Pentaweb."

Vicky, Kessley, Taylar, Dylan, Jeep, and Maël gather around me while I pull out my phone and open the Pentaweb app.

"Try 'horrible deaths,' plus today's date," Taylar suggests.

The web comes up with several headlines that make my heart stutter. I click the top one and start reading. *The elevator in a twenty-story office building in New York city plummeted down from the top floor today. Ten people were inside at the time. None survived.*

All I can do is gulp as I scan the next lines. Unable to read them aloud, I turn the screen so the others can read it themselves. The words swim before my eyes.

Doctors say the victims suffered tremendously, as the sudden drop would have caused their organs to keep falling while their bodies came to an abrupt halt.

I haven't read any farther, and I don't think I want to judging by the disgusted face Kessley pulls and the way even Maël's jaw trembles.

"What else happened?" I ask, unwilling to take my phone back to read the next news article but unable to control my curiosity at the same time.

Taylar goes back to the search results and clicks the next article. *"Six people quartered at a fraternity initiation near Paris, France,"* he reads out loud.

Kessley shivers. "Does that mean what I think it means?"

Taylar reads on. *"What started out as a dare for six so-called 'neophytes', took a horrific turn when one of them got quartered while tied to four cars. Although the surviving students are in shock, their statements are clear: they both claim the fraternity members suddenly went crazy, tying everyone to the cars one by one. The boys saw their friends die gruesome deaths. Local residents who heard screams of terror contacted the police. The two survivors and three police officers have been committed to the psychiatric ward."*

My whole body has gone cold. I snatch my phone back and press the home button frantically. "I don't want to hear any more."

It's as if my heart jumps out of my chest when my phone starts to play "Dancing Queen" by Abba. I set it as my ringtone after Mom fell into that hole in Purgatory, since it's her song. Now, it seems painfully inappropriate.

I pick up and a panicked voice answers me. "Dante? It's Wendy. Have you heard?"

"Yes, the book was used."

Wendy ignores the sadness and guilt in my voice. "We need to get it back, as soon as possible. If we can pinpoint the location of the last victims, we may be able to trace the book from there."

"Are you saying Gisella actually takes the book to those places?"

"She might. It's easier for an unexperienced spellcaster to be close to the people they want to cast the spell on. We're trying to find the location of the last victims as we speak. It's difficult, though. She moves from place to place fast, and the news doesn't always give an exact time of when it happened."

"We'll search, too. I'll also try scrying for her."

"That would be great. Let me know if you find

her."

"Will do. You, too."

We say goodbye and I hand the phone back to Taylar. "Try to find out where the last people were killed. If you find it, let me know immediately. I'm going to try and scry for Gisella."

Vicky follows me inside, where Mona and D'Maeo are sitting alone at the kitchen table.

"Did your friends go home?" I ask.

Mona nods. "Yes, they wanted to be close to their protégées."

"I understand."

I walk over to my usual seat at the other head of the table. Vicky pulls a map of the world from her pocket and spreads it out in front of us.

My fingers fumble to take the pendant from my neck and I hold the tiny athame above the map. With my eyes closed, I conjure a likeness of Gisella in my head. I hold onto the image of her dark face and look down at the colorful shapes that form the many countries. The pendant starts to spin on its own, in wide circles. Its movement stutters above South Africa, then moves along for another round. There's a pause above the same spot.

"She must be on the move. The pendant is searching."

The miniature athame slams down in Newcastle, England.

"Got her!" I cry out.

As if on cue, the others walk into the kitchen.

Taylar hands me my phone back. "The last known horror site was in South Africa. About half an hour ago."

"Yes, Gisella was there not too long ago, the pendant hesitated above the spot." My fingers wrap around the athame and I put it back around my neck. "She's in Newcastle now. I'll notify Wendy."

Jeep is still processing what I've told them while I type a message to Wendy. "Half an hour ago and she's already moved to the next place?" His voice rises in astonished revulsion. "What is she doing? Working her way through the book page by page?"

I put my phone down. "I hope not. What else did you find?"

Taylar sits down with a wary expression. "I thought you didn't want to hear about all the horrible deaths."

"I changed my mind. These people died because of our mistake. They don't deserve to be ignored."

The fierceness of Mom's indignant response startles me. "This isn't your fault. Nor is it Gisella's, even though she cast those spells."

I lower my head. "I'm not sure the victims of this killing spree will agree with you."

"They will," she says getting up from her chair. "Once they see what you've all done to prevent the world from falling." Her gaze lands on us one by one. "And once they see how many people you've saved and how bad the death of everyone you've lost hurts all of you."

Mom walks over to me and rubs my shoulders. "I wish we were able to save everyone, but that's unrealistic. We'll have to go for as many as possible. You all need to stop blaming yourselves for the people who died. You didn't kill them."

I grab her hands and squeeze them. "Thanks, Mom."

"So, tell me about the other news items you guys found," I urge Taylar.

He licks his lips. "Okay. The whole population in the village of Tata, in the Moroccan desert, died of heat stroke and dehydration when all their water dried up in the blink of an eye. More than eighteen thousand people perished due to the extreme heat."

Sorrow and rage pump through my blood. Eighteen thousand people dead. For what? To show how much power the book has?

"Then there was a flood on the Greek island of Crete. A strong current pulled about forty tourists into a cave. Abnormally high waves slammed them against the walls of the cave over and over. It's believed many of them died from internal bleeding before they had a chance to drown."

My hands ball into fists. "That is horrible. All those lives taken, without reason."

"There was one more," Taylar says. His face shows more pain than it did when he almost collapsed under the pressure of his unfinished business.

I brace myself.

231

"Two hundred sixty-eight people died from electrocution due to a system failure at a power company in China. For two minutes, every device in the building was electrified. Some people got away with mild burn marks. The electrical surge caused a fire, which spread through the building rapidly. This triggered the emergency system, which sealed off all the exits. The remaining three hundred thirty-seven employees died of smoke inhalation or burnt to death."

My hand flies to my mouth. Tears sting behind my eyes. I don't know what to say to this. I can't imagine what those people must have gone through. My lips move to let out the words "That's horrible" again, but they seem insufficient.

After a short silence, Maël stands up, pulls out her staff, and holds it out in front of her. We all get to our feet. "We pray for the lives that were lost today. We hope they will find peace and love in the afterlife. Their sacrifice will give us the strength to keep fighting until the end." She lifts her eyes to the ceiling, and we all follow her example, bringing our hands to our hearts.

As if on cue, a bright light descends through the ceiling. I squint and my heart nearly leaps out of my chest at the sight of a familiar grinning face. My concerns about Charlie were pushed aside by Gisella's killings, but they smoldered in the back of my mind. Now that I see my best friend again, tears fill my eyes.

Before Charlie lands on his feet, I've already

hurried over to him and started pulling him against me.

He chuckles. "Good to see you, mate."

Holding him out at arm's length to check him from head to toe, I cheer, "You're alive!"

"I'm fine now. I was out cold for… well, I'm not sure, a long time. When I woke up, two angels were sitting by my side."

I guide him to his chair. "They healed you."

He sits down and greets the others with a timid smile. "Yes. No need to worry about me anymore." All the affection coming his way obviously makes him uncomfortable. His hand keeps going through his hair and his cheeks are red. "Bring me up to speed. What happened while I was away?"

I exchange a quick look with D'Maeo. The old ghost shrugs.

Okay, no questions about his time in Heaven, I get it.

While we fill him in on everything he missed, he flexes his fingers. He seems a bit absent. Secretive, too. I'm not sure I like it.

Maël taps her wand against the table. "We should go, before Gisella casts the next spell."

Everyone except D'Maeo makes for the hallway.

"Is something wrong?" I ask.

"No. I was only thinking it might be a good idea to scry for her exact location. That might save us a long search and reduce her chances of surprising us."

Maël straightens her cape. "I agree. She knows we are trying to locate her. She might have set a trap."

I turn to Vicky. "Do you have a map of Newcastle?"

She shakes her head. "Sorry."

"I've got a better idea. One moment." Mom bounces up the stairs and comes back with a tablet in her hands. She taps the screen several times and places it in front of me. "This works too, right?"

I take my necklace off again. "I'm not sure, but I can try. I only hope it won't break your screen when it hits."

She waves my objections away. "Lives are more important than a simple device."

"Very true," Jeep comments, flipping his hat over in his hands nervously.

I hold the miniature copy of my athame above the map and think about Gisella again. The pendant starts to move. At first in wide circles, but soon in smaller ones. Then, it hits the right corner of the tablet. It leaves a small scratch on the screen.

Zooming in results in three street names. I grab a screenshot, and send it to Wendy.

After checking my pockets and waistband for my real athame, my foldable Morningstar, and my notebooks, I put the necklace back on. "Let's go."

After a quick kiss from Mom and a "Good luck" from Mona, everyone steps through the portal Taylar creates in the hallway.

Before I follow the others I put my hand on Charlie's shoulder. "Are you sure you're okay? You don't seem like... yourself."

He squeezes my hand. "I'm fine. Heartbroken, but I'll get over it. And," he leans closer and drops his voice to a whisper, "the angels boosted my power."

My lips form into a grin. "Really? What did they do?"

"I don't know, that's all they said. I guess we'll find out soon enough, right?"

"Right."

With a nod, I let him step through the portal first. Then, I shake off the last of my worries about him and cross the threshold to the United Kingdom.

It's a cold, somber evening in England. Everyone on the street has an umbrella, except for us. Of course, me and Charlie are the only ones getting soaked due to the relentless rain coming down from the gray sky. The others are invisible, which means it pours through them. One more upside to being dead.

There's no sign of Gisella or the demons. No panicked screaming, no shouts for help and no buildings seem to be missing some of their shadows.

"She's probably somewhere preparing for the next spell," Vicky says.

I check out the buildings around us. "Somewhere inside?"

"I think so."

"But, which one? There's no time to check them all."

Jeep is already halfway down the street. "We should walk through the streets the pendant landed on," he calls over his shoulder. "We might feel something off somewhere or see something weird."

We follow him, scan each window of every building, and grip our weapons in fear. No one is looking forward to fighting one of our own. Or having to face whatever Gisella is planning here. My hope is we'll be in time to prevent her from casting another spell.

We round the corner of the street and come to an abrupt halt.

"There." Taylar points at the third building on the right.

Immediately, I know he's right. A feeling of dread falls over me at the sight of it. It seems like an abandoned warehouse, placed between two shops. Worn bricks make up the front. A row of arched windows is covered in dust and grime. What's left of the white paint on the door is cracked and the window frames are all rotten. The musky smell of dust and dirt gets stronger with every step we take toward the building. Still, despite all the decay and neglect, there's something positive about it. When we pause to let a businessman with a suitcase pass, I notice what it is. The building isn't as gloomy as it must normally be. In fact, it's pretty light, because all of the shadows have disappeared. It's as if a single sunbeam falls upon it, even though the sun is setting.

The few people who pass it frown, noticing something off, but not knowing exactly what. To my relief, they all hurry along, eager to get out of the rain and home to their families after a long day's work.

We stop again the moment we reach the first shadowless bricks. I scan the windows. Some of them are broken and faint noises drift past the shattered glass. Growls and shuffling. And farther away, a familiar voice.

Charlie moves forward but I grab his wrist. "Wait."

"What for?" he grumbles under his breath. "We need to stop her before she kills more people."

"I agree, but you should calm down first."

"I *am* calm."

The trembling of his voice and his white knuckles say otherwise, so I hold onto his arm. I wait for him to look me in the eye. "It's not her fault, mate. She loves you, and she would never betray you if she had a choice."

He pulls his arm free and tosses his hair over his shoulder. "I know that. It's not her anymore. My Gisella is gone."

Maël leans forward and peers through the streaks of dirt on the nearest window. "She might still be in there. Don't give up on her yet."

Charlie shakes his head. "She's dead to me. I can't fight that thing in there if I think Gisella is inside her."

I exchange a worried look with D'Maeo. "Maybe you should stay here to keep an eye out for unexpected visitors."

He lifts an eyebrow before shrugging. "If you want

to waste time trying to get Gis back, be my guest. I'll wait here and take care of anyone who so much as breathes wrong. But I'm telling you, my girl is gone. There's nothing you can do about it."

He tries to sound tough and callous, but the edge in his voice betrays him. Fighting Gisella will destroy him, I know it. I can't let him go inside with us, even though we need every power we have to take her out and get the book back. We were very lucky to get Charlie back once, that won't happen again.

I pat his shoulder. "If there is a chance to save her, we'll do it. You can count on us."

He shrugs my hand off and straightens up. "Thanks. Now, go please. The longer we wait, the more damage she can do."

With a heavy heart, I let him turn away from me. There's nothing I can do to assure or comfort him. And he's right, we should hurry.

I grab my Morningstar more firmly and shake my unease off. "Everybody ready?"

They all nod and we tiptoe toward the door, which hardly looks solid enough to keep a two-year-old out. I start counting down from three in a whisper when there's a loud crash inside, followed by the breaking of glass and an angry shout.

One glance over my shoulder tells me everyone is thinking the same thing. We're too late.

CHAPTER 22

I knock down the door and we storm through a large open space, and straight into a spacious office. One half-rotten desk stands near the far wall, with two dead plants in large, modern planters next to it.

Dust billows up everywhere around us, making me cough as I breathe it in.

I bring my arm back to throw my Morningstar at the first person or monster to cross my path, but freeze. My friends do the same behind me.

The scene we've stumbled into is not what we expected. Gisella is not bent over the book casting some cruel spell, demons around her on the lookout. Sure, the demons are all present, but they're in the middle of a fight with a bunch of... soldiers?

Uncertain what to do, I take a step back and consult D'Maeo. "Should we join in? They look military, or something. Maybe we should stay out of it?"

A lasso lands an inch from my left foot, and someone materializes inside it.

"Definitely not the military," Jeep mumbles.

The woman who came out of nowhere picks up the rope around her feet, pulls it in at lightning speed and gives us a brief sideways glance. "Oh, hey, guys. Great timing," she chirps.

Then she dives into the fight, clicking her tongue.

As reddish smoke fills the air above the raging battle, and my mouth falls open.

"Was that Wendy?"

"I think so," Kessley whispers.

I squint at the figures jumping around. It *is* her. She's dressed in black and is wearing combat boots, like the other fighters. Her blonde curls are pulled up in a big bun. She's like a completely different person.

"Well, are we going to help them or not?" Kessley asks, her words coming from my right as well as my left now.

My gaze sweeps over each copy of her and I smile. "Of course we are." Then, I lunge forward into the fight.

This one is different from the ones I've been in up till now. The Keepers of Life move in a kind of blur. It's hard to pinpoint their exact location. One second, two are jumping a demon to my left, and the next, all three of them are gone.

Are they using portals to move around?

The thought is barely finished before another lasso

lands in front of me. A man in his mid-thirties appears inside it, picks it up, and raises a stick about six feet long to block a demon's path. Now, I notice all the Keepers have one. And they know how to use them. First, they confuse the demons by waving the sticks around, then they knock their twig-like legs out from under them. If the monster doesn't roll away fast enough, the stick gets wedged between the eyes or through the large open mouth.

It looks like they don't need our help. Except… the demons keep getting up.

I jump out of one monster's trajectory. I blast it backward with a lightning bolt and once it's down, I throw my Morningstar at it. The spikes lodge themselves into the middle of its face. For a couple of seconds, it lies there. It looks dead to me, but suddenly it moves again. The mouth opens and folds around the spiked ball. I feel it tugging so I put my weight behind it. When it growls, I push the button to reel in the ball. It comes back with so much force that it rips part of the giant mouth apart. With a tortured moan, the demon collapses. I shake the pieces of flesh from my weapon and approach the demon fast. It isn't breathing as far as I can tell, but I'm not taking any chances. With my Morningstar ready in one hand, I conjure a lightning bolt in the other. I lean closer to the open mouth, cringing at the foul smell rising from it. A chill creeps up my back when something in the back of the throat moves.

Is it coming back to life?

I'm not willing to find out what it feels like to have that hairy thing wrapped around my head, so I shove the lightning inside the mouth. I release it with a downward motion and step back. The head explodes, showering everything around it in pieces of red and black goo. Before I can wipe the remains off my bare arms, they turn to ash.

Ha, no coming back from that, you piece of Hellish crap.

My friends and the Keepers have also figured out a way to truly kill the bastards. One by one, they turn into clouds of black particles. I brace myself for the moment the dust literally clears, and we'll face Gisella. I wrap my hand tighter around my weapon and keep a lightning ball ready in the other hand. My friends draw closer to me, scanning the parts of the room visible between the dissipating ash.

There's no Gisella.

Wendy comes to the same conclusion a millisecond before my brain does. "She's not here. It was a decoy."

The other Keepers spread out through the building while my friends check every corner of the room. Vicky walks over to me and whispers in my ear, "She *is* here, cloaked by her shadows. Call everyone back."

"Where is she?" I ask, my gaze flitting left and right.

"North corner, close to the ceiling."

"Okay." I raise my voice. "Wendy?"

The young Keeper of Life walks over to us with a

concerned frown. "I can't believe we fell for this. We need to find her as soon as possible, Dante."

"Gather the Keepers. We need to come up with a new plan." I drop my voice back to a whisper. "Tell everyone Gisella is here. She's hovering near the ceiling in the north corner of this room. Be careful."

Wendy's eyes go wide for a second. She gives me a curt nod and takes off to inform her colleagues.

Pretending to be exhausted I rub my forehead and sigh. Meanwhile, I focus on a plan to take Gisella out and grab the book. I need something to restrain the shadows, since those are her strongest weapon. Unfortunately, I don't know what kind of offense strategies the Keepers of Life have up their sleeves, so it's hard to plan ahead. I guess we'll all have to give it our best shot and improvise during the fight.

Before I can come up with a way to take out the shadows, Wendy taps me on the shoulder. "Are you okay?"

A smile lifts the corners of my mouth. "Oh, yeah, sure. Just thinking."

A worried frown streaks her forehead. "We're ready to leave. Are you all coming?" She nods at my friends approaching us with hanging shoulders.

What she's really asking is: *Are you ready to fight Gisella with us?*

My jaw tightens at the thought of all the horrible deaths she's caused. My eyes meet Vicky's, and she winks. She informed the others. I nod at Wendy. "Of course. Let's go."

I'm not sure what the plan is, but I trust Wendy so I follow her. She walks to the front door and it takes all my concentration to pretend to be relaxed instead of on high alert.

Several thuds behind us make me whirl around. Tension builds up in the air as I aim my Morningstar and a lightning ball at the north corner. Wendy and my friends do the same. Now that I take a good look at the corner, I notice it's much darker than the rest of the room. All the shadows missing from outside have gathered here to hide Gisella from us.

Under it, several lassos slam down next to each other with loud thuds. In each of them a Keeper materializes, holding a copper ring with a diameter of about twelve inches. A metal line runs along the outside. In it, tiny yellow stones are placed, all the way around.

As one, the Keepers raise their rings and move their arms in a wide arch to the right. It's like the start of a dance.

The shadows move a little, but not enough to reveal the witch they are hiding. They seem nervous, though.

When all the yellow stones light up, I get ready to release my lightning and jump forward. I have serious doubts about our chances to defeat Gisella, but the weapons of these Keepers give me some hope.

"Surrender and we will spare your life," the Keeper in the middle says.

The shadows writhe and a hand becomes visible. It

points a finger at the Keeper of Life. "Mercy is for the weak."

At once the Keepers turn their rings and toss them in the air.

"Get ready," Wendy says, leaning forward on her stick, ready to join the fight.

I amplify my lightning ball and wait for our cue.

The glow of the stones spreads over the rings like fire. The air inside the rings changes. It's as if a shroud slides over the holes. It moves, as if it's breathing. Without a sound, they start to suck the shadows in and, bit by bit, Gisella becomes visible. Her skin is several unnatural shades darker than before, some of it covered in red fur. When her mouth twists into a menacing grin, I'm glad we left Charlie outside. This sight would break his heart even further.

"Give us the book," the Keeper in the middle demands.

Gisella rubs the cover of the Book of a Thousand Deaths pressed against her chest. I'm not sure how, but she's still hovering, her darkened red hair almost touching the ceiling. "This is mine now. But feel free to try and take it from me." She chuckles darkly.

The Keepers put away their ring weapons and pull out their sticks as one. Their battle cry spurs us into action, too. They use their sticks to force Gisella to the ground. Me, Wendy, and my friends do what we can to help from a distance. Jeep's army of resurrected animals has been waiting for his cue to attack. It's a small group, since we're near the city center, but it helps. Meanwhile, Vicky is using her new mindpower to try and move Gisella—or keep her immobilized, I'm not sure. At the same time, Maël tries to freeze the werecat-witch in time to give the Keepers the opportunity to grab the book. D'Maeo blocks as much of Gisella's powers as he can, his face scrunched up in pain with the effort. Taylar and Dylan pop up between the Keepers, slashing their swords and knives at Gisella. Taylar uses his shield a couple of times to protect one of the Keepers against the force fields she throws. They lose their balance, but at least they don't slam against walls. Which is also due to D'Maeo's efforts to block Gisella's powers.

While I try every weather condition I can think of to keep the werecat-witch busy, Wendy hurls some kind of boomerang at the north corner multiple times. I can see it cutting Gisella's arms and face, and I focus on ice filling up the cuts. That doesn't have any effect, so I try sunlight. The werecat-witch grunts but keeps fighting. She seems indestructible.

Kessley has changed into a slithering snake which wraps around Gisella's legs. She pulls her down an inch or two, and the Keepers move closer. I still wonder what they expect to accomplish by waving those sticks at her. They may have succeeded in skewering the demons with them, but the werecat-witch won't be so easy to defeat.

It's not until Gisella manages to get Kessley off

246

that I see the extra feature the sticks bring. The Keepers must have activated it when they faced Gisella. The top of each stick has split in two. From the hole a glowing arrow can be shot.

"What is that?" I ask Wendy while Gisella narrowly avoids getting her arm pierced by one.

Wendy catches her boomerang and answers me before she hurls it again. "The tips are dipped in holy light. If they hit someone evil, good will take over their minds for a couple of minutes. They can even tip someone over to our side for good."

"Wow, that's one awesome weapon."

She smiles. "It is. Unfortunately, we have a limited supply. And once they're fired, the light dies slowly. We can use them twice, at best."

The boomerang returns to her and I wonder what it does.

"If you keep fighting, I'll tell you what it can do," Wendy says following my gaze.

My cheeks warm up. One glance around the room tells me the sunlight I conjured has vanished. "Sorry."

I envision it filling up the room again and order it to burn Gisella, focusing on the wounds the others create.

"Each time my weapon comes close to its target, it attracts magical powers, like a magnet. During its journey back to me, it releases everything it captured. The magic it caught will return to its owner, but it weakens the target momentarily, making it less dangerous for the others to attack and easier to hurt our enemy."

As soon as she utters the last word, Gisella catches the boomerang and breaks it in two. She slams it toward the ground and leans left to avoid another bright arrow. "Enough!"

Wendy holds out her hand and the two wooden pieces that formed her weapon fly into her palm.

"Don't worry, I can fix it," she whispers as a response to my shocked expression.

With a violent arm movement, the werecat-witch creates a force field which throws us all on the ground.

When I sit up rubbing the back of my head, Gisella has opened the Book of a Thousand Deaths.

"I am done playing," she says darkly.

Monotone words slip from her mouth as she starts to read from the book.

"Stop her!" one of the Keepers yells, trying but failing to stand on her weakened legs.

A skeleton mouse jumps up onto the book and rips the page out before Gisella catapults it to the other side of the room with a flick of her finger.

"Well done!" I yell at Jeep.

My elation is crushed when the page on the floor evaporates and grows back into the book.

She starts to read again, and a burning pain wakes in the pit of my stomach.

What is she doing to us?

All the horrific deaths I've heard about flash by in a couple of seconds.

Please don't let that be our fate.

A lone arrow makes its way to the werecat-witch, who has increased the distance between her feet and the floor again. She's so busy reciting the spell in the book that she doesn't notice the arrow zooming toward her. The tip lodges itself in her ankle and she screams. Three Keepers jump forward. They pull the book from her hands and make their way to the other side of the room, while the rest of us form a line of defense between them and Gisella.

She lands on the floor and pulls the arrow from her leg. Her expression is murderous and black pulsing lines appear on her face and neck. Instead of better, the arrow seems to have made the situation worse.

She drops onto one knee and slams her hand down flat on the floor. The wood underneath her palm creaks and darkens. A crack appears and runs through the floorboards toward us with a trail of decay behind it. It crawls under the desk and onto the lone plant. The brown leaves change to black in an instant and crumble to dust.

The trail reaches the first Keeper, and his skin blackens. He crashes to the ground and coughs up blood and ash before going completely still.

"Move back," I warn the others. "She's spreading decay somehow."

Kessley transforms herself into a large owl and picks Taylar up a millisecond before the crack hits him. She drops him behind us and turns back into herself.

I try to create a wall of ice to stop it, but it moves too fast.

While the others do whatever they can think of, I try sunlight, water, wind… nothing works. Each failure pushes us back farther, toward the door.

CHAPTER 23

"Can you open a portal to get us out of here?" I ask Wendy and Taylar, our backs against the row of windows.

Wendy shakes her head. "We've been trying to. She's blocked our every escape somehow."

"She's grown stronger now that she has embraced her dark powers," Jeep responds, wincing as another of his zombies turns to ash.

D'Maeo throws out his arms to block Gisella's powers. Maël points her staff at the trail of decay. Finally, it slows down.

But it's not because of them.

Gisella claws at her leg, from which light is spreading.

"It's weakening her," I note. "We need to attack now."

With a shout, everyone pushes off from the wall

and windows. At the same time, Gisella pulls back her arms and throws them forward. An invisible force knocks most of us out cold. It feels like my lungs are squashed as I hit the wall, between two windows. I slump to the floor and force my eyes to stay open. Around me, everyone is quiet. Gisella is no more than a flash, moving between the still figures. She picks up the Book of a Thousand Deaths and strokes the cover with a creepy smile, unaware some of us are still conscious. Next to me, a female Keeper with straight black hair opens her eyes and gasps for air in silence.

The trail of decay has slowed down, but it's still moving. It crawls over the still forms of the other Keepers and my friends. Fortunately, its power has waned. It causes discoloration of their skin, but that seems to be all.

Still, I freeze when the crack continues its path toward me. I hold my breath, afraid any move I make will draw Gisella's attention. My muscles tense; I'm ready to jump up as soon as the decay closes the distance between us. What I'll do to defend myself against Gisella, I don't know yet.

The trail of withering wood comes ever closer, and then it stops an inch from my nose. I breathe out slowly and glance up at the werecat-witch standing so close to me I could touch her.

While she surveys the room, I snap my eyes closed and pretend I'm out cold like the others.

The sound of pages being turned precedes Gisella mumbling, "Now, where was I?"

A peek through my eyelashes reveals she has her back turned to me. From the corner of my eye, I see the dark-haired Keeper moving. I turn my head a little and mouth a *"No."*

She clutches her ring tightly, panic in her eyes.

"Can I borrow that?" I mouth, extending my arm toward it.

After a short hesitation, she hands it to me slowly.

I take a deep breath. What I'm about to do is risky since my knowledge of this weapon is close to zero. All I can do is guess how it works and hope I'm right. If it goes wrong, the Keepers of Life won't be very happy with me. Actually, they won't be anything at all, and neither will I. However, it's the only option we have. Even if it doesn't work, it might distract Gisella long enough for me to grab the book and stop her from casting another spell over us.

Without making a sound, I get to my feet and turn to Gisella. With all my heart I hope I can remember the movements the Keepers made. Arm up, then sideways in a wide arch. Sure enough, the stones start to glow.

Gisella stops flipping the pages and lets out a triumphant cry. "There you are!" She hasn't noticed me getting up.

I send a thought toward my weapon, *Capture Gisella. Swallow her whole.* Then I toss it upward.

A bright glow emanates from it and the inside starts to pulse.

So far, so good.

Gisella staggers and turns. The ring buzzes and the stones flicker.

"What are you—" Her question is cut short when the ring pulls her one step closer to it. She presses the open book to her chest.

"Come on," the Keeper next to me urges the ring. She has pushed herself up, too, and is grabbing her stick so hard it creaks in protest.

Gisella's expression changes from surprised to determined. The portal pulls at her, but not hard enough. She braces herself against it by placing her feet firmly on the ground. She holds out her free hand, extending her arm more and more toward the ring, no doubt planning to poison it like she did with the floor, the plant, and the Keeper.

I hit her with lightning, ice, and waves of water. Nothing stops her.

I need another ring. Maybe I can combine their power somehow, make it strong enough to pull her in.

I glance sideways. The Keepers and my friends are still unconscious. I start to lose hope of ever getting the book back.

Until hurried footsteps approach from behind me.

"Hold on, I'm coming."

I recognize Dylan's voice.

Relief rises in my chest when Gisella throws a look with a sliver of concern over my shoulder.

Dylan curses under his breath and his weight falls against me. I'm knocked forward, and the ground comes closer way too fast. My hand slams against the ring as I try to regain my balance. Thankfully, it doesn't shut down. If it does, Gisella will be free. She'll kill me in an instant or vanish with the book. Or both.

As I hit the ground and take a painful bump to the head, I focus on wind blowing through the cracked windows. Then, I order it to grab Gisella's ankles and pull. Caught off guard by my fall, she stumbles. The book slips from her hand.

Before she can reach for it, I grab the ring and slam it down over her head. The ring connects with the floor and her shocked scream is cut off abruptly. The light of the stones dies as I lift the weapon. There's no trace of Gisella.

I push up onto my knees, leave the ring on the floor, and pick up the book. Without even glancing at the spell, I slam it shut. It's heavy and cold in my hands, and it spreads a feeling of dread throughout my whole body. All I want to do is drop it, but my mind is stronger than my gut.

Dylan blushes when I help him up with my free hand. "I'm sorry about that. Stupid bad luck."

I stop him before he can utter another word. "Don't be silly. We caught her because you tripped. I'm glad your so-called bad luck finally decided to give a demonstration."

He gives me a shy nod and changes the subject. "Are the others okay?"

"I'm not sure." Saying it out loud makes the possibility of them never waking up quite real, and

I'm afraid to look. Instead, I focus on the dark-haired Keeper. She's squatting beside one of her colleagues. As soon as she touches his arm, the darkness on his skin starts to withdraw. A couple of seconds later, he opens his eyes and gasps for air. After some violent coughing, he seems okay.

Dylan raises an eyebrow at me, asking silent permission to touch one of our friends.

I nod, my chest tightening when he chooses Vicky, who's lying closest to him, on her belly.

He touches her cheek. The dark spots on her skin begin to disappear and her hand twitches.

Before I realize I'm moving, I shoot forward to kneel beside her. "Babe?"

Vicky gurgles and rolls onto her back. Her ashen face turns a shade lighter with every breath she takes. She keeps wheezing, so I pull her into a sitting position.

"Come on, babe, you're okay. There's no need to breathe, remember?"

She coughs and spits out bits of undefinable black. Dirt or insides, I can't tell. Either way, it shouldn't matter, since technically she doesn't have insides anymore.

She leans against my chest with a deep sigh. "That was awful."

I move the book a couple of inches away from her. "What did you feel?"

"It felt like I was choking. It didn't matter that I'm a ghost, I needed to breathe, and I couldn't." She shivers. "When the decay hit me, it felt like my organs were turning to mush. I felt it crawling through me and I couldn't move."

With my free hand I stroke her hair. "You're okay now."

"Yes, but we need to find a way to stop Gisella from using that decay on us again. If we come face to face with her without the Keepers of Life to help us, we're screwed."

There's no arguing with that.

While we get to our feet, the others are recovering. I'm relieved to see that all our friends are in one piece. Most of the Keepers are too. Only the Keeper who got hit first isn't getting up. Wendy squats beside him and takes all kinds of herbs and leaves from the pouches on her belt.

Pulling Vicky along I walk over to her, "Do you want me to try a spell? Or to call Mona or Quinn to heal him?"

Wendy doesn't answer. She lowers her head and whispers something in her colleague's ear. Then, she pours a little water into the cup of her hand, dips her finger in it and touches the middle of his forehead and his eyelids.

"Can I… help?" I offer again in a quiet voice.

Wendy presses her lips together, swallows, and finally looks up. "No, it's too late."

I push back the curse that rises in my throat and manage to whisper, "I'm sorry." With my eyes closed I bend over the man, and send my thoughts to him thanking him for fighting with us. Vicky does the same. The Book of a Thousand Deaths pulses and grows heavier, as if it can sense the evil inside the Keeper and longs to be closer to it. With the book stuffed under my arm I hold out my other hand to the water that's still in Wendy's palm.

She nods in surprise, and I dip my finger in and touch the Keeper's forehead and eyelids.

"Rest in peace," I whisper.

Vicky follows my example, and soon, the other Keepers, Dylan, and the rest of my Shield do the same.

Wendy, Vicky, and I step aside to give them some room and I gesture to two Keepers lying on the floor shivering and rolling their eyes restlessly. "What about those two? Should I get some help for them?"

Wendy shakes her head. "We've got our own ways of healing. They'll be okay. I'm not sure when, though, so we need to get back to our headquarters to discuss our next move. With three men down and danger closing in at frightening speed, we need to make sure all the objects under our protection remain safe." She shoots me a shy smile. "I'm sorry, Dante. I wish we could've done more to help in this battle, but—"

"It's fine, I understand," I interrupt her. "You have another role to play. Maybe our paths crossed to bring us together in this fight against Gisella. Now, we'll go our separate ways again."

Wendy holds out her hand, and I shake it. Hope

seems to light her up a little from the inside. "We will meet again."

"Good luck," I say.

"You too."

They prepare to leave, using their rings to open a portal that will take them home.

Dylan clears his throat. "What happens to the things pulled inside?"

The other Keepers gather around us. Their faces are grim. One of them steps forward and holds out his hand to me. Without hesitation, I give him the Book of a Thousand Deaths. He nods gratefully. His voice is lower than I imagined. He sounds like an old man, while he can't be more than thirty years old. "They are returned to their rightful place about an hour after they are captured."

My chest itches where I held the book and I rub the spot. "So, the shadows will return to their corners?"

"Exactly."

"What about Gisella?"

He shakes his head. The hair touching his shoulders doesn't move. There must be a ton of gel in it. "It's hard to say. She could pop up anywhere."

I sigh. "Great. Another chance for her to go on a killing spree."

"Yes, but at least the Book of a Thousand Deaths is safe. That's the most important thing."

"It is. I'm sorry we lost it."

He shrugs and his hair crunches a little. "Don't be

too hard on yourselves. Accidents happen, even when something is well-protected."

"Sure, but this accident caused a lot of deaths."

He wipes some dirt from his sleeve. "True, but everything happens for a reason. Don't beat yourself up about it."

His words amaze me. Somehow, I didn't expect him to be so forgiving. They take their job very seriously, as they should, and thanks to us everything went south fast.

The Keeper smiles and salutes us. "Keep the faith."

He waits for his colleagues to carry the two wounded Keepers through the portal before stepping through himself. Wendy blows us a kiss, and the portal closes behind her.

CHAPTER 24

When we step outside, the rain has stopped, and the sun is sending its summer warmth down. The street is more crowded now, filled with people going for a drink at a sidewalk café or getting some after dinner groceries. Charlie is sitting cross-legged with his back against the building, watching the passers-by and humming to himself.

I rub my neck and clear my throat.

Charlie looks up lazily. "Hey. I almost dozed off. She wasn't here, was she? Did you try to locate her again?"

My eyebrows move up. "What do you mean, 'she wasn't here'? There were demons in there, Gisella hid in a corner and attacked us. We almost died. Actually, one of the Keepers of Life did die. Two others got hurt badly."

Charlie's mouth falls open. "Are you serious? I

261

didn't hear anything. If I had, I would've come in to help." His eyes scan each of us. "Are you okay?"

Without a word I nod, still mulling over what he just told me.

"She must have put some sort of protection or shield around the building," D'Maeo says. "Something soundproof, to make sure passers-by wouldn't come in to check on the noise."

Charlie is wringing his hands. "You did find her, then?"

Unable to find the words to give him the bad news, I bite my lip.

"Was she…?"

"I think you were right," I say after a deep breath. "I saw no trace of our Gisella."

My best friend nods feverishly. "That's what I thought." He waves away my concerns before I even utter them. "It's fine. I'll be fine."

But he isn't. He looks tired and pale. I pull him into a hug. "We're all here for you."

"We did get the book back," Kessley says, trying to sound cheerful.

"And kicked some demon asses," Jeep adds, provoking a chuckle from Charlie.

"Call me inside next time you face some of those ugly bastards," he says.

I promise I will, and after some contemplating, we decide to go back into the warehouse for Taylar to open a portal.

Just as we're about to step inside, something

around us changes. Darkness falls over the building. People passing by glance up at it, but keep walking.

My heart runs wild inside my chest and I reach for my weapons.

D'Maeo puts his hand on my arm. "No need. These are only the shadows returning."

I drop my arms and follow the movement of the dark across the building. Cold fingers run up my spine.

What if Gisella returns with her shadows?

She doesn't, though. All the shadows do is slide into place and make the building look natural again.

We all exchange a small smile before filing into the building again. About a minute later, we're standing in the kitchen of Darkwood Manor. Mom and Mona greet us with equal amounts of relief and worry.

"Did you find her? Did you get the book?" Mom asks.

"We did," I answer sliding into my chair at the head of the table. Exhaustion falls over me. "The book is safe, but Gisella escaped."

"You couldn't get her back?"

I glance at Charlie, slumped in his chair. He doesn't even seem to notice the packet of cookies Mona sets in front of him.

Instead of answering, I give her a sad shake of the head.

"Well," Mom says with a sigh. "There's still time."

I'm not so sure, but I don't argue with her. Plus, she's right, we shouldn't give up on Gisella yet.

Mona walks around the table and touches everyone gingerly. "You've been hurt."

"We have, but we're fine," Vicky responds.

With a worried frown, Mona moves over to the stove. "I'll cook you all something nice."

I smile, because I have a feeling she's not only cooking for us to give us strength, it will also give her something to do while we wait for the inevitable.

The Devil will finish his backup plan to get to Earth soon. No doubt he's gathering his army while we sit here. The thought sends chills down my back and prompts my heart to go into overdrive.

Vicky moves her chair closer and strokes my neck. "Stay calm. We're ready."

I wish I could be so confident.

She places her hand against my cheek and pushes to make me face her. Then, she kisses me. For a couple of seconds, the rest of the world fades into the background. She pulls back and I keep my eyes closed to hold on to the tingly feeling inside me. Her voice tickles my ear. "You don't have to be confident. Determined is enough. And don't lose hope."

"I won't," I whisper back, and I bury my head in her shoulder.

When we break apart, I grab Vicky's hand and sit up straighter. "Listen up, everyone. This meal is probably our last together. The final battle is drawing near, and no matter how it ends, we will need to say goodbye to each other. Or most of us, at least." I rise to my feet and smile at Mona, who holds out a bottle of champagne, almost as if she's read my mind. I nod and her sparks put glasses on the table into which she divides the bubbly drink. Just a little for everyone.

We all pick up a glass, and a smile pulls up the corners of my mouth as memories flood my mind.

"I want to thank all of you, for standing with me. Cheers to your bravery, to all the good and bad times we've had together, and to our friendship. You will be in my heart forever."

"To friendship and victory!" Taylar calls out.

"Hear, hear!" we all answer and down our drinks.

Mona serves something delicious, as usual, and we laugh and joke about unimportant stuff. It feels good. Like a party. For half an hour, we push the pressure over saving the world to the back of our minds. The gloom may set back in once Mona's sparks have cleared the table, but everyone seems revived for now.

I thank the fairy godmother and stand up. "It's time we open the portal in the silver—"

"Wow, look at this," Charlie interrupts.

I squint at the phone he holds up to my face. "What is it?"

He turns the screen back to him and starts reading. "Thousands of people around the world are moving their families into World War II bunkers or homemade shelters after the gruesome series of deaths today. Followers of different religions are talking about an ancient prophecy that is about to come true. They speak of the rise of the Devil. He is said to come to Earth and kill everyone who defies him. When he crosses the border between Hell and Earth, the sky will turn black and then red. But all is not lost yet. The survival of mankind rests in the hands of a chosen one who has been preparing for this moment. Many could be killed in the oncoming battle between good and evil. Believers are summoning people to find a safe place to hide. Somewhere underground is recommended."

My eyebrows shoot up. "Could this be true?"

This would mean all those people didn't die in vain today. They were meant to die and serve as a warning for the rest of humankind.

Somehow, this doesn't make me feel any less guilty. Not all prophecies come true, after all. Maybe we could've prevented it and still saved everyone.

"Some parts are true for sure," Jeep says. "Satan is coming, and you've been preparing for it all summer. We can only hope that seeking shelter will prevent more deaths."

"And that people will listen to this advice," Vicky adds.

I close my eyes for a second and straighten up. "Either way, we need to defeat him as soon as possible. I don't want any more people to die because of a mistake we make."

D'Maeo is solemn as he answers, "Agreed."

I scratch my neck. "Not that I want to put any more pressure on all of you."

"Don't worry, we're fine." Kessley slams her fist

into her palm. "We're gonna crush this asshole."

Despite everything, a chuckle escapes my lips. "That's the spirit. So, is everyone ready to get the party started?"

Mom stands up, too. "We don't have much choice, do we?"

"No, we don't."

We file upstairs and into the secret room where I cast the spell to reveal the Bell of Izme and the porthole which leads into the silver mine. When I peer through it, I notice something.

"Is it darker in there than usual, or is it just me?"

"You're right." D'Maeo turns the porthole so we can check out the portal at the end of the secret tunnel.

I gasp. "It's already open!"

Jeep, on my other side, narrows his eyes. "The vortex is moving. I wouldn't be surprised if it opens into Hell on the other side."

A shiver racks my body. Images of Beelzebub coming through and almost killing Vicky with his deadly stare flash before my eyes. "What do we do now?"

Maël taps her wand against the porthole. "We open this, like we planned. Lead them straight into our trap."

Dylan scratches his head. "Shouldn't we set a trap first?"

Jeep turns to him with a grin. "We *are* the trap. We'll fight him on familiar ground and make him think the porthole was left open by accident."

"Yes," Kessley says excitedly. "He thinks he can squash us like ants, but we've got some surprises up our sleeves." She rolls up her imaginary sleeves and winks.

Jeep gives her a high-five. "Exactly, leopard girl."

A wave of uncertainty washes over me now that we're about to execute our plan.

Vicky comes up from behind me and wraps her arms around my waist. "Just do it. It's time. Trust yourself, trust us. We're as ready as we'll ever be."

"We can wait in the protective circle, if that makes you feel better," Mom offers from the doorway.

I send her a smile over my shoulder. "It would."

She holds up her thumb and goes back downstairs with Mona on her heels.

Sucking in a deep breath, I let it ease out. "Here goes nothing."

Then, I open the porthole.

The sound of the vortex inside the black void is thunderous. The whole tunnel reverberates with it. The darkness that normally keeps the portal closed now only covers a small part of it since I haven't used the Bell of Izme for a while. The swirling inside it is irregular. The vortex turns left, jams, and turns right again.

"I think they are indeed trying to get it to open into Hell." I hold up the bell. "Should I use it one more time? To make sure they won't think we're leaving both the portal and the porthole open on purpose?"

D'Maeo nods. "That sounds like a good idea. Just don't close it too far, or they'll find an easier way to Earth."

Reluctantly, I step into the secret tunnel. The comforting smell of smoke and tin has been chased away by a musty scent laced with a pinch of sulfur. I don't know what to cover with my free hand, my nose or my ears. Edging closer to the portal, I start shaking the bell. I want to get out of here as soon as possible.

The Bell of Izme takes over the movement of my arm, and the black mud-like substance in the corners of the portal starts to creep back to the middle.

"That should do it," D'Maeo says from behind me.

Although I try to stop, the bell has a will of its own. It wants to keep going.

"Dante? You can stop now."

"I know," I grumble. "I could use some help."

D'Maeo and Jeep apparate next to me. Jeep grabs my arms, while the old ghost wraps his hands round the bell one finger at a time.

"It's okay," he soothes. "Your job is done."

The numbness in my arm is replaced by a heavy feeling. D'Maeo takes the bell from me and I flex my fingers.

"This isn't working," I say, in case someone is listening from the other side of the vortex. "We can't keep this portal closed any longer. We need another plan."

D'Maeo nods his approval, and we climb back through the porthole.

For the first time, I hide the bell with a spell, but not the porthole. I create a small disturbance in the line of salt under it. Then, I look around and tap my chin. "Everything about this screams trap."

The tattooed ghost nods. "I agree. It's not very convincing."

"Do you think they'll care?" Charlie asks. "They're probably eager to finally take us out."

"But also careful," Maël responds. "They do not want to lose their master seconds after they escort him to Earth."

Taylar walks over to the porthole and looks up at the ceiling. "Sorry, house," he says. Then he brings his shield up, pushes off, and slams it against the ceiling. Dust rains down on his solid form. He jumps again, and this time part of the ceiling comes down. Wood lands below the porthole and one board scrapes the glass, leaving a scratch.

Taylar turns to us and spreads his arms. "There. Much more convincing." There's a flicker of darkness in his eyes which makes my jaw clench. When he grins at me, his pupils change back to their normal light blue. I try to relax, remembering Quinn's words.

Trust him.

The young ghost faces the ceiling again. "Please don't fix this until the bad guys walk into our trap."

The house lets out a soft groan in answer.

"Thanks," Taylar says and he walks past me, into the hallway.

Taking in his work I decide he's right. It does look much more convincing. As if part of the old mansion collapsed without us noticing.

"Let's go," I say to the others.

All the way to the kitchen a feeling of unease travels up and down my back. The hairs on my neck stand up, and a wave of cold hits me.

Is it happening already?

I suppress a shiver. Panic rises to my throat. When I walk to the back door and peer into the garden, the same panic is visible on the faces of my friends, waiting in the protective circle.

I join them, my expression as confident as I can manage. "Mona, can you rustle up the other godmothers?"

"Of course, they're ready. I'll go get them right now." She tries to sound calm, but I can hear the edge in her voice.

Above us everything turns dark. We all look up at the same time. My whole body goes cold as I remember the line in the prophecy: *"When he crosses the border between Hell and Earth, the sky will turn black and then red."*

Vicky takes my hand. "It's time, isn't it?"

The ground rumbles from deep within, shaking far below us. Screams drift toward us from a distance. The whole forest moves. Half of it tilts, while the rest of the trees sink several feet into the ground. An air-raid siren starts to blare.

I take a deep breath. "Yes, this is it."

CHAPTER 25

Our weapons drawn, we all hurry into the protective circle. My premonition told me it won't protect us for long, but we want our enemies to think we believe we are safe here.

Once we're all in the circle, we form a line and face Darkwood Manor.

"Don't attack too soon," I instruct my mansion. "Wait for the right moment to surprise them."

It remains silent, but I think it heard me.

Right now, the Devil is probably entering the secret room. The house doesn't even make a creak. Nor do our enemies. An eerie silence has fallen over us, only broken by the rapid breathing coming from me and my friends, and my own heartbeat performing a drum solo in my chest. No birds fly over the mansion and nothing scurries through the undergrowth. Not even the leaves rustle in the wind.

There is no wind. It's as if everything in our little bubble has come to a halt. Clouds no longer move above us, although that's hard to see now that the sun is completely blocked. The humid summer warmth has been replaced by a chilling cold.

Then, there's a crash from inside. Everyone stiffens. We raise our weapons.

"Some light, Dante?" D'Maeo whispers.

The lightning ball I throw up in the air comes to a halt between us and the back door. I glance at Mom, standing on my right. "What's taking Mona so long?"

"We're all here with you," Mona's voice whispers from behind me. She sounds much calmer than before, and that gives me hope.

A hideous, flat head peers around the corner of the kitchen. It blinks at us, lets out a longing moan, and licks its lips with a serpent tongue.

"Great, more demons," Vicky mumbles.

Kessley morphs into a lion with horns on its head. "We can take them. Bring them on."

The demon slithers onto the grass. Several other ones, some of which I recognize from the different circles of Hell, follow it. They watch us with hungry expressions but none of them attack.

Trevor steps out next. He surveys us, silent and calm until he spots Mom. His hands ball into fists and his lips move in a silent curse.

A sudden rush of boldness makes me call out to him. "It's not too late to join us, Trevor!"

Mom stands rigid beside me, and Trevor averts his

eyes.

More demons file out of the mansion. I watch every one of them, trying to remember each species' weak spot, while I wonder how many of them there are. Two rows of them have formed about twelve feet away from us when two dozen more creatures step outside. It's quite the collection of maleficent magical beings. Air, earth, water, and fire elementals, minotaurs, banshees, a dragon boy, and a ghoul. The Devil's servants are the same ones I saw in my premonition, but other things are different. Mona isn't visible and Gisella isn't standing next to Charlie.

Dylan curses under his breath from somewhere to my left. I can't blame him. These creatures look fierce and strong. But at least it's better than the Four Horsemen or Beelzebub. I can only hope we can take all these monsters out before we have to face Satan's strongest accomplices.

The last elemental takes his place in the line. The lightning ball between us dims. Goosebumps awaken on my arms and back as a cold current awakens. A large shadow falls upon the waiting monsters.

"Here he comes," I whisper, barely moving my lips. "Don't let him intimidate you."

My friends don't move a muscle.

Finally, the Devil shows himself. He's in his human form. Tall, dark-haired, and handsome, but creepy at the same time. His demon scales shine through the skin of his face more than the last time I saw him. His smile seems wider than possible. Flames flicker in his eyes. The fact that he has chosen to appear in his least impressive form gives me confidence. He thinks he can blow us away with a flick of his finger.

Ignoring the heat coming at me in waves, I nod politely as he walks around the line of monsters. "Lucifer."

"Dante," he says in a cheerful tone. "At last, we meet on Earth." He opens his arms wide. "I told you victory would be mine. All that stalling has done you no good."

Good, his words are different than they were in my premonition. We changed the chain of events leading to our defeat.

Casually, I toss my Morningstar from one hand to the other. "You haven't won yet."

"Oh, come on." With a huff, he waves my words away from his face. "You thought saving those souls would keep me in Hell. But each sin committed gave me enough power to tear a hole in the circle connected to it. It wasn't hard to find replacements for the sins you prevented." With a grin his gaze sweeps the line of demons by his side. "All I had to do was send some of my pets to keep you busy." He spreads his arms. Malicious delight flickers over his face. "I'm here on Earth now. The rest is just a formality."

"What's in a word," I answer with a shrug.

He chuckles and the ground under our feet shakes. "I see your confidence has grown. And you haven't lost your sense of humor or your boldness. I like that. My offer to join us is still open. Wouldn't it feel better to be on the winning side?"

"I prefer the good side," I respond, forcing my heartbeat to slow down to a normal pace. "Which is the same as the winning side in this case anyway."

Lucifer paces up and down the line of monsters. His head moves from side to side in mock disappointment. "Such a shame. You've got so much potential. Most of you do. Your love for the human race stands in your way of success." He tilts his head, as if a thought has occurred to him. "You know, you should take a leaf out of Gisella's book. She seems much happier with us." He pauses. "Oh, look, here she is now." Satan's voice rises with anticipation, and my heart all but stops when I follow his gaze to the back door.

Gisella walks out, followed by the seven rogue angels from my premonition. She's barely recognizable. The werecat-witch was always beautiful and unique, with her long, bright red hair which matched her red, leather catsuit, and her unsettling yellow eyes. Now, she's even worse than when we saw her in Newcastle. Her hair has turned pitch black. It hangs above her shoulders in greasy strands. The parts of her not covered in rags are drenched in a mud-like substance. Her eyes have changed into dark pits containing no emotions whatsoever. Her blades have replaced her hands and blood drips down from them. Under the mud, I can make out even more red fur than before. She's turning more and more into an evil cat.

Lucifer strokes her as if she's his pet. Which she is, in a way. "Isn't she gorgeous? My very own witchy werecat."

Charlie's heavy breathing reaches my ears. I hope he can contain himself. An impulsive attack will cost him his life.

"Is that it?" I taunt Satan, hoping my words will distract him from Charlie's imminent break-down. "You're not bringing in the heavy guns?"

Satan raises his eyebrows. "Oh, I'm sure this is heavy enough to defeat you. I sent my heavier guns, so to speak, to Heaven. Which, if I recall correctly," he taps his chin, "should also be under your protection."

As he utters his last word, the black sky turns red.

I flip my Morningstar like a professional knife thrower and conjure a lightning bolt in my other hand. "Let's get this party started then."

Satan simply smiles and beckons us. "Please do."

I grin back. "We're not falling for that. We can reach you all easily from right here."

He laughs out loud. The sound reverberates through my body. "Oh, come on, Dante. I know you're not a coward. Step out of that circle. Spare me the effort of breaking it down."

Instead of answering, I raise my lightning above my head. When I release it, several other things soar through the air. Grease balls form a wall around Satan fast. He's not making much of an effort to break it down. I know he can do so with one flick of his hand, or maybe even without moving, but I'm glad he wants to make a show out of it. While the wall blocks his vision, I pull out the Pearl of Arcadia and whisper the words to activate it: "Chosen ones, unite." Then, I place it in the middle of my palm and let my lightning consume it.

Soon, it turns into a blinding light. It hums and starts to ascent. It turns wildly in the air and colors shoot in every direction.

"What the…?" The grease wall melts into a puddle at Lucifer's feet. He narrows his eyes at the marble, hovering above the edge of the circle. For a moment, astonishment takes over his face. Then, he holds out his arm and balls his fist.

Nothing happens.

"You piece of…" He swallows the rest of his words and tries to regain his calm demeanor.

The angels behind him freeze for a couple of seconds. I'm afraid the monsters will kill them before they have a chance to get to our side, but none of them seem to know what's going on. They're waiting for their master to give them an order. The Devil's stunned moment of silence gives the angels the chance to listen to the message recorded in the pearl. Their faces become lighter, and the darkness slips from their eyes. The hatred in their expressions flows out of them. One by one, they spread their wings and zoom past Lucifer to our side. In their flight, they shed the darkness clinging to their huge wings. Just like in my premonition, they land softly behind us. At once, the air feels cooler, and everything is lighter.

Satan snaps out of his confusion. "You might be able to get the angels back on your side, but it won't be enough." He gestures at the sky impatiently. "Hundreds of my brothers are dying up there as we speak. You really think a few more angels will make a difference, boy?"

Suddenly I'm fed up with all his manipulation and misguided confidence. Sure, he's the Devil, he's strong and scary and everything. But almighty? No way. He's been beaten before. He has been locked under nine layers, nine circles, for centuries. And now that he's managed to break through them, he thinks he can take what he wants with a snap of his finger?

I ball my fists.

"What were you thinking, Dante? That you could stroll into this battle and do what your ancestors never could?"

I envision a bright beam of sunlight cutting through the red sky and hitting him in the face. "Would you finally… shut up!"

It wasn't meant as a cue, but as soon as Lucifer lifts his hand to shield his eyes, the fight flares up again.

The sky lights up with magic. I keep the sunlight aimed at Lucifer. It annoys the hell out of him. He keeps squinting to see something. Charlie is throwing grease at him, trying to stick his arms to his side, while Kessley transforms into a kind of porcupine that can shoot a seemingly endless supply of thorns.

Five of them hit the Devil square in the face, and I look up to check on the Pearl of Arcadia, afraid someone will knock it out of the air. But it moves lazily to all sides, evading everything that tries to hit it with ease.

Something slams into me, and I tumble backward. I scramble to my feet in a hurry. The sunbeam is gone, and Satan's face is inches from mine. "Give up now and I won't torture you for eternity."

I force myself not to move a muscle. He can't hurt me inside the circle. "You can stop talking. You know the answer. I'm not crossing over to your side, and I'm not giving up." With my arms crossed over my chest I raise one eyebrow. If he wants to play mind games, I can play along a little longer. "I understand you're getting nervous. This is the first time you're facing the chosen one. You know I'm strong, but you're not sure what I can do exactly." I give a curt nod to my friends. "Or what they can do." The cockiest smile I can manage lifts my lips. "I made a lot of friends while you were trying to kill the nine souls. And I saved most of those, by the way. That should give you an idea of the outcome of this battle."

The corners of Lucifer's mouth twitch. They move up more with every word I say.

He's actually enjoying this. Does he like these mind games this much, or is he distracting us while he waits for more backup to arrive, just like me?

"Actually, the fact that I'm standing here," he says gesturing at his black leather shoes, "despite not taking all of the souls, gives you the best idea of what's coming." He leans closer and the flames in his eyes flare up. "You see, even if you saved all the souls, I still would've broken through the circles. You know why?" He sticks his finger against my chest and a burning sensation shoots from my heart to my toes and back. I grit my teeth and force myself to stay upright. He can't really hurt me as long as I'm inside the circle.

The pain subsides and Satan throws more bravado at me. "Because I'm always prepared. My backup plans have backup plans. No matter how hard you try, you cannot surprise me."

"Oh yeah?" The humming above my head ceases and the multicolored light changes back into white. My hand opens at my side and the Pearl of Arcadia lands in my palm. "How's this for a surprise?"

With a speed I didn't know I possessed, I bring my hand forward and shove the pearl into his mouth. Then, I punch him in the face with my other hand.

He swallows on instinct, just like I hoped. His eyes bulge, and he starts to cough. Trevor steps forward and puts his hand on his shoulder. "Are you alright, my lord?"

Satan lights up from the inside. His legs twitch. It sounds as if his insides are torn apart.

A frown pulls at my forehead.

It can't be that easy, can it?

"We should take him out now," Vicky whispers.

My hand shoots up. "No, wait."

A lightning ball soars toward the Devil. At the last moment, I send it to the right with a flick of my hand. Satan spreads his arms and closes them with force in front of him. A rush of air hits us, but not nearly strong enough to blow us off our feet.

The Devil coughs up the pearl and it zooms back to my hand when I stretch my arm.

"You didn't fall for that," he says in mock disappointment.

I rub the pearl with my shirt. Bright balls of light approach in the corners of my eyes.

The other angels. The humans given the choice to serve Heaven and humankind after their deaths, called to us by the Pearl of Arcadia to take on their angel forms now and stand with us.

My heart beats faster as I count the times I feel something light touching the ground behind me. One, two, five, twelve, eighteen... they keep coming, and all Satan does is watch. He doesn't seem worried at all.

Does he have backup waiting somewhere, too?

Twenty-two, twenty-five... twenty-seven. More than we expected.

I try not to grin as I put the pearl back in my pocket. With my Morningstar raised I crack my neck. "Well, what are we waiting for? Enough chitchat, right?"

A shadow falls over his face. "You're right. I'm

done playing. It's time for you to get out of that circle. I've got more important things to do than fight you."

I know what's coming next, and so do my friends. We talked about my premonition several times. We all know what to do.

"Get ready," I say. Then I turn around to welcome the angels with a grateful nod.

Some of them, mostly the younger ones, are visibly nervous. I can't blame them. Their world has been turned upside down. They found out magic is real, and there's a Heaven and a Hell, a God and a Devil, and now, no more than a few minutes later, they're in their angel form, facing the darkest evil in the universe.

Nervous or not, they shine like newborns. Their light is even brighter than Quinn's. I'm grateful for it. It makes this whole situation a bit less dark.

Movement close to my feet snaps me out of my thoughts. Just like in my premonition, the outline of the circle vibrates. The man in front of me grows until he looms about six and a half feet above me. There's nothing handsome about him now. Flames burst through his face, melting away the skin and revealing the pointed bones of his sharp jawline. Two large, red horns sprout from his skull. His eyes are now nothing more than holes with fire inside them. Steam rises from his nose.

His chest grows wide, ripping his shirt to shreds. His hands form into sharp claws.

Here we go.

He throws his huge claws forward and the rocks that form the protective circle go up in dust. Flames spread through the ditch, turning the salt inside into liquid. Another push of his arms and it all goes up in smoke. He roars and spits a huge flame in my direction.

Reflexively, I conjure a block of ice and order it to protect my face. It drops down in front of me in the nick of time. The flame slams into it and melts it within a millisecond. I order the water to attack, and that's when all hell breaks loose.

CHAPTER 26

Everyone moves at the same time. As both sides collide, all the shapes seem to melt into one. There's no time to keep track of my friends. Of Vicky. Of Mom. I need to trust in them, and in the fairy godmothers protecting us, to hold out. To handle themselves.

In the middle of the noise and chaos of soaring light, shadows, cries of anger and pain, clanging of metal against metal, and sounds I can't place, Satan rises. He only has eyes for me, and weirdly enough, it doesn't scare me that much. Whether it's because I'm now confident about my powers or because I can feel the light of the angels behind me, I'm not sure. I do know he's eager to end me. And to cause as much pain as possible in the process, no doubt.

The water I send his way rises to his waist and onward, toward his chest. The flames around his bones pull back with a violent hiss and he shakes the water off.

No, stay where you are. Crawl up and into his mouth and nose, I order the water.

It obeys, albeit with difficulty, pissing Satan off along the way.

"You stupid boy," he growls. "Do you really think a bit of water will stop me from squashing you like the annoying bug that you are?"

"Of course not," I reply calmly.

I lean to the left to avoid a vortex before it knocks me down. At the same time, my focus shifts to the sunlight piercing through the red sky above us. A strong beam shoots down, blinding Satan for a second. I don't even need to order the angels to attack. They move with me as if they're a part of me. As if we share one mind.

Keep blinding him, I say to the sunlight. And then, to the water: *Lift me to his face.*

While I bring my Morningstar down between his horns, I envision the bottom of the wave freezing. The cold spreads all around the giant legs.

The spiked ball turns when I jerk it to the right, and bits of bone fly around my ears.

Satan hisses and reaches up to grab me. Three balls of light grab each hand and force it down again.

After tearing my weapon from his skull, I bring it down once more, but he shakes his head. I lose my grip and soar through the air. As fast as I can, I conjure some wind to catch me.

The Devil roars in anger. The flames bursting from inside him grow into an inferno. My balls of light burst into a trillion tiny spots which fizzle and vanish. The ice around his legs melts, and I quickly order the water to keep him in place.

Storming forward, ready for another attempt at restraining him, a sudden feeling of unease hits me. I come to a halt and look around. With a yell of surprise, I duck as a blade scrapes my shoulder.

Gisella.

My eyes narrow when I turn to find a trace of her. She's moving so fast I can only see a flutter in the air.

"Keep her away from me," I tell two angels hurrying to my side. "And watch out, she's strong."

They nod and spread their wings, forming a barrier between the werecat-witch and me.

I turn back to Lucifer, and something hot hits me in the face. The water I conjure washes it away, but some of it has crawled into my nose. It's making its way toward my brain and I shake my head to get rid of it. The pain is excruciating. It's as if my skin is burned away from the inside while hot knives pierce every part of my brain. The pain blocks out every rational thought and stops me from sending any kind of order to my limbs. All I can do is scream and shake my head, my hands pounding aimlessly on my skull.

"Stand still," a tingly voice whispers in my ear.

As soon as I obey the stabbing inside my head turns into a sort of wriggling which makes me shiver. A picture of a thousand worms crawling through my brain hovers in front of my closed eyes. I want to push my hand through my skull and pull them out. To my relief, with each worm that crosses from one side to the other, more heat is flushed away. I can think straight again.

I blink in time to see Satan smirking at me.

"*Mmm*," he says smacking his cracked lips and running his forked, black tongue over them. "Your brain tastes delicious."

"Enjoy it," I say, my voice hoarse from screaming. "Because that's all you'll ever taste of it."

It takes me a millisecond to envision a storm above his head. Hail, rain, wind, thunder, and lightning, the whole shebang. It wraps around his head at my command.

He thrashes to get it away from him, smashing an angel's head in the process by accident.

Keep him busy, I tell the storm. Then I conjure another huge wave to tug at his legs. He sways and another pull takes him down. Just in time, my friends standing behind him dive out of the way—courtesy of the godmothers no doubt. Some of our enemies aren't so lucky. An earth elemental and a banshee get squashed under the giant body.

The wave turns into thick ice and once his feet are stuck, I start to work on his arms. But each time I shift my focus to another part of him, something else melts. Meanwhile, the storm is weakening, and somehow Satan is pushing it away from him. I glance around, trying to see how the others are doing. A skeleton grizzly bear is stomping through the battlefield that was my back garden minutes ago. A flaming zombie deer knocks over the elemental that set it on fire. Jeep must be doing okay.

My eyes search for Vicky. I find her side by side with D'Maeo, who's deflecting all powers aimed at them both, while my girl lifts a minotaur from its feet with her mind. She shakes him wildly in the air before using him as a bowling ball, knocking several demons over.

My instincts tell me to focus on my own adversary. He's managed to get rid of the storm blocking his view. Harmless melted ice splashes around his legs as he rises without using his arms.

I fling my arms forward. "Huge gust of wind!"

To my surprise, the Devil waves his arms to keep his balance.

"Give up, Dante!" he bellows, straightening up and spitting a giant flame at me. "You can never win."

I duck to avoid the flame and roll over when Lucifer reaches for my throat. He grabs my leg and lifts me into the air. I try freezing his claw, but he simply shakes the ice off and brings me closer to his face.

His disgusting tongue slithers over his lips as if it has a mind of its own. "I'm going to enjoy devouring you."

The heat rising from his red skull scorches my skin. Blood drips from his horns. I quickly cover my face and neck with a layer of ice. Heat and fear block my ability to think.

Lucifer lifts me above his head and opens his mouth.

Stay calm. Focus. All I need is a distraction.

Below me, an air elemental, half changed into a tornado, is struggling with Maël's time-bending powers. It's turning at half speed, its face becoming solid every couple of seconds.

Dangling upside down, I focus on it. It *is* made of wind, after all.

Fly up here.

With a shriek, it ascends. Maël lifts her head, sees me, and turns away to focus on another enemy.

Oh, great. Yeah, I've got this. Don't worry. You go help someone else.

The air elemental turns back into full wind mode in an attempt to break free from my power. It doesn't realize this only makes it easier for me to control it. The more wind, the more control.

Satan's open mouth is coming closer at an alarming speed. I need to act fast, but now the stench coming from his throat fogs up my brain. With my powers focused in full on the elemental, there's no ice left to protect my face, which means blisters are starting to appear on my skin.

I push through the pain and envision the tornado slipping into Lucifer's mouth, funnel first.

With a jerk, the air elemental swerves left and drops down between the torn lips of the Devil. There's a scream of fright and pain, followed by a cough and a lot of wheezing. Satan brings his hands instinctively to his throat, dropping me in the process. I tell the water at Lucifer's feet to catch me, and land on my feet.

While Satan bends over, spitting pieces of air elemental, I look around for Taylar. The stone shield covers his face and heart. He's got the ghoul pinned to the ground, and is about to stab it in the heart when a demon knocks him over.

A second later, a cross between a troll and a wolf stomps on it with its giant foot, turning it into instant black smoke.

Taylar turns back to the ghoul, but it's gone.

He searches for something else to attack, and his eyes meet mine. I beckon him with my head, and he appears at my side in a flash. I nod at Satan, still coughing his guts out. "I can't beat him. The best we can do is stall him until we're ready to... you know."

Taylar nods. "Okay, I'll help you. What's the plan?"

He raises his shield at something, and I turn with a lightning bolt in my hand. A demon with a split head and three, uneven legs slides over the grass toward us, it's mouth open and showing its glistening, long teeth. Its humanlike feet are covered in Charlie's grease. I release my lightning at it and Taylar hits it in the ugly head when it tries to dodge my attack. The demon's legs give in, and the young ghost brings his shield down onto the neck, separating the head from it with one, clean slice. It goes up in smoke, and Taylar turns back to me.

I drop my voice to an almost inaudible whisper. "Remember where I went recently? That copy?"

"Yes."

A couple of paces to his left, Gisella somersaults over Dylan's head, her blades ready to cut off his head. I conjure lightning and aim for her fur-covered form. Before I can throw it, Jeep's hat zooms past. Its sharp rim hits the werecat in the leg. She changes her trajectory and lands neatly on her feet. Dylan lashes out and cuts deep into her leg, provoking a hiss from her.

"Can you take us there, but make sure he doesn't notice?" I continue, "And once we're there, get us some backup from another world?"

I lift my Morningstar and he ducks. I release it over his head, and it cuts the legs out from under a demon that leaps at Mom.

Taylar gives me a blank stare through the black smoke it turns into. "Other worlds?"

"Like the one with the beetle-bees, can you get them to help us?" Another idea hits me. "And the mist from the Underworld. It can help us here."

He clenches his jaw. "I'll do my best." His eyes grow wide as Satan moves behind me. "You distract him, and I'll open a portal. Make sure he follows you through it."

That shouldn't be a problem. He's so eager to kill me, I doubt he's paying much attention to his surroundings.

While the flames around his red bones flare up

again and he pounds his chest to get rid of the last bit of air elemental stuck in his lungs, I whisper to my fairy godmothers, "Tell Mom to create the illusion of everyone leaving through a portal, once Satan and I are in the copy world. Leave me and the backup armies in there. Come get us when Vicky is ready."

A soft whoosh is their answer and I turn my attention to the monster before me.

Satan wipes his nose and grunts. "That was a nice move. But, it's not enough. You can't kill me, boy. Nobody can."

"Maybe you're right," I answer with a shrug. "But I'm going to try anyway."

"I admire your guts," he growls. "I'll enjoy the taste of that when I devour you."

I smirk at him. "No, you won't. The only thing you'll taste is the sour flavor of defeat."

He shakes with laughter and the ground trembles with him. "You're the funniest adversary I've ever had. You're inches from death, and you still think you can win."

Lightning comes to life in my hands and I hold it up. "It's not what I think that matters, it's what I know."

For a second, confusion flickers in his eyes. I guess he's not immune to prophecies after all. Or to a bit of manipulation.

Behind Lucifer a portal appears. I blink and it's gone again, but I know it's Mom shielding it with an illusion. I remember its location. All I need to do is lure the Devil through it, and the world is safe. For a while, at least. Long enough for us to defeat all of Lucifer's helpers and for Vicky to get ready.

Something big storms straight at me in the corner of my peripheral vision and I swerve left to avoid it. A stone hand hits my shoulder. I recognize Trevor. Dylan is right behind him, a rock in each hand and murder on his face.

Before I can decide whether to help him or not, a shadow falls over me. Without looking up, I drop down on one knee and roll over. Fog rises around me and Satan, a perfect copy of the image in my head. His claw reaches for me, missing me by a hair.

Reach up and distract him.

While the fog obeys, I scramble back to my feet and move behind Satan. That's when I realize I have no idea where the portal is anymore. Moving around made me lose my focal point. With my arm out behind me, I search for a shift in the air. My eyes never leave the monster in front of me. He's getting angrier by the minute and I'm afraid of what he'll do once he's tired of playing. He might be able to scorch us all with a single flame if he gets desperate enough.

With a new wave, I grab his right ankle and pull, but not hard enough to make him fall over. I just need to get his attention, so I can dive through the portal and make him follow me.

If I can find the portal.

Lightning sparkles in my right hand while my left is still probing the air.

Then, I feel it. A slight drop in temperature, a change in the air current. In a flash, I pull back my arm and take a step left before hitting Satan in the back with lightning. It covers him head to toe, and sends as much electricity through him as possible.

The Devil growls in pain and whirls around.

"Coward!" he thunders. He bends over and his foul breath hits my face, sending me back in an involuntary stumble. "You dare to strike me from behind?"

His voice is so loud my ears ring. I've really pissed him off now. Of course, this makes it much easier to pretend I'm scared shitless. With my heart pounding deafeningly in my ears, I scramble back on hands and feet. My surroundings change, and yet, they don't. I'm still in my back garden, but this lawn is empty. Still, it's as scorched as the one I've just pushed off from. It looks like this second Earth copies all the changes, too. Everything is the same, except for the people in it.

"Are you finally ready to surrender?" Satan bellows through the opening he can't see.

I need to get him through the portal fast, or he'll notice something is off.

Mom, please remember to put a copy of the battle in here, or he'll never fall for it, I beg her in my head.

A loud clicking rises from the grass to my left. I look down and find myself staring into another portal. A horde of beetle-bees shoots up into the garden. The bright red lights on their bellies pulse and they slam their fangs together violently.

Great job, Taylar!

Shooting a wink at the bee leader hovering in front of me in the middle of the army, I start to push myself back, a panicked expression plastered on my face.

Satan's laughter shakes the ground in both worlds.

Ignoring him, I get up, nearly tripping over my own feet in the process, and start to make my way to the forest straight ahead. Without hesitation, the beetle-bees give chase. Inside, I'm cheering. The leader understood my plan.

And sure enough, it works. A growl turns the air around me hot and the ground moves once again. This time because Satan is coming after us.

"He's mine!" he bellows.

The beetle-bees don't miss a beat. Their clicking noise only seems to become louder, as does the flapping of their transparent wings.

I come to a halt at the line of trees and glance over my shoulder. At first, I'm confused.

Did I run out of the portal and back into our world?

Everywhere I look, angels and ghosts are fighting monsters of all kinds. Vicky has joined Dylan and Jeep in their battle against Gisella. Maël uses her staff to bash in the head of a banshee. The dragon boy spits fire at Charlie, and D'Maeo blocks it with his power of deflection. A second later, the dragon's face is covered in grease. He yells and claws at the gel melting into his eyes. D'Maeo grabs his sword and stabs, but the boy spreads his wings and takes off.

Six Kessleys have surrounded a water elemental. Angels and demons clash.

It dawns on me what has happened. Mom copied everyone inside her illusion.

She did it!

Now, it's up to me to make the next part convincing.

I look up at the beetle-bees hovering above my head and say loud enough for Satan to hear, "Keep him busy, so I can get my friends out of here."

The leader lets out a confident sounding wail, followed by a loud buzz. As one, the whole horde turns back. Without any fear, they attack Lucifer's face.

He swats at them and flings a couple of them into the trees. Several others cling to his claws and push his arms down with the forceful flapping of their crow-sized wings.

I swerve around them and search for Taylar. The real or the fake one, I don't care. I'm sure he can hear me even if I speak to the wrong one. A demon's claw misses my face by an inch when I duck and come to a grinding halt next to the young white-haired ghost. "We need to get everyone out of here, everyone on earth. Can you open a portal and suck everyone but me and Satan in?"

Taylar nods. "I think so."

"Good. Do it now."

He salutes me, slams a demon in the face, and

storms off.

I make my way back to where the beetle-bees are fighting Lucifer. Several squashed and burnt ones are lying in the grass, their bellies no longer lit. My heart aches for them.

A handful of wind wraps around the Devil's head and I pull.

With one arm still held to his side by the bees, Satan struggles to get the wind off. He roars and grows several inches. Most of the bees lose their grip.

Rain, I need rain.

It appears and I let it fuse with the wind. An image of a water tornado wrapping around the Devil pops into my head, and it instantly becomes reality.

"Get everyone out, Taylar, now," I call out.

Illusions run past me with fake evil creatures on their heels. They vanish through the portal, which closes behind them.

Lucifer opens his arms and the waterspout grows wider. When his arms are stretched, he slams them back together. The twister is catapulted forward. It hits me like a ten-tonner. Water flows into my mouth and nose. The wind knocks me over.

Help me up, I order it, coughing and spluttering.

Satan is rubbing his hands, ready for another round.

I try not to panic, but it's hard when you're out of ways to surprise your opponent. Especially if that opponent is the darkest and strongest creature in the universe. My heart goes into overdrive, while the last part of my brain freezes. I have no idea what to do now.

CHAPTER 27

"Don't worry. We're still here."

A disembodied voice whispers in my ear and calms my heartbeat in an instant.

My fairy godmothers. They stayed with me.

"Of course we did, but you've got this. There's more to you than your meteokinetic powers. You're one of the strongest mages alive, Dante. Have faith in yourself."

More to me than my meteokinetic powers? Like what?

"Like spellcasting," she answers.

I back up when Lucifer takes a step toward me.

Casting a spell will take way too long. Besides, I don't have any ingredients here.

"You still think you need all that?"

Lucifer shrinks back into his human form and tilts his head. "What? No more fighting? You think you can kill me now that you've transported every human on earth to another realm? Which I don't think you did. You only made sure your friends are safe. And even that went wrong." He snorts and steam rises from his nostrils. "You do know…?"

I block out his voice. Words shoot through my mind like fireflies. It takes mere seconds to grab the right ones and put them in a logical order:

"Voice of Satan, you are weak.
Now, you can no longer speak."

The words are muffled. It's more of a test for me than a real attack since this will fuel his anger if it works. I can always come up with better ones.

I shake my head as if to get rid of something inside. "Sorry, what was that? I missed some of your rambling there, I'm afraid."

He opens his mouth to answer. No sound comes out and his face contorts into a mixture of astonishment and frustration. His hands go to his throat before he sends me a burning look. His lips move, and I can make out something like, *"You did this."*

My shoulders move up in a casual shrug. "It's much better this way. You shouldn't talk so much."

The fire in his eyes burns so high it touches his forehead. The red of his bones shines through his face as his mouth twists to produce an angry growl. He holds out his arms and pushes flames out from under his skin.

With some conjured ice I block a huge flame.

Water drips down my arms. I'm preparing to fling the ice at him, when something grabs me from behind and pulls me back. In a flash the edges of a portal pass me, and then I'm back in Darkwood Manor's back garden. The real one, I presume. The arms let go of me, and I scramble upright. One look around tells me Vicky is far from ready to create the circles of Hell.

Taylar is standing behind me, ready to close the portal.

"What are you doing?" I dive toward the gate but he shuts it with a fast hand gesture, leaving me staring at him in shock. "Why did you do that? I was keeping him occupied until it's time to…" The rest of the sentence is left hanging since our plan needs to remain a secret. "You know."

A banshee drops down on top of us shrieking so loud I have to cover my ears. Taylar pushes me out of the way just in time to avoid her sharp claws. Charlie zooms by and shoots grease balls which cover her mouth. Then, they explode, and her head is blown off. I'm not sure who did that, but I'm fine with it. One less enemy to worry about.

Charlie walks through the black smoke that remains of the banshee, comes to a halt next to me, and points up at the sky. "Heaven needs our help, now. We can't wait any longer."

My eyes follow his pointing finger, and my breath gets caught in my throat. The sky is still red. It seems a bit lighter now than before, more bloodlike. Right above us, there's a giant rip in the air. Bodies fall from it. An explosion lights up the sky and sparks set the tilted trees in the distance on fire. If I block out the noise of the battle, I can hear screams, sirens, the shrieking of panicked animals, and the crackling of fire. The air-raid alarm has changed into a sad, broken whine.

A yell pulls me back to the fight. "Dante? We could use a little help here."

I turn toward Vicky's voice. She and the rest of my Shield are fighting the last of the elementals while the angels are busy taking out the demons.

The sky rips even further and debris tumbles out, creating two camps again. What our enemies don't know, is that we've still got the surprise of a living house waiting for this exact moment. As the line of monsters moves back a little to avoid the bits of Heaven crashing down on them, I see three familiar faces from the corner of my eye. They step out of the kitchen, determined expressions on their faces and weapons in their hands. Kasinda, Chloe, and Ginda.

I can see Kasinda's gaze moving over all of us, then checking out our enemies. She stiffens for a second when she spots her niece on the wrong side. She pulls another weapon from her belt and nods at the two witches next to her. Chloe, the Mahaha we saved recently, seems to turn a shade bluer. She stretches out her arms, and her fingers and nails grow. Ginda, Chloe's friend and a chlorokinetic witch also known as a plant manipulator, holds a spiked flower in each hand.

As one, they leap at the demons at the back of the group. Without hesitation, the rest of us attack from the other side.

Hearing a *whoosh* above my head, I duck. Just in time. The house has stood up, and its arm made of the upstairs annex slams into five demons at once. They are catapulted backward. As I dive forward to take them out completely, a foul-smelling creature knocks me over. My feet push it away mid-roll and stand up in one movement. My right hand scrambles for my athame and I hold it out toward the ghoul. It hisses at me, and the stench gets worse. Saliva drips from the many sharp teeth sticking out of its wide mouth like toothpicks. Vapor rises from the hole under its gleaming white eyes.

I lash out and scratch the top of the elongated bald head. Long nails dig into my shoulder, making me yell. My athame slips from my fingers and the ghoul is on top of me in a flash. It shivers with delight and leans forward to place both claws next to my head. The nostrils around the gap which serves as a nose flare as it breathes in my scent.

Two beams of sunlight stream down on its right arm. It pulls away, and I roll out from under it and push it over. Now on top, I place one hand on each side of its head and send lightning through it. Its whole body convulses. Its teeth fall out and electricity shoots over the exposed bones in its arms. It splutters and twitches. As soon as I release it, the body goes up in smoke.

Without warning, Trevor lands on me. His stone body pushes the air from my lungs. I try to hit him with something, but he pushes my arms down and leans over, bringing his face close to mine. "What did you do with Lucifer?"

I force a grin onto my face and wait for him to give me some room to breathe, so I can answer. "I killed him."

Trevor shakes his head. "No, you didn't. We would've known." He tilts his head. "You locked him up somewhere, didn't you? Thought you could keep him there until… what?"

My eyes unintentionally flit toward Vicky, who slices off a demon's legs and jumps on top of it to finish it off.

Trevor follows my gaze. "I see, your plan is to have Vicky create nine new circles of Hell." He throws his head back and laughs hard. "I'm guessing you don't know she must awaken the powers she needs for that. Which isn't easy. But it doesn't matter, because she'll never create those circles." He lets out a dark chuckle. "Oh, how disappointed you will be when Vicky chooses our side, just like Gisella did. And like your mother will."

His words fuel my anger which I use to kick him away from me. He's on his feet swifter than I anticipated, but so am I. Expecting him to try and knock me over, I brace myself.

He doesn't charge, though. Instead, he turns and

makes his way through the battlefield. With one well-aimed blow, he smashes in the head of a skeleton boar. Several steps farther he pushes an angel out of the way, saving the life of one of his elemental brothers. Then, he walks past two Kessleys and a banshee rolling over each other in the grass. He ducks to avoid a splash of angel blood that Taylar aimed at a demon. He searches for something in the air and, once he finds it, takes a step forward, glances over his shoulder to meet my eyes, then salutes. A moment later, he vanishes.

I curse under my breath. He must have stepped through a portal. He left the battle to search for Satan, and I let him get away.

"Dante?" Kasinda comes to a halt next to me, panting hard. "What's wrong?"

"Nothing. We need to hurry. Heaven needs our help." I look at the weapons in her hands. One is a spear and the other a sort of rope. Both are drenched in blood and some sort of goo I don't want to identify. "Thanks for joining us."

"Just because I don't have any magical powers anymore doesn't mean I'm helpless. Of course I came." She jots her spear sideways into a small tornado, which turns back into a human woman. With the press of a button on the heft, the air elemental explodes into a trillion pieces.

I cover my head as they rain down on me. "Nice toy you've got there," I say. Then, I wink and dive back into the battle.

Our enemies are falling quickly now that they're outnumbered and missing two of their strongest fighters. The house has taken out a lot of them, too, and it's still swallowing demons two at a time. Taylar has opened a portal to the Underworld, letting the mist seep through and cling to anyone who feels fear. Soon, three of the remaining five elementals are on the ground, wriggling and screaming as the mist starts to bite into their flesh. Two of them turn into water, and one into fire, but the mist has a strong grip on them. It feeds on them and pulls their remains back to the Underworld.

Taylar closes the portal and moves to Dylan's side in front of the mansion, which is searching for more "food." Maël has frozen the dragon boy in time and one of the angels drops a light into his mouth, which consumes him within seconds.

Mom is facing the last minotaur by herself. I want to run over to help her, but a demon blocks my way. It has a broad body and a head just as wide. The scales on its shoulders and legs glint in the red light from above. The rest of it is covered in ice and it spits drops of cold water in my direction.

An ice demon from the ninth circle of Hell.

I remember what the drops can do. They paralyze and sting the skin, making one scream in pain.

But not this time.

As I envision sunlight streaming down on the demon, it squeals and moves aside. Under my order, the beam follows the demon and heats up. The ice starts to melt. I turn up the temperature, and water gusts down its body like sweat. It tries to shoot icicles at me, but there's no ice left inside it. As a last resort, it throws itself at me.

While it soars through the air, I summon some wind and order it to catch the demon and twist as fast as it can.

Water sprays in all directions. The demon shrieks and flounders, then it's ripped into a thousand droplets of water by the mini tornado I've created.

It doesn't die, though. I'm trying to come up with a way to kill it when a large blob of grease lands on it. The pieces are pulled apart and then, without warning, they blow up. I duck and cover my head, but nothing lands on me. I look up to find only smoke.

Charlie jogs up to me and holds up his hand. We exchange a high five.

Only now do I understand he was the one who blew up the banshee. "That's your new power? You can blow up your grease? That's awesome, man."

His grin stretches from ear to ear. "I know."

Seeing him makes me wonder what happened to Gisella. I haven't seen her since I came back from the copy of Earth. My chest tightens at the possibility that someone killed her. Underneath all the evil that consumed her, she's still our friend.

But first, I need to make sure Mom's okay.

A bit disoriented from the fight with the demon, I turn until I find her again. She's standing perfectly still. A sword is in her hand, raised to eye level. A minotaur approaches. It doesn't seem to notice her. It keeps turning in every direction, grunting in frustration, and moving its arms in front of it, as if it can't see.

Mom must have created an illusion around the creature, and she's luring it toward her. Once it reaches her, she brings her sword down between the two horns. Its legs give out under it and it slumps to the ground. She pulls her sword free and slides it into the minotaur's right eye. It goes up in smoke while pride runs through my veins. The mansion lets out a disappointed grunt watching its last bite get carried away by the wind.

Having checked everyone else around us, the question I have to ask Charlie is forced through my lips. "What happened to Gisella?"

Charlie's eyes sweep the garden. Our friends are all still standing, albeit with scratches, cuts, and bruises, and covered in sweat, blood, and dirt. Most of them circle one of our enemies. It's only when we step closer to them, that I see they've captured Gisella.

As soon as I recognize the contorted, almost black face with the livid expression, I hold out my arm to stop Charlie. "You stay here."

"What? No way, I can keep going."

To our left, the mansion groans. Giving it a brief glance, I turn my head to my best friend. "Can you please go check if Darkwood Manor needs help?"

With a frown and a huffed protest, he takes off. A relieved sigh escapes me before I carefully approach the circle with Gisella at the center.

The werecat-witch is hunched over on the grass. Shadows whirl around her in slow motion. Dylan and Taylar have their sword tips aimed at her but seem to lack the courage to get closer. Maël's lips are moving fast, and the tip of her staff is glowing. D'Maeo has positioned himself half in front of her with his arms outstretched to block any sudden attack. Jeep is moving his hands, forcing half-collapsed skeleton animals onto their feet. Two Mahahas are standing side by side, their faces a deep blue and their claws ready to rip out Gisella's throat if she moves. One of them must be Kessley. I can't tell which one. Ginda urges beanstalks to rise from the ground and hover over Gisella threateningly. Vicky is standing rigid beside her, her hands balled by her sides and her gaze locked onto the werecat-witch.

Kasinda is the only one not ready to strike. Her hands are clasped over her face as tears stream through her fingers.

Frowning, I watch them all for a moment, wondering why no one is attempting to take Gisella out. Are they clinging to some far-fetched hope of getting our friend back?

When nobody moves, I conjure a lightning ball and step forward, ready to push past the Mahahas. "I'll do it."

"No, wait!"

The panic in Taylar's voice makes me freeze.

Gisella grunts and he aims his sword at her again.

"Keep her there." His words are probably meant for Maël, whose lips seem to move even faster.

"What are you waiting for?" I whisper to the young ghost.

"Two angels tried to kill her already. They died horrible deaths."

Searching the ground ends with no trace of them. Maybe it's for the better.

"What did she do to them?"

Taylar's eyes go dark. "The decay. Her touch poisoned them. Evil crawled into them and ate them from the inside."

I swallow the nausea in my throat and blink several times to lose this image.

The grass around her comes into focus. It's turned brown. Dozens of insects lie belly-up between the dry hay. "So, what's the plan? Capture her?"

D'Maeo, Taylar, Vicky, and Jeep shake their heads at the same time.

"That's too dangerous," D'Maeo says.

So Maël is keeping the werecat-witch trapped in time, while the others are trying to think of a way to kill her.

The first thing that comes to my mind is to burn her. A better way would be to tear her apart, like I did to the demon. But underneath all that evil, Gisella is still our friend, and I wouldn't want to do that to her. Or to Charlie.

I guess the others are struggling with the same problem, or they would've killed her already. Together, they should be strong enough to take her on.

I clear my throat. "Guys. Heaven needs our help, *now*. We can't afford to wait any longer."

A loud high-pitched whine echoes through the forest. It is answered by the same cry from all sides. The sound makes my skin crawl. "What was that?"

Vicky clenches her jaw. "Cats. She's summoning them for help."

One of the Mahahas looks over her shoulder with a panicked expression. "What? I'm not killing any cats!"

"I have a feeling we'll have no choice, Kess," Taylar says without taking his eyes off Gisella.

"Sure we do," Vicky says darkly. She turns to the left and her gaze locks onto the tree line. "Step aside."

Jeep, Ginda, Chloe, Kessley, and Kasinda move away from her, creating a large gap in the circle.

A tall pine tree starts to tremble. The earth at the base of it moves. Roots rip through the surface and the whole tree rises into the air.

I hurry out of the way as it soars toward me.

Just in time. The tree slams into Gisella, hard. Turning my head the other way, my eyes squeeze shut. Silence descends on us. Even the mansion stops squeaking and grunting.

When I find the courage to turn back, the tree is lifted again, slowly this time. Maël resumes her mumbling. We're all on high alert. The cats' yowls change into woeful meows.

Kessley tilts her head. "I think they're retreating."

"She's still moving," Jeep remarks.

I want to argue. There's no way the unrecognizable flattened form is still alive. But then the arms twitch and she raises her half-squashed head. The circle of decay around her widens.

With a roar, Vicky sends the tree back down. It slams onto Gisella, two, three, four times, each pound harder than before. Blood and black drops drench all of us and we shield our faces. The shadows shoot out of her body and flee back to where they belong. The tree is lifted again. Bile rises to my mouth at the sight of the strips of flesh stuck to the bottom of the trunk. Blood drips from the roots.

I retch and avert my eyes. What I see now isn't much better, though. Vicky's face is a mask of fury and loathing. She clenches her jaw so hard I can hear it squeak in protest in the sudden silence. The tree seems to tremble with anger as much as Vicky herself.

"Enough!" D'Maeo's shout catches me by surprise and I sway on my feet.

A shudder goes through Vicky and she shakes her head as if to get rid of something. Her gaze falls upon the remnants of her rage and her hand flies to her mouth. The tree drops from the sky like an invisible string is cut.

"Oh, my god," Vicky pants. I hurry over to her and she closes her eyes and buries her face in my chest. "What have I done?"

I stroke her hair and kiss the top of her head. "You did what you had to do."

"And so much more," Jeep states dryly.

Kasinda steps out from behind him and walks over to her niece. She kneels at Gisella's side, brings her hand to her heart, and then to Gisella's. "Rest in peace," she whispers. Her lips tremble, but she bites back her tears, stands up, and turns away from the broken body.

Vicky is crying in my arms. I try to comfort her, but I'm not sure what more to say.

Suddenly, she lifts her head and stiffens in my arms. "Oh, no. Charlie." She breaks free from my grip and strolls past me. "Don't!" she calls out to him. "Don't look."

But Charlie keeps walking toward us.

Vicky grabs his shoulder and tries to push him back. It's no use.

"I need to see her, Vicky."

"No, you don't." Her voice rises in desperation.

Mom comes over, too, and I cross the distance between us in a millisecond. "Can you create an illusion to soften the blow for him? Make her look a bit more like herself?"

"Sure." She turns toward the hole with the bloody mess in it.

It changes before my eyes. Gisella's body seems to inflate. She's still covered in blood and black drops, but she looks kind of peaceful now. Her face is no longer torn and distorted with anger or covered in dark lines. Some of her natural, bright red hair shines through the dark strings. The tufts of cat fur look soft.

"Let him go, babe," I tell Vicky. "Give him a chance to say farewell."

Charlie pushes past her. The closer he gets, the bigger his steps become. He stumbles into the hole the tree created and drops to his knees. His hands wrap around hers and he lowers his head. A river of tears falls onto her face.

"I'm so sorry I couldn't save you." His voice is no more than a hoarse whisper, but it rips my heart out nonetheless. I've never seen or heard my best friend like this. He's been sad before, but this is so much more. He's broken. Even if his voice hadn't shown this, his body would have. It's trembling with grief and misery. His back is bent forward so far, it's almost as if it's literally broken.

"You're the best thing that ever happened to me. I will miss every second not spent with you." Charlie presses her hand against his closed eyes, pushes himself up onto unsteady feet, and staggers back onto the lawn. He stands there frozen, not seeing us or anything else. Then, he throws his head back and lets out a howl which shatters what's left of my heart.

I rush over to him and put my arm around him. When I try to pull him close, he pushes me away and wipes his cheeks vigorously. "No, I'm done crying. I want to kill the bastards who made this happen."

I slap him on the back. "I'm with you, mate."

Taylar's arms fly around in rapid movements. "I'll open a portal to Heaven."

Surprised at how easy magic has become for him, I

nod. After decades without it, he has adapted to his new powers so fast they now come natural to him. The same way Mom has taken to her abilities, despite being a non-magical. One would think I'd be able to control my powers a lot faster than them since I'm the chosen one, but no.

The appearance of a portal cuts of my moment of self-pity. At least it distracted me from Charlie's grief, and my own, long enough to pull myself together. What I see on the other side doesn't do my heart any good, though. While we jump through one by one, I tell myself it's probably not as bad as it looks.

It's no use. One glance around is enough. There's no denying it—Heaven is on the verge of destruction.

CHAPTER 28

My friends have fallen silent and I can't blame them. There are no words for this.

I still see my version of Heaven, with the clouds and the blue sky, but it's all... wrong. The sky is as red and broken as the one we saw on Earth. The sun has dropped. Half of it is hanging sideways about an inch from the ground, a lava-like stream gushing from it. Fragments of scorching hot light are scattered everywhere, burning holes into the clouds making up the ground. The clouds untouched by the heat are no longer soft and white. They are torn in half, have sharp, smoking edges, and the whiteness is tainted with a dark red.

Blood.

But this is not the worst of it all.

I swallow, wishing I could block out what I'm seeing. If only I could turn back, walk into Darkwood

Manor, and never come out again. This is worse than what the spells from the Book of a Thousand Deaths caused.

Bodies of angels lie everywhere. Most of them aren't in one piece anymore. Their wings are snapped or torn off, faces have been burnt away, robes shredded by claws. Limbs have been tossed aside. Some of the heads are turned in the wrong direction. Empty eye sockets stare back at me, and there are dark holes in almost every chest. A river of red makes its way through the gruesome scene.

It's a massacre.

The gates—strong, high, and impressive in my memory—have been taken down. Their iron is bent in several places and half of a fallen gate disappears into the torn ground.

Kessley shivers. "I thought angels only left a sort of shadow when they died? Like the one we found in Shelton Banks' basement."

D'Maeo kneels next to one of the bodies. "These died not long ago. They will most likely vanish after several minutes."

"Does that mean the killers are close?" Chloe sounds as scared as I am.

On instinct, everyone reaches for their weapons.

Two figures emerge from a cluster of clouds, and I grip my athame tighter and conjure a lightning bolt. "Very close."

The sight of Trevor a few seconds later makes me groan.

How did he get here so fast? And why isn't he out looking for Lucifer?

A restless feeling settles in the pit of my stomach.

Taylar stiffens beside me.

"It's Shelton Banks."

Only now does my gaze move to the second figure. It is indeed the mage who ordered the pixie to kill Taylar and his brother. The man who killed me by shoving my astral form with his mind.

I try not to shiver and remind myself, *I'm not alone this time.*

Before I can even finish the thought, Shelton moves his hands the same way Taylar does when he opens a portal. Sure enough, a light appears at his side.

"Come fight for me," he barks and about a dozen pixies fly through the portal, followed by a small army of trolls.

"Where the heck did he find so many new ones to work for him?" Jeep whispers.

The pixies and trolls form two rows, above each other, then approach us with a calm disposition. They look beaten up and tired. Half of the pixies have trouble staying in the air and some of the trolls are limping. They're all covered in scratches, dirt, and blood.

"Go on!" Shelton shouts. "What's taking so long? Attack them!"

The creatures look sad and not in the least bit eager to fight us. It makes me feel sorry for them, and it crosses my mind they might not be so evil by nature after all. They're following orders, and against their will, by the looks of it.

Guilt burns in my stomach at the thought of the massacre we caused in Shelton Banks' manor. It wasn't so different from what we're seeing here.

My hand closes around the lightning in my palm. Involuntary words tumble from my mouth. "I'm sorry we killed your sisters." The trolls grunt impatiently. "And your brothers. We should've given them a chance to surrender, or at least given them a choice to join our side."

The pixies' small faces turn from tired to angry. Their wings flutter faster, and they show their tiny teeth.

In the middle, a pixie raises her hand. "Wait." She flutters closer to me. I stand perfectly still while her eyes bore into mine. A tiny frown appears in her small forehead. "He is sincere." She returns to the line of waiting pixies, who relax a little. "It is not our choice to be part of this battle. We do not belong on any side. We do not want all evil vanquished, nor do we side with Lucifer. We are impartial."

Moving my athame to my left hand, I rest my right hand on my heart. "You have a choice, you all do. If you do not fight us, we will leave you alone. We have no intention of wiping out all evil. All we want is to prevent Lucifer from ruling over Earth and Heaven."

The flying creature bows. "Then, we will retreat."

"You most certainly will not!" Banks bellows. "I

told you to attack."

As one, the pixies and trolls turn to face him.

Fear flickers across his face.

"We will no longer be your slaves," the pixie tells him.

Trevor changes into his full earth elemental form. "Do as he says," he snaps. "We need you in this fight. Dante and his friends will kill us all if we don't kill them first."

Half his words get lost in the noise of the charging creatures. Shelton is overrun and, for a moment, I think they must have torn him apart. Except, he's a powerful mage. Killing him isn't so easy. Trolls and pixies are tossed aside, and Shelton is pulled to his feet by an invisible string. He opens his arms, mumbles something, and the trolls all fall flat on their faces. With a screech, the scattered pixies dive down again. Trevor snatches a couple of them out of the air and squeezes them to a pulp.

"That's our cue," I say, releasing a lightning bolt which hits the side of Trevor's face, making him miss the next pixies he wants to grab.

Charlie has already crossed half the distance between us and Shelton. Several grease balls hit the mage in the face and explode. Banks lets out a pained cry and topples backward. He's covered in trolls and pixies again before he even hits the ground.

The rest of us follow Charlie, while Mom, Maël, and Ginda stay behind to control the fight from a distance. Kessley changes into a bigger version of the trolls and slams into Trevor. Chloe jumps on top of him and breathes in his face. As ice covers the creature, Kessley opens her huge mouth to bite his head off. At the last second, he rolls aside, sending the Mahaha flying. He grabs the Kessley troll by the throat and squeezes. I'm about to envision wind to pull his legs out from under him when Taylar comes rushing by. The stone shield Trevor unintentionally gave him covers his face. He headbutts the elemental, and Kessley lands on the clouds back in her human form. The expression of surprise on Trevor's face is priceless.

Deciding the three of them should be able to handle Trevor, I join the fight against Shelton. I'm glad to see Ginda's flowers and beanstalks sprouting from the clouds around Shelton. Several crushed pixies and trolls with empty eyes are on the ground next to him. His head turns in every direction, but he doesn't appear to see much.

Did Charlie blind him? His face doesn't look burnt.

As if on cue, Charlie throws more grease at him. The blobs hit his face and blow up. He's like a human torch. My friend jumps him and several trolls and pixies follow.

I want to join in, like Dylan and Vicky, but without warning the fire from his head expands. Flames scorch my hands and neck, sending me back in a stagger.

D'Maeo removes his tailored jacket and covers a pixie with it, smothering the fire that's about to consume her. Then, he holds out his hands to block Shelton's power. The fire dies.

Shelton's face becomes visible again, still unburnt.

He can withstand fire? How is that possible? He's not a fire elemental.

Then, I see it, tracing the outline of his cheeks and hands. A slight tremor in the air, and the casual flicker of blue light.

"He created a shield around himself."

D'Maeo's face scrunches up as he tries to hold back Shelton's powers. "Break it with a spell, we'll distract him."

I take a couple of steps back and my place is taken by more trolls and pixies. Dylan and Kasinda move in a careful circle around the mage, thrusting their swords forward every few seconds. Vicky tips Shelton off balance with her mind, and Jeep aims his hat at the mage's throat. It hits its target flawlessly, but the sharp rim bounces off without causing harm. Kasinda picks it up and flings it back at Jeep.

Meanwhile, words are tumbling through my mind again. There's not much time to think of a spell, so I call out the first thing that sounds logical:

"Powers of All, hear me pray.
Take our enemy's protection away."

The blue layer peels away from the mage like a second skin. It bursts into a thousand tiny lights and rains down on him.

Banks screams and his hands fly up to his eyes. At first, I think something hit him in the face, but nothing even got close. He rubs his eyes, blinks several times, and turns his head in all directions. His gaze doesn't lock onto anything. It's like he's gone blind.

A grin spreads with my understanding.

Mom.

I turn to give her a thumbs up, and she grins back.

Shelton waves his arms and flames shoot up from the clouds. Some of the pixies' wings catch fire and they tumble to the ground.

He prepares for another attack, but now everyone dives at him at the same time. They stab, punch, kick, and bite. I join them and fill the gashes my friends make with lightning. Shelton's body crackles and convulses. Still, his lips are moving, casting spells to paralyze my friends. They fall sideways like puppets without strings. Until a black chrysanthemum sprouts in his mouth. He tries to spit it out, but the petals lodge themselves into his cheeks. He turns his head wildly, struggling to breathe. I reach Charlie and pull him up. The others are stabbing at the mage's body again. Blood flows out of him from all sides.

Trolls and pixies crawl onto him, driving my friends away. The flower turns into dust as Shelton moves his fingers. He opens his mouth to cast a spell but, this time, his former slaves are faster. One of the trolls shoves a fist inside while a small army holds down his arms and crushes his fingers. The sound of breaking bones makes me flinch. Shelton roars with pain and anger. He manages to shake his attackers from his right arm and brings his hand up to use his powers. Kasinda, Dylan, and Charlie jump onto the arm at the same time. The trolls hurry back to help. Vicky steps up to his head and stares at him hard. I'm not sure what she's doing to his emotions, but his eyes grow wide, and he starts to thrash. When I get closer with my athame raised, in case she needs help, bubbles appear under his forehead.

She's using more than just her empath powers.

It looks as if his brain is boiling. The skin rips with a nauseating sound and his brain explodes, splattering pink mush over everyone who's nearby.

With a mutual shriek of joy, the former slaves fling themselves onto him. My friends let go of his arm and back up. The sound of teeth ripping through Shelton's flesh is even worse than that of breaking bones.

I turn away from the feast, wipe the gory gunk from my shirt, and spit some of it on the ground. "Yuck."

With a simple shake, Vicky turns back into her beautiful, unscarred, clean self. "Sorry about that. I had to make sure he wasn't getting up again."

Charlie chuckles. "Well, you succeeded."

A scream from behind spins me around. Taylar, Kessley, and Chloe have forced Trevor to the ground. Eager to get farther away from the sound of gnawing, I hurry over to them.

Trevor is about to bring his leg up to kick Taylar in the crutch. Before I can stop him, his leg is forced down by something invisible.

I don't pause to wonder who it is. Words leave my mouth before I even realize they were in my head:

"It's time for Trevor to say farewell.
Take him now and lock him in Hell."

The clouds under him come apart and he drops with a frightened shriek. Taylar, Kessley, and Chloe hover safely above the gap until the clouds return to form the broken path.

Taylar and Kessley hug, and I hold out my hand to help Chloe up. "Nice job."

She shoots me a shy smile. "You, too."

"You need to hurry," Quinn's voice says in my head. "Trevor and Shelton were put there to slow you down. The others are heading toward God's tower. We need you to stop them, before it's too late."

"They're going after God himself?" I say out loud, shock drowning out the relief I felt at the sound of my friend's voice. I'm afraid to ask who "the others" are.

Quinn reads my mind and answers the question. "Prepare yourself. You will need to face the Four Horsemen and Beelzebub. And, eventually, the Devil himself."

"Did he escape the copy world?"

"Yes, Trevor found him and brought him here."

A curse slips out, and the others gather around me. Only now do I notice that all the bodies around us are gone. Dead angels have left large shadows everywhere, wings spread wide as if they want to touch each other. A heavy sigh pushes away the tightness in my chest.

Without sugarcoating, I give my friends the bad news about what's coming next. Their expressions change from relieved to fearful.

"Well," Jeep tosses his hat in the air. "We always knew we'd have to fight them again. I guess we're as ready as we'll ever be. Don't forget the surprises we still have in store." He nods at Vicky and Maël.

Taylar lifts his shield with a determined look on his face. "I just had an idea how to keep Beelzebub busy while we fight the Horsemen."

"What about the Horsemen? I'm not killing their horses." Kessley folds her arms.

D'Maeo shakes his head. "Don't worry, we won't have to."

"And if we…" Kess pauses. "I mean, once we've defeated Beelzebub *and* the Horsemen, how do we keep the Devil busy until," she licks her lips, "you know."

Taylar leans toward the middle of the group with a malicious grin that makes my insides turn. "I've got a plan for that."

CHAPTER 29

After Taylar and D'Maeo's explanations, I address Quinn again. Automatically, I look up, even though I'm in Heaven myself now. "Quinn, are you still there?"

"Yes."

"Can you come and fight with us?"

"I'm sorry. I want to, but I've been ordered to guard the door to God's dwellings. Mumiah is here with me. We're the last defense that stands between the survival of Heaven and Earth and total destruction, if you fail."

"We won't fail. But, we could use some help."

"Help is already on the way. I've pointed some wandering souls in your direction. They should arrive any second now." He pauses and I can hear him swallow his emotions. "Good luck, Dante. I'll see you soon."

As I'm about to answer, the sound of voices reaches me. I whirl around and my mouth falls open. A group of soldiers too large to count marches toward us. They're see-through, but that doesn't make them any less impressive.

Dylan cheers and jumps up and down in a Kessley imitation. "It's Armando Accardi, with his army from Salvatorum!"

I gasp. "The soldier who accidentally killed you?"

"Yes. He promised to come and help us, but I wasn't sure if they could make it, so I asked Charlie and Gisella to keep that quiet. I didn't want to give you all false hope."

Charlie is smiling, too. It looks a bit sad, and I want to hug him. *"Sorry,"* he mouths.

I swat his apology away and mouth, *"It's fine,"* back.

I should never have doubted him, not even for a second, even though I knew he was hiding something from me. Charlie is incapable of doing anything evil.

As the soldiers approach, I see something strange. The one leading the group is not human. It's an ent. Although he's much taller than the soldiers, he's also more transparent than the rest, which explains why I didn't notice him until now.

Vicky presses herself against me and searches for my hand. "Is that…?"

Emotions block my throat so all I can do is nod. Relief, joy, and gratefulness all fight to get out.

Finally, the group comes to a halt, and the white

tree in front bows. "My friends. It is an honor to see you again."

I bow back, and so does everyone behind me. "Althan. I am so happy to see you."

"We never got the chance to thank you for saving our lives. Again," Vicky adds.

The white tree moves his branch arms to place his hands together. "It was my pleasure."

Vicky and me exchange a quick baffled glance. We both find it hard to believe the tree who saved our lives when we froze in that strange and dark world, and who fell to his death when we escaped to the next world, is standing in front of us. He has healing powers even stronger than Mona's. And more faith in the written word than any creature I've ever met. He sacrificed himself for us, based on a prophecy.

As I struggle to find more to say to him, he stretches his arm out to his left. "Meet Armando Accardi. I met him on my way here. We should all be honored to have him on our side. He's worthy of such a strong name."

I frown.

Strong name?

Althan notices my confusion and bends over to whisper, "His name means brave soldier."

"I see." I thank Althan with a nod and hold out my hand to the young man. "It is an honor to meet you, and all of your friends."

Armando looks tough. He has a two-day stubble, and his camouflage suit fits tight around his chest. His eyes bore into mine. It's clear he won't let anyone mess with him.

His whole face changes with a smile, and I relax. "We're happy to help." He makes a quarter turn and gestures at his army. "We also brought you another surprise."

Two by two the soldiers step back, creating a path between them. I hold my breath.

Another surprise?

The last soldiers make way and there, at the end… is Dad.

I can't help the tears gushing down my cheeks as I make my way toward him, breaking into a run. I nearly push him over when I reach him. His laugh carries me back to a much happier time, before Mom's fits, and before the Devil decided to ruin all of our lives.

"Hello, son."

It feels so good to hold him again, to feel his strong arms around me, and I can almost fool myself into believing he's still alive. The last time I saw him was so tense; our conversation was filled with doubts, fear, and warnings. This time, I don't want to waste a second.

"I'm so glad you were able to escape again," I say forcing myself to let go of him.

"Me, too. The Horsemen have been busy preparing for the battle. They forgot to watch me."

"Quinn told me they will attack God's tower."

Dad's nod is solemn. "Yes, but I have some inside

info we can use to stop them."

We walk back to the front of the group, where Mom waits for us, wringing her hands. We stop before her and I step aside.

"Susan." Dad's eyes glisten with sorrow and shine with love at the same time.

"John." Mom's still fidgeting with her fingers. "I-I'm sorry for—"

"No." He takes her hands and pulls her closer. "*I* am sorry, for not telling you what was going on. I tried to protect the both of you by keeping you out of it. I failed to see that bringing you in could've saved us all."

"It doesn't matter anymore. I understand why you did what you did. And I'm grateful for it."

They stare at each other for a couple of breathless seconds. Then, they hug so hard they almost melt into one person.

Vicky leans against me as I wipe away my tears.

After not nearly enough time I clear my throat. "We need to go. Tell us what you know about the Horsemen, Dad."

"Killing their horses isn't the only way to defeat them. Severing the bond between them and their riders should weaken them enough to beat them."

Maël slams her staff into the clouds. "How do we separate them?"

Dad puts his hand in his pants pocket, pulls out a small blade, and unfolds it into a spear the size of his arm with a strong flick of his hand.

Maël and D'Maeo gasp at the same time.

"The Lance of Michael."

"The archangel?" Ginda asks, and Dad grins.

"Yes. The one he used to send Lucifer to Hell. Michael locked some of his divine light inside the runes on the heft."

Hope sparks in my chest. "Can we use it for that again?"

"No, Lucifer's powers have grown, and the power of the runes in the lance have weakened over time. The longer it is separated from its master, the less power it will have."

Jeep puts his hat back on his head. "But it's still enough to sever the bond between the Horsemen and their horses, right?"

"Exactly."

"Great. Let's kill those bastards, then."

Jeep strides off and, when I nod, the rest follow him.

Dad grabs my wrist while we make our way to a flickering light in the distance. "You'll need to use a spell to make the bonds visible. Can you do that?"

My heartbeat quickens from fear and at the same time hope rises. We can do this. "No problem."

He slaps my back. "I'm so proud of you."

We come to a halt when a bright white tower suddenly rises above us. Seconds ago it was at least a mile away, now we're only several feet from the huge entrance. The building is shaped like a triangle. The top of it disappears into the cracked red sky. With windows covering it from top to bottom, it looks like a modern office building. Except the whole thing sparkles. Looking at it brings my heartbeat down and clears my head.

My gaze falls upon the figures standing at the entrance. They take their time to turn around, as if they have nothing to fear from us. Four men on horses, and in the middle, the giant form of Beelzebub.

Satan's right hand looks even more terrifying than the first time we met him. The crooked horns on his head seem to have grown. An oily black substance drips from the sharp tips onto his arms, burning away the last of the shredded flesh on his bones. His long neck consists of pulsing veins, and through the holes in his chest I can see his insides writhe.

Next to him, the Horsemen look small and insignificant. The White Horseman sits straight on his horse, his bow and arrow strapped to his back. He looks like a mighty warrior, but his white uniform with the golden belt has not even a speck of dust or blood on it. As if he presents himself as a warrior, but has no wish to fight. The Red Rider is dressed in a suit of armor and covered from head to toe in dirt and blood. The sword he has drawn is scratched and dented. The Pale and Black Horseman look almost fragile, one without skin wearing a tattered cloak, the other so thin his motorcycle clothes almost slide from his bony body. It's easy to think they could be mowed down with one strike of a blade. I know what powers lie within them, though, and I can feel it deep within me, too. They can cause famine, war, destruction, and disease. They will tear us apart from the inside if we lose focus for even a second.

"We can't let you go any farther," I declare making my way to the head of the group.

The Pale Horseman snorts. "You can't *let* us? Boy, if you still think you can defeat us, you must be delusional. Have you seen the army of angels who thought they could keep us out?"

"We have, and you will pay for that."

The Red Horseman raises his sword. "What are you waiting for? I'm always ready for another war."

I take my athame out and nod at Taylar. "So are we."

We charge as one. The noise of stomping feet, war cries, and magic fills the air.

Black flames burn holes in the clouds before my feet. I jump over them and avoid getting hit on instinct. Or should I say: thanks to my fairy godmothers.

D'Maeo leads a group of ghost soldiers who protect Taylar. Vicky, Dylan, Charlie, and what remains of the angels approach Beelzebub in hopes of distracting him from the real threat. Meanwhile, the rest of us focus on the Four Horsemen.

Five Kessleys form a line between them and us. "Go on then, give it your best shot," she provokes them.

They narrow their eyes and stare hard at her. Soon,

the eager expressions on their faces are replaced by frustration.

All the Kessleys giggle as one. "I told you your tricks don't work on me." Five Kessleys become ten. "Your powers can't latch onto me. They lose grip because I can change shape and multiply."

While she keeps them busy, Dad and I sneak to the side.

Dad holds the Lance of Michael firmly in his hand. "Are you ready?"

"Yes."

I come to a halt and concentrate on the right words to use.

"Powers of Heaven and powers of Earth,
show me now your greatest worth."

Dad pushes me aside and a dark flame passes an inch from my head.

"Keep going!" he yells above the racket.

"Stop the boy! Take his voice!" one of the Horsemen calls out.

The clouds under my feet tremble and rip. Energy seeps from my body and a sharp pain shoots through my stomach. It feels as if I haven't eaten in a month.

Maël appears next to me and grabs my arm. "Ignore the pain. You are strong, you need to keep fighting."

Another invisible stab, this one in my chest. When I look down, I catch a glimpse of something dark crawling under my skin. The stench of rotting flesh and blood makes it hard to breathe.

"Ignore it, Dante. Finish the spell!" Dad bellows.

My legs give in, but someone catches me. Leaning on my friend, I try to remember the rest of the words. They come out in a mumbled whisper.

"There is a bond that shouldn't be,
between the riders and their steeds.
Find the ties and make us see,
so we can set these horses free."

Four strings of light become visible. The piercing pain in my gut stops. I thank Kasinda, whom I recognize now as the one holding me up, and regain my balance. Dad is already on his way to the nearest Horseman, his lance held high and his expression murderous. He's in the center of a group formed by Ginda, Chloe, Jeep, and several angels. Althan has stayed behind with Maël, who is awakening the remnants of the black tree inside her.

My gaze moves farther and I freeze on the spot.

"What's wrong?" Kasinda asks.

"Vicky." I pick up my athame, which I must have dropped when my legs gave in, and start to make my way toward my girl.

She's standing in front of Beelzebub, immobilized.

He seems immune to the soldiers attacking him. Charlie is pulling and shoving Vicky, trying to get her to move. Dylan holds his hands in front of Vicky's face to break her eye contact with the man-monster.

The White Horseman of conquest leads his horse next to Beelzebub and looks down with disdain. "That won't do you any good. You can never fully break free from him. Vicky is Lucifer's great-granddaughter. She belongs with him." He tilts his head and moves his gaze to me. "But you already knew that deep in your heart, didn't you?"

Rage and despair build up inside me. I envision wind and make it push the Horseman from his horse. As soon as he's falling, I hurry over to Vicky and help the others to move her. She doesn't budge. It's as if she's glued to the ground. Her pupils are empty and lifeless, except for darkness growing within them. Black lines under her cheeks tell me Beelzebub is waking up the slivers of evil that must remain inside her.

She was never fully cured. But I won't give up on her. I'll lose her anyway, but not before she saves us all. She has a part to play in all of this and betraying us is not it.

"Wake up, babe. Please." I shake her shoulders. "Let the good drive out the evil inside you. I know you can do it."

A sharp pain hits my back and I double over. I gasp for air, and Vicky finally moves. She looks down at me with eyes as dark as oil. *Please come back to me,* I beg her in silence. Without a word, she turns her head and walks toward Beelzebub. She takes her place between the hell beast and the White Horseman, who has pulled himself back onto his horse.

"No..." I moan. In my mind our whole plan shatters. Without Vicky we have no way to defeat Satan. Our whole plan is built on her.

I'm about to roll over and give up when I see Dad approaching from my peripheral vision. To distract the Horseman, I drop onto my knees and retch.

"That's it," the White Rider says. "You puke your guts—"

His sentence is cut short as Dad brings his lance down, cutting the string of light. It vanishes with a hiss. The Horseman screams and slides off the back of the animal as if an arrow has hit him.

Beelzebub roars. I stand up and prepare to attack. Then, I hear Taylar's voice. "Hey, asshole!"

Everyone turns to look at him. He moves his hands, and a portal appears under the beast's feet. Beelzebub falls into it with an astonished growl.

Now free, Vicky dives out of the way and makes for the tower.

Taylar moves his hands around again, and another portal appears about ten feet above the first. Beelzebub's feet come through, followed by the rest of his ugly body. His skin shreds even more when it touches the edges of the portals. In vain he grabbles for support and disappears into the lower portal. Seconds later his feet appear again in the top one. Taylar did it. He trapped the man-monster in a never-ending plunge.

There's barely time to feel triumphant about it. A blast of light accompanies a thunderous explosion.

We all duck to avoid getting hit by flying debris. The horses stagger and I look up. Part of the base construction of the tower is gone. The whole building sways on its foundation.

"The end is near!" the White Horseman calls out in triumph. "Soon God's tower will fall, and the Apocalypse will begin."

"No, it will not." Maël apparates next to him and grabs his head with both hands. She brings her face close to his.

Althan comes up behind her and slams his branches together. "That's it, Maël. Do it now."

Her forehead touches the rider's and dark twigs burst through her curls.

The Horseman's eyes grow wide. "No... That's impossible."

The twigs shoot forward and pierce through his eyes. His scream is lost in the sound of the collapsing building.

Althan looks over Maël's head and moves forward with haste. Instinctively, I follow him. He comes to a halt before the hole in the tower. "We need to save this building."

"Yes, but how?"

Althan's mouth twitches. He sighs, then rises to his full, impressive height. "This is why I am here, Dante. I will hold the building up." He shoots me a sad smile. "If you can hold it up for me for a minute?"

The tower is starting to tip over.

How will I be able to hold that up?

Althan is already walking toward the gap. "It's too heavy for me to lift, but I can merge with it once I'm under it. Use a spell to lift it."

Of course. A spell.

Afraid of something sneaking up behind us, I check for incoming attacks. No one seems to notice us. Maël and the White Horseman are still face to face. My other friends have created a barrier between them and the other three Riders. In the meantime, Dad is moving in to cut through another bond.

Maël shudders violently, as if ten thousand volts go through her.

I take several steps back. "Mom, enhance her powers!"

She nods and flexes her fingers.

Meanwhile, Beelzebub has managed to grab onto the edge of the lower portal. My heart skips a beat.

"Taylar!" I call out. "Did you bring holy water?"

"Yes!" he shouts back without breaking the line of defense.

"Use it on Beelzebub, and hurry!"

After one glance over his shoulder he darts toward the beast. He pulls a bottle from his pocket and throws the contents at Beelzebub. The man-monster roars in pain and lets go. He plummets into the portal as Taylar keeps watch beside it.

"Dante!"

Whirling back around, I find Althan has moved under the destroyed side of the tower. The building is tipping faster now and the ent is about to get crushed.

"Shit!" I squeeze my eyes shut and beg the words to come, hoping I can fix it without using Althan.

"Take this building, save its soul,
put it back and make it whole."

With a grinding noise, the tower straightens up. Althan stands tall, his branches above his head to fill the gap. Before I can tell him to get out of there, the building starts to repair itself. The debris is pulled back in. It builds a wall around the white tree. Soon, I can only see his face.

"Oh, no." I hurry over to him and try to punch a hole in the wall to free him.

"Don't. I can hold it."

I shake my head. "No. It will be fine without you. I can get you out with another spell."

Althan's face changes. His eyebrows drop and the white bark turns red. "Listen to me, Dante. You need to go inside. Go now. Make sure Satan never reaches God."

The resolution in his voice makes me drop my arm.

I still don't understand why we need to save God. Why isn't he fighting with us? He's all-powerful, right? Why doesn't he save us and himself with a flick of his wrist?

"Because he is busy saving people from the earthquakes and floods Lucifer caused," Quinn's voice says in my head. "Don't let that be for nothing,

Dante."

"Go," Althan begs me. "Leave me. It's okay. This is my destiny. Now, go and fulfill yours."

I bite back my tears. "Thank you, Althan. For everything."

He smiles and a second later he turns solid. His curled-up lips solidify while his branches crunch as a cement-like substance covers it. The trembling of the tower stops.

"Thank you," I whisper again, and then I set off toward the high doors.

CHAPTER 30

The entrance is huge. There are no floors, except for one at the very top, which I can barely make out from down here. In the middle of the hallway there's a column with an elevator inside. Around it, dozens of lights in all colors of the rainbow float up in an endless stream of beauty.

There's no time to admire it, though. My gaze is pulled to the red beast pounding on the elevator doors.

I hurl a block of ice at him.

He stops pounding and turns to face me. His ugly mouth forms into a grin. "Dante, you little trickster. How lovely to see you again." His forked tongue darts over his lips. "Just in time for the grand finale."

He shrinks to his human size and steps aside to reveal Vicky. "I'd love to have her kill you. What sweet torture that would be. But," he sighs dramatically, "we've had enough delays. It's time for me to take the throne."

Anger boils to the surface at the sight of Vicky next to him. I take three steps toward him, another block of ice in my hand. "You will never—"

"Dante! Watch out!"

With the ice in front of me for protection I whirl around. Several figures soar toward me. There are open maws, sharp claws, oil-dripping fur, and wriggling tentacles. It's too late to avoid them. I'm a millisecond away from being devoured by demons. As I order the ice to expand, my eyes lock onto something else. Amid all the snapping jaws and extended claws, I can make out blond, blood-streaked locks cascading over a Hawaiian shirt. Blobs of brown gel hit two of the demons in the face. Then, his body connects with mine. The force knocks me back. Charlie takes my place in the midst of the hungry horde of monsters. One hand shoots out to stop me from sliding farther away from them, while I lift the other to fire lightning balls. I conjure wind to pull them away from Charlie. When it doesn't work, I add water. At the same time, I jump forward and slash as much skin as I can reach with my athame. Explosions rise from the mess of limbs and teeth, but the demons who fall are replaced by others before I can even blink.

"Enough," the Devil says calmly.

The demons retreat, and I drop down next to my best friend.

His shirt is ripped to shreds, his hair now more red than blond. Deep gashes run along his cheeks and chest, and blood oozes from the wounds. He's gasping for air.

My fingers ache as I tear pieces from his shirt to stop the bleeding. It's no use. There are too many holes to cover.

"Hold on," I plead. "I'll call for help." My voice is so hoarse and my heart beats so loud in my ears that I can barely hear myself.

His breathing steadies and his eyes lock onto mine. "This is where we part ways."

"No, Charlie. Don't give up." My hands press on the gaps in his chest. The cloth is already soaked; blood seeps through my fingers.

"We needed a sacrifice, remember?" He lifts one corner of his mouth into a crooked grin. "I knew it would have to be me when Vicky almost killed me."

I try to tell him how sorry I am about that, how sorry *she* is, but he cuts me off.

"No need to feel guilty. Quinn couldn't heal me completely. He sent me back with enough time to fight by your side. I'm grateful for that."

"The godmothers can heal you," I insist.

He closes his eyes for a second. When he looks at me again, there's resignation as well as sadness in them. His hand goes to mine and he pulls it from his wound. "No one can heal me, mate. I'll be reunited with Gisella. The real Gisella." His smile is genuine now, no trace of sorrow in it anymore. A pool of blood forms between us. "The moment someone dies, only the powers they were born with stay with them. She'll be herself again, Dante. You have to let me go."

He coughs, and blood wells over his lips. He opens his mouth again to speak. His voice is weak, the slow and forceful rising of his chest pushing the words out in a stutter.

Bending over him, I bring my ear close to his face. His breath feels warm on my cheek. It takes me several seconds to realize it was his last one.

A storm awakens inside me. The pressure behind my eyes makes my head hurt. My blood pumps through my veins with so much force I'm afraid they'll burst.

I grab Charlie's head and shoulders and press him against my chest. I want to tell him I love him, let him know how much joy he has brought into my life. Whenever I was sad, his smile and sense of humor kept me going. When my friends betrayed me, he stayed by my side. Nothing could get boring with him around.

"Oh, how sad," Satan whines. "He gave his life for you. And for what?" He lets out a low chuckle which makes the whole tower vibrate. "You'll die anyway. I'd say you have about…" he pauses, then snaps his fingers. Claws scrape the floor as the demons scramble up. "Two minutes to live."

I lay Charlie down gently and conjure up every weather condition I can think of. Rain, hail, snow, wind, sunlight, it all comes down at the same time. While the monsters fight to get through it, I move back, toward the open doors.

Charlie's death will not be in vain. No matter how hopeless things get, I will not give up.

There's a growl behind me and I freeze. With a slow turn, I'm face to face with two more demons.

"Farewell, Dante," Satan says.

The demons leap. All I can do is duck with my weapon above my head.

Nothing hits me, though. When I look up, both demons are pulled back by ropes.

"Someone called?"

I blink several times. The girl in front of me doesn't change. She's really here. Limping and bleeding, but real.

"Wendy?"

"Yes, sorry we're late. We had to get rid of some demons ourselves, to make sure the book and the other objects are safe. We came as soon as the light of a sacrifice reached us." Sorrow shines in her eyes. "I'm sorry for your loss."

"Move," someone yells from behind her, and we dive in opposite directions.

I get to my feet and find myself back to back with another familiar face. "Soimane?"

"Hey, Dante." For the first time since I've known her, the leader of the iele is panting. "We saw the light from the sacrifice. Need some help?"

"We do. We need to prevent Lucifer from

reaching the top floor."

"I'll see what we can do."

She rises above my head and gathers more iele than I can count.

"Wait," I say piercing a demon's eye with my athame when it leaps at me.

Soimane raises an eyebrow.

Lowering my voice, I explain, "Try not to kill Vicky, please. We need her."

She makes a small bow. "Of course."

That doesn't sound comforting, but it'll have to do, because another monster jumps me. Its momentum carries us both through the open doors. Once we land, my feet push it off, and I grab my Morningstar, letting it unfold. The spikes hit the demon in the chest as it soars backward. I pull my weapon in and cut the monster's head off with one clean slice. An oily substance sprays from its insides before it goes up in smoke. Too late, I close my eyes. Darkness covers my vision. My body feels almost weightless and I'm unable to move. From a distance I can hear shouting followed by an angry roar. I conjure water and let it flow over my eyes. The oil stings like crazy, but bit by bit my surroundings take shape again. My limbs, however, don't cooperate yet. All I can do is lie still and wait.

About five feet away from me, the bodies of two Horsemen appear lifeless. The other two are trying to keep Maël at bay. Dad burns any demon who dares to come close to her. I think they can handle themselves.

What I'm worried about, is the fact that Beelzebub has somehow broken free from his two-portal prison. What remains of my friends are fighting him. By the looks of it, Mom is using every illusion she can think of to confuse and distract him. However, my friends seem just as confused, stabbing in the wrong places and leaping at thin air. Ginda creates beanstalks around his feet to pull him over. At the same time, two stems pop out of the ground behind the chlorokinetic witch. As they wrap around her neck and squeeze, she grabs them with both hands. Taylar rushes to her side and cuts the stalks.

Kessley changes into a huge snake-like monster and lets out an angry hiss.

"Go on," D'Maeo says. "I'll block his powers."

Panic grips my throat when I realize what Beelzebub is doing. I struggle to find my voice. Parts of my body respond to my pleas for them to obey. With my hands balled into fists, I squeeze the words out. "Stop! He can absorb the powers we use on him."

To my relief, D'Maeo lowers his hands. The next moment a black flame hits him. He's lifted off his feet and thrown to the ground several feet away. In full control of my body again, I jump up and rush over to him.

"I'm fine," he says, already getting to his feet. "I can take a hit."

While the others engage in the fight again, this time without using their powers, I lean closer to the old ghost. "I've got a plan. We need Mom and Chloe for it."

He nods, vanishes, and appears again with the two of them by his side. "Tell us."

I talk faster than I've ever done before. Jeep yells with pain, making me cringe. "Do it. Do it now."

D'Maeo goes invisible and almost at the same time Chloe changes into his mirror image. After a nod at Mom, I set off to execute my part of the plan.

"This will never work!" I scream at my friends, taking my place at their side. "We'll have no choice but to use our powers. Without them, we can never defeat him." I face the giant beast, lightning in my hand. "See if you can handle this."

I make a throwing motion but keep the lightning in my hand. At the same time, D'Maeo's form jumps between me and Beelzebub. "Watch out!" He stretches his arms to block an attack, then pushes off and lands on the beast's waist.

Beelzebub roars with delight as he absorbs the powers. The fake D'Maeo lets go and returns to my side with a couple of somersaults.

"Stand down," I tell the others.

"What did you do?" Jeep asks turning his hat over and over in his hands. "Now he can block our powers."

"No, he can't." Mom lifts the illusion, and I grin.

The fake D'Maeo turns back into Chloe, and Jeep's mouth falls open.

Over my shoulder, I nod. "Enhance his power,

Mom."

"Gladly."

D'Maeo joins us as we watch Beelzebub shiver and wriggle.

"What's happening?" Dylan asks wiping sweat and blood from his forehead.

"He absorbed Chloe's powers."

The ground shakes as Beelzebub drops to his knees. His already torn skin ruptures even more while ice bites its way through his insides.

Kessley's mouth falls open. "What the…?"

"He's made of fire, just like Satan," I explain. "Chloe is frozen. Those two don't go very well together." I turn to Taylar. "Do you have any holy water left?"

"A little bit."

I hold out my hand. "Give it to me."

"No." He cracks his neck. "I'll do it."

Without hesitation, he walks up to the man-monster, kicks him in the face, and forces his mouth open. "Enjoy," he says and pours the holy water into Beelzebub's throat.

Beelzebub's whole body convulses. His arms and legs twitch. Taylar's shield drops down over his face and he jumps out of the way.

The beast creates dark flames in his hands and presses them against his body. The ice on his torn skin melts. He tries to hit Taylar, who goes invisible to make the flame shoot through him. He reaches the monster's neck, raises his sword, and brings it down with all his strength.

Beelzebub gurgles as his arms flail and smoke rises from his nostrils.

Taylar lifts his sword again. This time the head comes off. It rolls into the still open portal and with a simple hand gesture the young ghost closes it. Then, he jumps down from the body before it goes up in smoke.

"Wow. Well done!" Kessley cheers.

They manage a brief hug before a shriek of pain rips through the air.

A ghost soldier doubles over. The Black Horseman laughs and aims his powers at the next soldier.

I grab D'Maeo's arm. "Time for your backup plan."

Kessley sucks in a sharp breath. "Don't tell me you're going to—"

"We have to."

Simultaneously, D'Maeo and I bring our arms back and throw our weapons at the red and black horse. They hit their targets on spot.

"I'm sorry," I whisper, my heart contracting with pity.

The horses neigh and fall sideways. At the same time, their riders gasp.

Without hesitation, the soldiers take their chance to seize them. With Dad still by her side, Maël kneels beside the Red Horseman, who tries to pull himself free. His eyes are fuming, but he's too weak to use his powers.

I address Armando Accardi, who's holding down the Black Horseman. "Can you handle them from here?"

"Yes, thank you."

"Good." I turn back to the others. "We need to get back inside to stop Satan and get Vicky back on our side."

We make our way to the doors. I can see the battle raging on inside. Behind the Keepers of Life and the demons, the iele are keeping Satan busy. Vicky seems okay, as far as I can tell.

Taylar stops me at the doors. "Remember what Quinn told you about me?"

I frown.

Why is he bringing this up now?

"Do you remember?" he presses.

"Yes, he said I could trust you."

He nods. "Keep that in mind."

"What—" There's no time to finish my question because Taylar has already run off. He blends into the battle, and I lose sight of him.

I scan the moving figures to see who needs my help. One of the Keepers is holding a small device, like a button. A blue light shining from it is wrapped around the elevator shaft, all the way to the top. It's like a shield or something. About a dozen demons surround the Keeper, eager to take the button from him.

I'm about to throw myself into the fight when the

floor shakes violently. The walls tremble and several windows fall down. The remaining Keepers and iele scatter to avoid the glass. A huge flame shoots over our heads, followed by a blast that makes my teeth chatter and my head spin. The world turns sideways, and I hit the ground. All around me bodies drop like flies. A heavy weight presses me down, and something growls close to my ear. I lift my head an inch and see the demons placing their paws or whole bodies on each and every one of my friends. The blue shield dissolves and an eerie silence descends, only broken by the heavy breathing of the monsters.

Footsteps approach until a dark figure looms over me. "You won't escape me again, Dante." He gestures at the floor around us. "No more armies to help you."

Vicky steps up from behind him. Her face is now a dark mask which has chased all of her beauty away. Her blonde tips have turned black.

"Are you sure you don't want to join our side?" she asks in a low voice.

My lips press together and I blink back tears of frustration.

"He'll never turn, Vicky," Satan says.

"Pity," she answers.

Holding her gaze, I say goodbye to her in my head. While I'm telling her, without words, how much I love her, her eyes change. The black pulls back… and she winks. In another blink she returns to her numb hypnotized state. But it was real, I know it was.

She's pretending.

"*I* will join you," a voice on my right says.

Both Satan and Vicky look up. The Devil steps over me and Vicky follows him.

"What was that?" Satan asks.

"I said I'll join you," Taylar repeats.

Cold trickles into my veins at the sound of his voice. It was the same way when he turned evil at Shelton Banks' mansion. Carefully, I turn my head. The demon holding me down snarls but holds back at a "Not yet!" from Satan.

He gestures at the demon on top of Taylar. As soon as it lets go, Taylar stands up and faces the Devil as if he has nothing to fear. His face is just as tainted as Vicky's, and despite what he told me moments ago, my heart beats wildly with worry.

"So, you are Taylar. The one I was warned about."

The young ghost frowns. "Really?"

"Yes, really." Lucifer's hand shoots out. He grabs Taylar by the throat and lifts him up to his face. "Tell me. Do you think you can trick me?"

"Not at all," Taylar splutters.

Lucifer grows into his beastly form. Flames lick Taylar's face, but he doesn't even flinch. "Should I be impressed by you, then? The one who can trick me with his power. You don't even have a power of your own, so I've been told. All you have is what you stole from Trevor."

The white-haired ghost remains calm. His eyes turn even darker. "If you don't believe me, look into my soul. You can sense evil, can't you?"

For a moment, Lucifer is silent. Then, he sets Taylar back on his feet. "Very well." He shrinks and looks Taylar in the eye. As his body goes rigid, his pupils start to swirl. Even the demons are quiet now.

It takes mere seconds, but it feels like an hour. Satan stands up straight, lets out a sort of surprised huff, and slaps Taylar on the shoulder. "Wonderful. Welcome to the team."

Taylar grins back. "I am honored. Is there anything I can do for you, my lord?"

My teeth hurt from how hard I'm gritting them.

Trust him? Really, Quinn? If it wasn't for your reassurance, I would've flushed the evil out of him before this battle started.

There's no answer.

Lucifer has something to say, though. "I would enjoy watching you kill your friends."

My eyes close. This is it.

"They were never my friends," Taylar answers. "It would be my pleasure."

"Wait," Vicky's voice interrupts. "If you don't mind, I would like to do it. After all, wouldn't it be better if someone in the family got rid of the chosen one?"

Satan laughs hard at that. "It would be," he says, each word shaking with laughter. "Please, go ahead. And make it a good show, will you?"

I lift my head as she turns to us. Her gaze sweeps the many people on the floor. Her mouth forms soundless words. Numbers. *Three… two… one.*

As one, we all push up, sending the demons flying. My first lightning ball is aimed at Taylar, but I squash it after one look at his face.

It's normal again. How is that possible?

Not even a hint of darkness rests in his eyes, no evil crawls under his skin.

He turns to the Devil, who is frozen in astonishment. "Surprise!"

Then he pulls his sword from his back and drives it into Satan's chest.

Lucifer stumbles back, both hands reaching for the heft. "This can't be. You're evil. I saw it. I felt it."

Taylar tilts his head and sticks his lower lip forward. "Oh, I'm sorry. Didn't they tell you my dormant power woke up? Didn't you know I can switch from good to evil whenever I want to?"

While he keeps the Devil talking, I turn to Vicky. "Start now." Then, I pick up my weapon and do something that wasn't part of the plan. "Mona, send all fairy godmothers to protect Vicky. We need to keep her safe, at all costs."

The Keeper of Life next to me touches my arm and assures me, "We'll keep the demons away from her."

I smile, grateful for their help.

He yells an order and it's like everything wakes from a frozen state. As if someone pressed play and all the characters start moving again.

Ignoring the pain of what are, no doubt, several

bruised or broken ribs, I hurl the demon who kept me down over my shoulder and press a ball of lightning into its mouth. When it goes up in smoke, I hesitate. Do I stay close to Vicky in case something slips past the Keepers? Or do I join Taylar, the iele, and the rest of my friends in their fight against Lucifer?

D'Maeo makes the choice for me. He apparates to my side and positions himself between Vicky and the raging battle. "Go on," he says. "I've got her back."

"Thanks."

I weave my way past extended claws, jaws that snap shut, wheezing magical rings, clouds of poison, and waving swords toward the spot where Satan is pulling Taylar's blade from his chest. Eight of the iele folk circle around his head. They've linked hands and are preparing to hit him with a force field, like they did when Beelzebub came through the portal in the silver mine.

Maël has joined us. Her eyes are focused on the sword she's keeping locked in time. No matter how hard Satan pulls, it won't budge.

Giant flesh-eating plants sprout from the floor and snap at Lucifer's body. Even though they're tearing the flesh from his legs, revealing the bright red below, he ignores them.

Dad moves to my side and burns a demon mid-leap.

A hand pulls me away with a, "Step back."

Recognizing the iele Mandre, I obey, grateful for a chance to catch my breath.

The air ripples and a blast of energy hits Lucifer from all sides. The force of it nearly knocks me over, even from several feet away.

Satan's body ripples, just like the air did a second ago. Waves move under his skin. They reshape him from the inside, pushing his torso out of proportion. His cheeks seem to collapse and his chin droops.

A brief flash of light to my left catches my attention. I turn my head and stop breathing.

Vicky is hovering in the air, spinning with her arms wide and her eyes closed. The light shining from within her spreads farther and farther. She's more beautiful than ever, her face soft and peaceful. With each turn her arms go higher, as if the light carries them up. Although her lips move, her words are so soft I can't hear them.

A sound like thunder startles me and something slams into me. A body. I cry out in pain as another rib cracks. One of the fairies lands at my feet like a bag of garbage, bleeding gashes running over her whole body. The remaining iele from the circle crash to the ground all around me. In a flash, I see Soimane's face among them, her beautiful features burnt, her white gown covered in red.

The Devil grows larger than I've ever seen him. Flames burst from every pore in his red, skinless body. Horns sprout from the top of his head and grow until they're as big as his bulky legs. He stomps on the floor and cracks run along the tiles.

"You think you can hold me down?" he bellows.

361

"You think the snippet of magic inside you that you call power will kill me?"

"Not really," I confess, reaching sideways to support Dad, even though the pain shooting through me almost makes my knees buckle. I wait until the first ring of light comes alive around Lucifer. A copy of the ones Isabel created in the memory I saw. "But those snippets of power distracted you long enough for Vicky to create a brand-new prison for you."

The baffled look on his demonic face is one I'll never forget. The flames engulfing him seem to lose their glow.

Vicky turns so fast it's difficult to see her. Words drift through the smoke-filled air, some of which I recognize from the memory Charon showed me. "Pagans… seal the circle… sinners…"

"How do you know that spell?" Lucifer screams, clear panic seeping through each syllable. "How are you able to do this? I cursed you. I killed Isabel's powers inside you. You can't have woken them up, I would've known!" He slams his fists down onto the circle of light that holds him.

It glows brighter and a second circle appears under it as the first one hovers up to a point above his head.

Dad gives my hand a comforting squeeze.

Satan wheezes. "No, you can't do this. I was meant to rule the universe."

After checking for any surviving demons, I put my athame away. "Not today."

Another circle blazes to life around the Devil's

feet. Tiny sparks fly from the first circle. They cover Lucifer from head to toe. Then, with a crackle, the top circle solidifies. The ground rumbles and the tiles crack beneath the beast before he sinks about a foot into the floor.

Vicky keeps turning. Circle after circle is created. Each time one solidifies above Satan's head, he drops deeper into the floor. Soon, he's out of sight. This time, he doesn't fight it. He doesn't beg for Vicky to stop. He doesn't threaten to kill us all once he's out. He knows he's defeated and there's no way any soul of a sinner will help him escape this time. Vicky will make sure of that.

Now that everything is silent, save for the crackling of the circles and the soft whoosh of Vicky's turning, we can all hear her words clearly.

"Acts of violence will be punished
in this circle night and day.
Sinners will be trapped and guarded,
for their errors they will pay.

Build a circle full of souls.
Close it tight and lock the holes.
Keep out those who don't belong.
Punish those who have done wrong.

Acts of treachery will be punished
in this circle night and day.
Sinners will be trapped and guarded,

for their errors they will pay."

The last circle forms and Vicky slows down. Remembering Isabel's collapse when she finished the spell, I hurry over to Vicky and catch her before she hits the floor.

She smiles up at me, exhausted but with determination in her eyes. "Almost there."

I block out my own pain and let her lean against me. "You've got this."

She moves her arms gracefully and once more a light awakens inside her. At her silent command, the Devil rises out of the hole. He's helpless as he floats within the nine glowing circles. His eyes are fuming, but still, he doesn't make a sound.

Vicky pushes the light out of her body. A soft humming escapes her lips, entwining with the light and encasing the structure of circles Lucifer is inside of. One at a time, the circles disappear into the hole. The last one drags Satan down with it. In a final attempt to escape, he goes wild. He changes back into his beastly form and lashes out all around him. His hands claw at the lines now keeping him trapped. Although he breathes fire at them and tries to rip them apart, the circles resist every attack. The Devil squirms, curses, and roars. Without the slightest hesitation, the last circle drops out of sight. Tiles close over the hole, and Satan's last frustrated roar fades. Vicky's song comes to an end.

CHAPTER 31

We all watch the spot where the greatest evil in the universe stood mere moments ago.

Mom is the first one to move. I hadn't even noticed her standing behind us. She wraps her arms around us and holds us tight, making me flinch. "I am so proud of you both."

Dad joins us in silence.

I give myself a few seconds to enjoy this feeling before I break free and look around. Inside I'm cheering and crying at the same time. "Does anyone need help?"

The fairy godmothers show themselves. They look tired but determined to assist anyone who needs them.

When I turn to where I saw Soimane fall, two figures are bent over her. Sfinte and Mandre have kneeled at her side, their heads bowed. Tears drip onto the iele leader's tainted body.

"Mona!" I call out, rushing over to them. "We need you here."

Mandre grabs my hand and shakes her head. "It's too late, Dante."

"And it's okay," Sfinte adds, wiping her cheek. "Soimane was the one who brought the iele back to Affection and made them see how we had strayed from our path of peace and love. Her task has been fulfilled. She is happy now."

I show my last respects to Soimane by bowing and thanking her for everything she has done for the world. Then, I leave her friends alone to mourn.

Vicky is at my side before I can decide what to do next.

"We did it," I whisper. "We defeated him."

She sighs. "Yes, but so many have died."

My gaze glides over the bodies of angels, Keepers, and iele. Charlie lies in the midst of it all. I can't bear to look at him. My eyes flick over the ones who are still standing. All our friends look exhausted. Beaten up, drained and dirty, but still with us.

Vicky's lips meet mine as soon as I turn to her. She grabs the back of my head to pull me closer and I grunt.

"Are you hurt?"

I wave her concern away. "I hit my head a couple of times and I cracked some ribs. Don't worry, I'll be fine. Mona can heal me once I'm back home."

The implication of the word *I* hits us both hard.

Vicky bites her lip and turns away to hide her tears. "How long do you think…?"

My hand caresses her back while I shake my head. "I don't know. Not long."

One by one, the members of my Shield look up, as if they can feel the moment of our goodbyes drawing near.

I want to talk to them, but Wendy blocks my way. She looks ghastly. Her clothes are torn, her right eye is one big bruise, and her hands tremble. "We're going back to our headquarters to look after our wounded and check on the objects we're sworn to protect." She holds out her hand, and I shake it. A smile breaks through the scratches and bruises on her face. "It was an honor to fight by your side, Dante. I'm sure we'll meet again."

"The honor was mutual. Be safe, Wendy."

She nods to Vicky and returns to her colleagues. Soon, they vanish inside their lassos.

The sight of the many fallen fairies makes me swallow hard. Most of the ghost soldiers are still standing, plus a couple of angels.

I clear my throat and address them all. "Dear allies."

All eyes turn to me. In them pain and grief swirl, but no fear. Not anymore.

"We lost a lot of great people today. Brave souls who will never be forgotten. I have no words to express my gratitude for how you were all willing to fight by our side. I wish you all peace and happiness.

The fallen ones will be loved and honored forever. May they rest in peace." My words are followed by a deep bow to each body in the room.

When I straighten up, tears well up in my eyes. Every single person in the room copies my gesture. Their last bow is for me, which I answer with my hand on my heart. The bodies of those who have died are lifted by strong arms and carried through portals opened by Taylar. A glimpse through the portal to Affection shows me that all the flowers by the side of the roads there are hanging their heads. Even though we won, it's a sad procession that leaves Heaven.

Me, Mom, Dad, Mona, Dylan, Kasinda, Ginda, Chloe, the fairy godmothers, and my Shield are all who are left behind. Chloe is leaning heavily on her best friend.

"Are you okay?" I ask.

She shakes her head. "My wounds are…" Her breathing is shaky, irregular. "Fatal."

"Are the godmothers not able to heal you?"

"Maybe. But I don't want them to." She sends me a sad smile. "I never belonged in this world, Dante. You and your friends gave me purpose, and I'm grateful for that. I'm ready to move on." She coughs and her face crackles. "I'm taking my best friend out for a drink for the last time."

She sways and Ginda keeps her upright.

I hug them both at the same time. "Thank you, we couldn't have done this without you. I hope you find peace."

When I let go, Chloe is sporting her bright smile.

Taylar opens a portal to the Winged Centaur and we all wave goodbye.

"We should go, too," the fairy godmother with the short black hair says. "Lots of people on Earth need our help. Not only for healing, but for comfort, too."

Pressing my hands together, I bow again. "Thank you for all the protection you gave us." I hear Charlie's voice in my head and repeat his words out loud. "And for being awesome."

They bow back and go up in colored sparkles. Mona stays behind.

The air is thick with sorrow when none but the regular gang is left. Save for two members.

"Do you think he's happy?" Mom asks, gesturing to the top of the tower with her eyes.

"He must be," Jeep answers, rubbing his tattoos nervously.

"He is." Quinn's voice floats down. "I was asked to thank you for him, since he's still busy saving people on Earth. He will send you a message soon, though; to thank all of you personally."

Mom rests her head against Dad's shoulder, and I quickly look away.

"So, now what?" I ask.

Quinn sighs. "Now, it's time to say goodbye."

A lump rises in my throat, and I swallow. The sound of splashing water reaches my ears. We all turn to see where it's coming from.

I can't help but smile through my tears at the sight

of Charon. Of course it would be him who came to collect my friends.

Vicky reaches for my hand and our fingers entwine.

"My friends," Charon says with his deep voice as his boat comes to a halt in front of us. "You have exceeded my expectations."

"Thank you," I say.

He gestures at the dark world on the other side of the portal. "It is time for your friends to come with me, Dante. I will give you a moment to say goodbye." He leans on his oar while we decide silently who will say goodbye first.

It is Maël who steps toward me before anyone else does. "I have known many kings, but none as brave as you. It was an honor to fight with you, master."

"And for me, Maël. I'm glad you'll finally be reunited with your tribe."

She pulls me close and when we break apart, she hands me her staff. "I will not need this anymore. Can you keep it safe?"

Stunned into silence, I take it and hold it against my heart.

The ghost queen adjusts her cape and turns to the others to say goodbye. I place the staff on the ground.

Jeep is next. He takes off his hat and flings his arms around me. "What a ride, huh? Much more exciting than the circus."

I grin, thankful he's using his sense of humor to break the emotional moment, and pat him on the back. "Say hello to your wife for me. And try not to smooch too much."

He throws his head back in laughter. "Not a chance."

We hold onto each other for several more seconds. His laugh changes into a hiccup that's more like a sob. He turns away to hide it, and I let him go.

Taylar and Kessley approach me next, and I take a deep breath. "Are you looking forward to your new afterlife together?"

Kess shrugs. "I don't know. I liked it here. You welcomed me like a family, and here I mattered."

Taylar pulls her closer. "You matter to me wherever we are."

She blushes and starts to giggle uncontrollably. "I'm sorry," she exclaims. "I can't help it."

We all laugh.

My arms wrap around them both. "I'm so proud of you. You both showed your worth when no one seemed to believe in you." I rub the back of Taylar's head. "Your brother will burst with pride when you tell him everything."

His eyes twinkle. "I can't wait to see him."

I let go of them. "Enjoy your time together. Be happy." The last words come out choked; the corners of my mouth refuse to turn into a smile.

"We'll miss you," Kessley says.

"I'll miss you, too, crazy leopard girl."

In an attempt to collect myself, I let out a slow breath and lower my gaze to the floor for a couple of seconds.

Dylan comes up to me next. He trips over his feet and bumps against me. We chuckle and turn the awkward collision into a hug.

"Thank you for giving me a chance to prove myself, and for me to make a difference in the world."

"You keep forgetting, you were always important to the world."

He blushes, gives me an awkward salute, and walks away.

My gaze falls upon Mom and Dad and a lump rises in my throat. They're like a statue, clinging to each other in desperation. When they share a passionate kiss, I avert my eyes. No matter how much I swallow, the emotions keep rising to the surface. Soon my cheeks are drenched.

Dad walks up to me. "Son." He holds me at arm's length. Each time he blinks, tears fall.

My lips are pressed together in a tight line. I can't speak anymore.

After staring into each other's eyes for what seems like forever, but is way too short, he pulls me against his chest. "There are no words to express how proud I am. And how much I wish I could stay here with the both of you."

I splutter against his shirt. "We'll meet again."

With a smile, he wipes his cheeks and then mine. "Yes, we will." He places both hands against my face. "I love you."

"I love you, too, Dad." My eyes are getting wet again, and I bring my hand up to wipe at them.

He turns away, blows Mom a kiss, and walks over to Charon's boat.

Mona and D'Maeo are at Mom's side in the blink of an eye and she accepts their comforting arms gratefully.

My breath comes in gasps. My chest hurts as it contracts. Thinking of the last person to say goodbye to, my legs turn to jelly. I slide onto the floor and hide behind my hands for a moment.

Soft, warm fingers pull them away and the most beautiful, mesmerizing blue eyes stare into mine.

"We knew this day would come," she whispers.

"That doesn't make it any easier." There's more I want to say, but the words get stuck in my throat.

"We'll be together again someday, babe. And then, it will be forever." Her lips find mine and electricity fizzes between us.

It seems to last forever, but she still pulls back too soon. I press my forehead against hers and close my eyes. "I can't do this."

"You have no choice."

"Yes, I do. I can come with you."

She shoots straight up, anger written on her face. "No. We talked about this. You're not doing that. You deserve to live."

"I don't want to live without you."

"There's no other way."

As I hold her close my tears run free. "I love you.

Forever."

"I love you, too."

Over her shoulder I can see Dad, Maël, Jeep, Taylar, Kessley, and Dylan standing in the ferryman's boat. They're ready to set off to Tartarus. I should let Vicky go, but my heart stutters at the thought.

On the other side of the portal, I see Charlie and Gisella in the distance, standing hand in hand on the shore of the river Lethe. They wave and it takes all my strength to lift my arm and return the gesture.

Vicky uses the moment to break free. She walks to the boat and places her hand on the side, ready to hop in.

"One moment," Charon says. "There's one problem."

"A problem?" the two of us say in unison.

"If I take Vicky, the balance in the universe will be disturbed."

A frown pulls the corners of my mouth down. "What do you mean?"

"She's the descendant of Lucifer. Her soul is part evil."

"So? She can control it. You saw, right?"

The ferryman nods. "I did. And that is why I will not take her with me."

My heart stops beating altogether. I don't understand what's happening.

Charon shows me his lipless smile under his hood. "You know part of my job is to keep the balance in the universe."

I nod.

"When you took down Trevor, Shelton and their friends, a lot of evil was removed from Earth. To maintain balance, there needs to be some evil in your world. Which is why I will leave Vicky with you. Together, you can keep the evil inside her dormant."

"You what?" My heart stutters back to life. The beating is so irregular it doesn't pump enough oxygen into my brain. I must be hearing him wrong.

Vicky takes a step away from the boat. "Are you serious? I can stay with Dante?"

Charon leans forward, letting his oar support his weight. "Very serious. Do not disappoint me. If you let the evil take over, I *will* come and get you. And I won't be so friendly then."

Vicky turns around with her mouth open. My heart goes into overdrive. It takes several tries to form words.

"But, I chose for D'Maeo to stay. Does this mean he has to go now?" I turn my head to where Mona, Mom, and D'Maeo are wrapped up in a group hug. No matter how much I love Vicky, I can't let Charon take the old ghost instead of her.

Tears form in my eyes as I face the ferryman again.

He shakes his head. "Someone in Heaven decided he can stay. It has little to do with the balance, which means it doesn't concern me. It doesn't change my decision concerning Vicky."

Time seems to slow down as both Vicky and I leap forward. I catch her and fling her around with a hysterical laugh. The rest of my Shield cheers and whistles.

When Charon clears his throat, I set Vicky down. We both approach the boat and bow.

"Thank you so much. Thank you, thank you." I keep repeating it, unable to come up with any other words.

Charon gives us a small nod. He places his oar in the water and pushes off.

Slowly, the boat with our friends and loved ones in it is carried into the Underworld.

Arm in arm, Vicky and I watch them go, waving until the portal closes.

I turn to my girl and let her black-and-blonde locks slide through my fingers. "I guess forever starts now."

The End

CAST OF CHARACTERS

First, let me present to you my Shield of ghosts, consisting of:

*D'Maeo – the "father" of the ghosts, about sixty years old in human years. He wears a dark suit and has gray hair down to his shoulders and sideburns connecting to his beard and mustache. He has the power of deflection. Recently, we freed him from the Black Void which had clung to him, trying to turn him evil, ever since it killed him.

*Maël – the "mother" of the Shield. The oldest of the female ghosts, although she can't have been more than thirty-ish when she died. To me, she looks more like a goddess than a queen, with the golden headpiece on her black curls and the golden cape moving around her black dress with golden flowers. The staff she always carries helps, too. With it, she can influence time. She's also able to sense evil in places and people. She was the queen of a country in Africa a long time ago. Her whole tribe was poisoned and she was tortured to death.

During our first visit to the Shadow World, Maël was captured by the black tree, which is connected to the Black Horseman—the four trees are connected to each other, and to their respective Horsemen. We freed her, but a remnant of the tree is still inside her. We're hoping to use this against them.

*Jeep – necromancer. Around forty years old, I'd say, ghost years not counted. Tattoos cover his arms all the way up to the rolled-up sleeves of his burgundy buttoned-up shirt. There are pictures in his neck as well. He has a dark beard, mustache, and sideburns. Once, ghost mages were trapped under his tattoos, but they escaped. We defeated them, save for one mage who turned out to be benevolent (Dylan). Jeep's hat can be used as a boomerang. The rim is extra sharp.

Jeep was married to one of the strongest magicians who ever lived: Charlotte.

*Taylar – our youngest ghost. He was about fourteen years old when he died. His powers are dormant, and we don't know what they are. We've seen evil in him, which worries me a little; although, I try not to think about it.

His hair is a deep white, like his translucent skin. Taylar is our strongest fighter when it comes to non-magical fighting. His shield is his favorite weapon.

*Kessley – Taylar's girlfriend, and the only ghost I

added to my Shield myself. She is something else. Not only is she a shapeshifter, but she can also multiply. She makes us laugh whenever the alcohol takes over—a result of her dying while drunk—and she starts her overenthusiastic hopping and exclamations.

Kess is British, has bleached hair, and is dressed in a tight, short, leopard skin dress. She's about my age and died recently.

*Vicky – my girl. I could go on and on about her, but I'll try to keep it short. Vicky is awesome, gorgeous, and tough as hell. She's a magical empath, which means she can read other people's feelings and also influence them.

Vicky is a couple of years older than me, nineteen would be my guess, I never asked. She's great with a sword, and probably the bravest of us all. And did I mention she's awesome?

Other important people, in alphabetical order:

*Armando Accardi – the soldier who accidentally killed Dylan (see below). He is now the leader of Salvatorum, a place between Earth and Heaven where soldiers with unfinished business go. They can have a peaceful afterlife there, but most of them choose to travel to Earth on a regular basis to save people in need.

*Beelzebub – Satan's right hand and his strongest

warrior. He is a huge man-monster with shredded skin, a round mouth with small, pointy teeth, and glowing yellow eyes.

*Beetle-bees – creatures from one of the strange worlds we visited while we followed the Beach of Mu to Purgatory. They helped us fight some monsters.

They look like a cross between stag beetles and bees, and they're the size of guinea pigs. Their transparent wings are as large as a crow's, with pulsing red veins. Their razor-sharp fangs make a loud clicking sound when they slam together, and a soft red glow illuminates their bellies.

*Charlie – my best friend. A cheerful, easy-going guy who eats a lot of junk food to fuel his magical grease balls. He looks like a surfer dude with his long blond hair and dressed in shorts and a Hawaiian T-shirt.

*Chloe – the seventh soul, a Mahaha. Mahahas are people who froze to death and came back to kill others by freezing them. They are ice-blue and cold to the touch, with hair that is long and frozen stiff. They wear ragged pants and usually no shirt. Mahahas are often evil, but Chloe is nice.

*Dad / John Banner – vanished ten years ago without telling us anything about magic. He's a pyrokinetic. I inherited Darkwood Manor and my Shield from him. Killed by one of the Four Horsemen, he has been trapped in an in-between world with them. He managed to escape not long ago, and told us the Devil has a backup plan to break through the nine circles without using the nine souls.

*Dylan Maylord – the eighth ghost mage who escaped Jeep's tattoos. He's about fifteen years old, and his powers consist of lifting curses and undoing spells. Bad luck followed him around when he was alive, but it turned out it actually saved a lot of lives. He was killed by a soldier named Armando Accardi, by accident. To solve his unfinished business, Dylan searched for Armando. He found him, but didn't move on, which probably means we need him by our side.

*The Four Horsemen – strong warriors who fight with the Devil and are not easy to kill. They are each connected to one of the trees in the Shadow World, though, and also to their horses. Maël has a piece of the black tree inside her, which she will try to use on the Horsemen when we face them again. The Red Horseman of War is the only one we haven't met yet. We got away from the other three by tricking them. They are: the Black Horseman of Famine, the White Horseman of Conquest, and the Pale Horseman of Pestilence.

*Ginda – Chloe's best friend. She is a chlorokinetic witch, which means she can create and manipulate plants. She helped us defeat the ghost mages who escaped Jeep's tattoos.

She is slender, has lots of freckles in a kind face, and brown hair which moves on its own.

*Gisella – Charlie's girlfriend and a striking appearance. She has long, bright red hair, yellow eyes, and is usually dressed in a shiny red catsuit. She's half werecat, half witch. The werecat half translates into amazing athletic abilities, like high jumps, extremely fast movements, and somersaults, plus hands that turn into blades. Her witch-side is part evil. It gives her the power to control shadows and throw force fields. She can also heal. She absorbed the evil powers of her aunt Kasinda (see below), which are sometimes hard to control.

*The iele – a fairy kind with the skill to create powerful objects to ward off evil. The iele don't like to be seen. Everything they touch becomes dangerous for humans. However, it wasn't always like that. Once upon a time a powerful mage captured one of them and forced her to teach him all she knew. Since then, the iele want nothing to do with humans or other magical creatures. Which is why every good thing they create turns bad when another creature touches it. The Bell of Izme, which I have to keep the black void in the silver mine closed, was made by the iele before they turned against humanity.

So far, we've only met three iele: Soimane-the

leader-, Sfinte, and Mandre. They are gorgeous women with long, white gowns. Their white hair tends to flow up and down in an invisible current, like the hems of the garments which cover their feet.

*John Banner – see 'Dad'

*Kasinda – Gisella's aunt, and a powerful Black Annis witch (a dark witch). A plump middle-aged woman with multiple layers of clothes. Her hair is the same bright red as Gisella's, but she's got streaks of black in it.

*The Keepers of Life – a secret organization tasked with keeping the Book of a Thousand Deaths safe. We're not sure if they have any other tasks, but they probably do. I only saw a Keeper of Life once, in a memory my Shield showed me of Dad attacking one because he wanted the Book of a Thousand Deaths while under the influence of one of the Four Horsemen.

*Mom / Susan – the only non-magical person in our party, and therefore the one we will try to transfer Charlotte's powers to. She's skinny and has blonde hair.

*Mona – Mom's fairy godmother and best friend, who also keeps an eye on me. Like all fairy godmothers, she can do amazing things with her sparks. Heal, take away fear, set the table... I sometimes compare her to the Stepford Wives because of her too blonde, too straight, short hair, too much make-up, and her perfect, unwrinkled skin.

She and D'Maeo fell hard for each other. Since she's always cooking up something magical, she has no regular seat at the kitchen table. Usually, she sits on D'Maeo's lap.

*Quinn / Qaddisin – one of my close friends and one out of two who didn't betray me. He's an angel, part of the Council of God, and the right hand of God himself. Like all angels, he is strikingly handsome. His skin is dark, he has short curls, a solid chest, and huge shoulders. He can read thoughts and he can speak inside someone's head even when he's far away.

*Shelton Banks – a powerful mage and rich businessman who works for the Devil. He's responsible for Taylar's death and that of his brother. We've been trying to get him in prison for that, to resolve Taylar's unfinished business.

*Susan – see 'Mom'

*Trevor – Mom's old neighbor who has had a crush on her since they were young. He's an earth elemental and works for the Devil. He often leads the hunt for the next soul needed to break through the corresponding circle of Hell.

Make a difference

Reviews are very important to authors. Even a short or negative review can be of tremendous value to me as a writer. Therefore I would be very grateful if you could leave a review at your place of purchase. And don't forget to tell your friends about this book!

Thank you very much in advance.

Newsletter, social media and website

Want to receive exclusive first looks at covers and upcoming book releases, get a heads-up on pre-order and release dates and special offers, receive book recommendations and an exclusive 'look into my (writing) life'? Then please sign up now for my monthly newsletter through my website: www.tamarageraeds.com.

You can also follow me on Facebook, Instagram and Twitter for updates and more fun stuff!

Have a great day!   Tamara Geraeds

Found a mistake?

The Ninth Angel has gone through several rounds of beta reading and editing. If you found a typographical, grammatical, or other error which impacted your enjoyment of the book, we offer our apologies and ask that you let us know, so we can fix it for future readers.

You can email your feedback to: info@tamarageraeds.com.

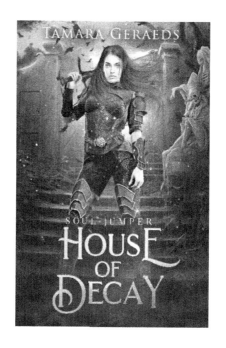

SOUL JUMPER
HOUSE OF DECAY

Welcome to Vex Monster Tours.
Please press PLAY to watch this video.

PLAY

Loading….

Loading….

Loading….

"Hi there, and welcome to Vex Monster Tours. If you're looking for an adrenaline-filled adventure, you've come to the right place. My name is Vex and…

You're laughing, aren't you? I don't blame you. I would too if I were you. But it's not my fault that I'm called Vex. My parents had a great sense of humor, or so they thought. They were both Soul Jumpers, of course, like me, and thought it was ironically funny to name me Vex, since they trained me to be a nuisance to any kind of monster.

Anyway, in case you don't know what a Soul Jumper is, I'll explain it to you briefly.

A Soul Jumper is a human with special powers, born and trained to kill monsters. We are stronger and faster than regular humans and have more endurance and agility and some other extras. When we touch the last victim a creature killed, a connection is made with the next target of that monster. When that target is attacked and about to lose the battle with the monster, our soul jumps into the target's body. From that moment on, our natural strengths are doubled, as are our senses. This gives us the power to defeat the monster before it kills another person. While we're inside the victim's body, they have no control over their moves but can still feel everything and talk to us. If they die, we jump back into our own body, which is protected by a flock of birds. Hawks, in my case. We have special Soul Jumper battle outfits, like I'm wearing now, connected to our souls to make them jump with us. They have some neat gadgets as extra back-up.

So, where was I?

Oh yes, Vex Monster Tours offers you the chance to see and fight any evil creature up close. To increase your chances of winning without my help, you get a day of training. That doesn't sound like a lot, but I'll give you a cupcake that contains a special mixture. It will give you the ability to pick up everything you learn a lot faster, and it builds up muscle at triple speed.

A blood vow is made between me and the monster of your request in which we agree not to attack before the arranged time. I will protect you the best I can while letting you fight the monster for as long as possible. Sounds cool, right?

But why, do you ask, would a monster agree to fight two people? Well, for one, most monsters are cocky, and two, these days, there are so many hunters roaming the streets that they have a hard time finding a quiet place to attack. They think they have a better chance for a meal when they're just fighting you and I... but we'll prove them wrong.

Have any questions? Feel free to email or call me!"

CHAPTER 1

I sense something off even before I see it. My muscles tense at the feeling that I'm not alone, like I should be.

Custos lands quietly on my shoulder while I peer left and right. Everything seems normal. There are no odd sounds, no footprints on the path or in the earth around the trees.

Then I notice it. The door to the training barn is ajar. It's just a crack, and there isn't enough wind to make it move, but I know something is wrong.

Custos cocks his head when he notices it a second later. He nudges my neck with his beak, as if to say, 'Go check it out!'

Slowly moving closer, my mind whirls around the possibilities. *Did I fail to properly close the portal after the last training session, making it possible for the monster to escape?*

I shake that thought off. Even if I didn't close it completely, the portal only lets monsters cross halfway. It's not really a passage; they can't get through to this world.

With narrowed eyes, I watch the creak in the door. My ears try to pick up a sound, any sound, that could give me an indication of what to expect. When they finally do, just as my hand moves to the doorknob, I freeze.

Custos lets out a disrupted croak as the pained whimper drifts toward us.

"That sounded human, right?" I ask him quietly.

He nods, and I wrap my fingers around the doorknob. "Good. That rules out the worst."

Before I get the chance to pull the door open, the leader of my protective kettle pulls my hair.

"Ouch," I whisper. "What was that for?"

The hawk swoops down to the ground and pulls at my pant leg.

A smile creeps upon my face. "Oh yes, good thinking, Custos."

I pull out the short blade hidden in my boot and wait for Custos to settle back on my shoulder.

"Ready?" I ask, and his talons dig into my shirt.

With one fast movement, I pull the door open. It takes me a millisecond to realize I won't need my weapon. No one is jumping out at me. The whimpering has stopped, but there's no doubt where it came from. Several of the traps that line the walls have been set off. Whomever broke into my barn managed to avoid the first trap, judging by the three arrows lodged into the wall on my right. Dodging them slowed him down enough to get doused with flammable liquid and set on fire.

I scan the floorboard in front of me. Yep, burn marks. The trail of black spots leaves no room for doubt about the intruder's next move. He dove for the bucket of water on my left, that has tipped over and is still dripping.

"And there it is," I say manner-of-factly.

Three small steps take me to the edge of what is normally a pretty solid wooden floor with no more than slits showing the dark void below. Now, the boards have moved aside and down, creating a large hole with a view of the endless blackness. Inches from the tips of my shoes, bloodied fingers are straining to hang onto what remains of the floor.

I lean forward so I can see my unwanted guest. "Hello there. How can I help you today?"

The man attached to the fingers is about nineteen years old. He has black hair covered in grease and green eyes that look up at me with a mixture of relief and despair. Scorch marks decorate his arms and face, and there are burn holes all over his shirt.

I study him shamelessly while he searches for an answer.

Custos scurries over and softly pecks at one of the fingers.

With a squeal, the man pulls back his hand, swinging dangerously by the other before wrapping it back around the floorboard five inches further to the right.

"Help me, please," he finally manages.

"Sure!" The fake smile on my lips almost hurts.

I squat down in front of him. "But first, I'd like to know what you're doing here."

One finger slips, and he groans. "I'll tell you everything. Please help me up."

"I will," I answer, examining my fingernails, "after you tell me."

"Fine." His voice goes up a couple of octaves. "I was hiking in the forest when a bear attacked me." My gaze drops down to his green shirt, which streaked with red between the holes. There's a gash in the side that could've been made by a bear's claw, but it could also be the result of climbing the fence around my premises.

I frown. "Where's your backpack then? Did you drop it?"

"I did." He nods. His dark eyebrows are pulled together when he sends me a pleading look. "It fell into the pit. Please don't let me fall too. Please."

He sounds convincing, yet something about his story is off.

"Tell me exactly what happened with the bear."

He groans. "Please pull me up first. I can't hold on for much longer."

I stand up and take a step back. "I'm sorry, but I don't trust you. Your story doesn't make sense."

"Why not?" he exclaims. "I encountered a bear; I swear! I've never seen one so big in my life."

"What kind of bear?"

"A black bear, of course; it's the only one that lives here."

"Hmm." Anyone could know that.

And then it hits me. The thing that doesn't add up in his story.

"Bears never come close to my home. They sense

the monsters that visit frequently."

The muscles in his arms are starting to shake from the effort of holding on. "Please… I don't know what it was doing here. I'm telling you, it attacked me, and I figured climbing over your fence was my best shot."

I tap my lips with my finger. He is so full of bull that it's almost funny. Even if a bear would come close, climbing over the fence would trigger my alarm. *What are the odds of a bear approaching and my alarm failing on the same day?* And I'm not even counting the tripwires set up everywhere.

I cock my head. "You don't seem surprised to hear that monsters visit me on a regular basis."

He focuses on his fingers, trying to get a better grip. His breathing is fast, and sweat trickles down his temples and over the stubble on his cheeks. "Monsters are everywhere, why would that be a surprise?"

"No…" Slowly I shake my head. "You know who I am, what I am. You know what I do."

He clenches his teeth. "I swear-"

He yells in panic as his other hand slips from the edge. I drop back down quickly and grab it.

"Didn't your mother teach you not to swear?" I say. My voice is low with repressed anger. My patience has vanished. "Now, tell me the truth, or I'm throwing you in."

"All right, all right!" He swallows and licks his lips. His weight pulls at my arm, and I grunt.

"You better hurry."

"I know who you are. You're Vex Connor, a Soul Jumper, *the* Soul Jumper." He gives me a sheepish grin. "Everyone admires you. I just wanted to see how you did it all, you know. What kind of tools you use, how you live…" His voice trails off, and he breaks eye contact.

After a short silence, I shrug. "Well, that still sounds crazy but much more plausible than your other story." I grab his arm with both hands and haul him up.

He collapses on what remains of the floor and clutches his hands to his chest.

Custos shrieks, and I nod at him. "Yes, turn off the traps for a minute, please."

The hawk flies to the other end of the barn, close to the ceiling to avoid the booby traps that are higher up on the walls. I block the intruder's view as Custos picks up a rope, drops the loop at the end around the handle of the device I built and pulls.

With a sound like a collapsing bookcase, the floor boards pop back up until the black void below can only be seen through the cracks.

I stick out my hand. "Let's go. I'll give you a cup of coffee before you leave. You can wash up while the water boils."

* * *

Want to read on? Order this story on Amazon now!

IMPORTANT NOTICE

All *Soul Jumper* stories can be read in random order. You can start with the story that appeals to you most. It is, however, recommended to start with Force of the Kraken.

I hope you enjoy them!

ABOUT THE AUTHOR

Tamara Geraeds was born in 1981. When she was 6 years old, she wrote her first poem, which basically translates as:

A hug for you and a hug for me
and that's how life should be

She started writing books at the age of 15 and her first book was published in 2012. After 6 books in Dutch she decided to write a young adult fantasy series in English: *Cards of Death*.

Tamara's bibliography consists of books for children, young adults and adults, and can be placed under fantasy and thrillers.

Besides writing she runs her own business, in which she teaches English, Dutch and writing, (re)writes texts and edits books.

She's been playing badminton for over 20 years and met the love of her life Frans on the court. She loves going out for dinner, watching movies, and of course reading, writing and hugging her husband. She's crazy about sushi and Indian curries, and her favorite color is pink.

BOOKS BY
TAMARA GERAEDS

The Cards of Death series

The First Demon
The Second Premonition
The Third Sin
The Fourth Soul
The Fifth Portal
The Sixth Ghost
The Seventh Crow
The Eighth Mage
The Ninth Angel

The Soul Jumper series

Dream of Death
Force of the Kraken
House of Decay
Flames of Fury
Fog of Deception
Demon of the Shadow
Rage of the Siren
Curse of the Coven
Wrath of the Gargoyle
Tree of Terror
Mask of Mutation

The Soul Jumper series is available in paperback
under the titles *Soul Jumper Collection #1 and #2.*

Printed in Great Britain
by Amazon